NEPTUNE ISLAND

A LINCOLN MONK ADVENTURE

BY TONY REED

PROLOGUE

Undisclosed island, Pacific Ocean
Two years earlier

The fishing village rested in the shadows of the mountainside, overlooking the calm waters of the Pacific Ocean. Dozens of huts and assorted shacks dotted the dusty track, the village's only road to the ocean's edge and to several dilapidated fishing boats lining the town's weather-worn pier.

The stilted longhouse with thatched roof and bamboo walls sat at the far end of the sandy trail facing the village, the beach, and the ocean beyond. The moon was high in the night sky, its dancing light reflecting across the bay's tranquil waters.

The islanders were celebrating in the longhouse and enjoying the evening's meal when the first tremor coursed through the island. The chatter stopped. Laughter and conversation from the day's events died away.

The longhouse shuddered from a second tremor—stronger, deeper, louder. As the walls shook, floorboards convulsed beneath their feet. A mother grabbed her infant and ran for the door. Others followed, charging the only exit, desperate to escape the unknown. Terrified, the villagers abandoned the longhouse and scattered in all directions, some vanishing into the jungle, others taking shelter behind shacks and outbuildings.

The horrifying roar of earth tearing apart reverberated through the air, followed by a barrage of rock, mud, and battered jungle foliage thundering down the mountainside with the force of an out of control freight train, destroying everything in its path. The northern face of the mountain broke away in a tidal wave of sludge and dirt rushing inexorably toward the village. Bamboo walls exploded as the sea of debris slammed through the longhouse. The landslide slammed onward, relentlessly consuming the hapless village.

Frantic islanders raced down the main street toward the ocean in hope of escaping to the open harbor. They never stood a chance. Their screams of terror silenced as the face of the deadly wave swallowed them all, and the rumbling subsided. Apart from the odd wail of a seagull, a deathly quiet filled the night air.

Ocean waves crashed upon the remnants of the landslide that had now reached the beach. The surge continued, devastating the shoreline and fishing boats tied to the solitary jetty. In time, the mud, foliage, and debris would drift with the ebbing tide.

A Eurocopter EC155 sat on the plateau of an adjoining mountain. The rotor blades turned lazily as the moonlight glistened on its polished black frame. Two figures stood beside the chopper gazing through state of the art night vision binoculars. The trim African American in his mid-forties lowered his binoculars. Billionaire Jonathan Kane needed to see the devastation with his own eyes. The man in the white shirt and two-piece Armani suit, was Kane's loyal chief of security Leon Maxwell.

Kane leaned against the chopper leisurely, while Maxwell's gaze darted about as he scanned the scene below. The fishing village and shoreline no longer existed, buried beneath tons of rock and jungle terrain. In its place was a swirling cauldron of debris and mud the size of ten football stadiums.

"Most impressive." Kane's tone was detached.

Maxwell swung his binoculars to the side and pulled out a small electronic tablet. He viewed the screen's data and then rechecked it. The figures displayed were not the expected results.

"Was velocity achieved?" Kane asked.

"John ..." Maxwell's voice trailed off, not wanting to finish the sentence.

"Well, was it?"

"All data is within thirty percent of the estimated parameters," Maxwell said.

Kane ran his hand over his short-cropped hair. "Only thirty percent? We need *exact* velocity and mass volume data. You know that!" Kane surveyed the carnage below. "It appears the prototype has performed quite poorly."

Maxwell had seen that expression of frustration and disdain many times.

"I trusted you, Leon, to hire reliable people who could get the job done. It appears you have failed again."

Annoyed at himself for having failed his old friend and mentor, Maxwell lowered his head to avert eye contact. Sensing the distress the poor results and his exasperated response had caused his loyal and long-time friend, Kane threw his arm around Maxwell's shoulders. "We need people who can get results now."

Eager to please, Maxwell nodded with enthusiasm. "I'll get on it right away," he promised.

Kane returned to the destruction and carnage before him. Moonlight illuminated the shattered landscape, revealing a nightmarish scene from the apocalypse. Faint cries and screams reverberated up the mountainside.

"Thank you," Kane replied to their echoes of despair. "Thank you all for your sacrifice. Your deaths have not been in vain. You are the first step." Kane's sincere tone switched to indifference. "Leon, find me another island."

"Of course."

Kane smiled at his old friend. "I'm hungry. Shall we get something to eat?"

A rat scurried between Maxwell's feet. He glanced down and, without hesitation, crushed it beneath his shoe.

As the men climbed aboard the chopper, Kane gave the pilot a whirling signal to indicate take off. The turbines roared. Moments later, the rotors whirred to life. The chopper thundered as it lifted up into the night sky.

• • •

Agrihan Island, Pacific Ocean; Northern Mariana Islands chain
One month later

The diver broke the surface, shattering the tranquil water. He flipped back his goggles and removed his regulator. "We found it!" he exclaimed, grinning broadly and giving a thumbs-up.

The diver had surfaced beside a sleek black cruiser with *Christina* painted on the bow. The cruiser drifted lazily, anchored only a few feet from a sheer rock wall rising from the ocean three hundred feet above the boat and running the circumference of the island before disappearing sharply around a knoll at the south end.

A slender woman in a white bikini leaned over the cruiser's side rail, her waist-length auburn hair pulled back in a ponytail. Her Asian heritage complemented her white bikini perfectly, further enhancing her natural beauty. Her gaze, behind chic sunglasses, never left the diver as he swam to the back of the boat and climbed aboard.

The diver sat on one of the deck benches mounted opposite each other and removed his goggles. He unclipped the scuba tank's harness and resting the tank beside her. Then he pulled a towel from under the bench and wiped his face. "Two weeks of searching, but we finally found it."

"Where?" Christina asked.

He finished drying his face and threw the towel aside. "The fissure's about twenty feet down in the rock face—wide, too. You could fit an ROV in there no problem, even a small bathyscaphe if necessary."

"Anything else?" she asked.

"The geologist was right. The fissure leads to a subterranean chamber. It's massive—the biggest cave I've ever seen."

"Both of you have seen it?"

"My partner saw it first."

"And where's your partner now?"

"He's right behind me. He'll be up any minute."

Christina walked to the front of the cruiser. She opened a small fridge and removed a bottle of chilled champagne and three flutes. After popping the cork, she returned to the stern.

"It looks like congratulations are in order." She handed the diver a flute and filled his glass, glancing over the side to where the second diver was making his way to the surface.

Christina placed her empty flute on the bench and pulled a phone from her carry bag. She tapped GPS LOCATION LOCKED, then dropped the phone back in her bag.

The diver, who had been ogling Christina's slender figure, slapped her lightly on the rear saying, "Let's get this party started." At his touch, Christina's muscles flexed and her body tightened.

The diver raised his champagne flute, and then noticed that Christina hadn't poured any for herself. "Not drinking?" he asked chirpily, energized from the find and what was to come. He licked his lips in anticipation.

Christina pulled a Sig Sauer P238 handgun from her carry bag. She took aim at the diver's forehead and fired. Blood and brain matter exploded from the back of his head as the diver slumped back against the railing. Christina lifted his legs and flipped him over the side.

The second diver broke the surface at the stern. He was midway up the ladder when Christina fired a round into his forehead. A small red dot appeared in the center of his brow as the back of his head burst apart and he fell from the ladder into the sea. "Say hello to your partner," she murmured.

Emotionless.

Detached.

Another day, another paycheck.

Her gaze followed the corpses as they drifted with the tide, the blue water around them transforming to crimson. In no time the bodies would spark a feeding frenzy among the sharks.

Christina surveyed the surrounding waters. The ocean was empty: no charter boats, no fishing trawlers—no prying eyes. Satisfied, she slipped the handgun into her bag and entered the cabin. Through the plexiglass windscreen, she spotted several fins slicing through the water toward the cruiser.

"Bon appétit," she said to no one in particular. She tapped a button on the console, throttled up, and the cruiser motored away.

• • •

Las Vegas, Nevada
Two weeks later

La Casa Di Ninetta was Eddie's favorite restaurant for two reasons. Situated behind a shopping mall two streets back from The Strip, tourists were less inclined to frequent it. Only the locals who worked in the district knew of the eatery, and that's the way Eddie liked it— away from watchful eyes. The other reason? The great Italian cuisine.

The meticulously dressed man appeared next to his table during his second serving of spaghetti Bolognese. Eddie eyed the man warily as he finished a mouthful of pasta and wiped a spot of sauce from his chubby chin. "Can I help you?" he asked, washing the pasta down with a swig of beer.

"Yes, you can." The stranger gestured to a chair. "May I?"

"It's a free world." Eddie tried to sound nonchalant as the man sat opposite him. With his immaculate grooming and perfectly trimmed beard, the man didn't appear to be one of Tony's goons. His tan was not the work of a salon, and his Armani suit was tailor made. Even his black leather shoes had a gleam only money could buy. The only clash with his fastidious appearance was a jagged scar running down the side of his neck. Eddie took another sip of his beer and continued eating, but he eyed the man for sudden movements.

"My name is Leon Maxwell, Eddie." Maxwell adjusted his suit for comfort. "You graduated high school with top honors and received a grant to attend MIT. However, your theoretical work for the application of quantum computations was largely ignored, and after two years—and several altercations with staff and students— you were asked to leave.

"Nevertheless, your work drew the attention of a local think tank that paid you handsomely. You quickly squandered the money on all the clichés: gambling, illicit drugs, women … Your work suffered because of these distractions. Your theories remain largely unproven, and you cannot pay your gambling debts. Worse, your termination left you with your concepts and ideals still unrealized. You currently reside in a mobile home just outside the city limits. Because of your temper and failure to get along with others, work opportunities have not been forthcoming. Your gambling debts exceed eighty thousand dollars, and—believe me when I say this— men have been buried in the desert for a lot less."

Eddie finished the last of the pasta and wiped his hands down his oversized Hawaiian shirt. He sighed and looked at Maxwell with world-weary eyes. "So you know all about me—warts and all," he added sarcastically.

"Your papers were dismissed by your peers as nonsense, as pie-in-the-sky rubbish." Maxwell eyed him narrowly. "Why?"

"The equations were sound. It's the real-world application that's tricky. That's what those idiots didn't get."

"So it can be done?"

"Of course." When it came to his scientific and mathematical abilities, Eddie was arrogant.

Maxwell scrutinised the obese man. Clearly he was a slob with control issues. Nevertheless, his answer to the question rang true, and his facial movements and demeanor also indicated that he was telling the truth. Maxwell pulled out his cell phone, tapped a few keys, and slid the phone across the table. "My employer needs people with your skills, Eddie. Competent people with drive, people who can work to a deadline and understand non-disclosure agreements. My employer has instructed me to make you an offer."

Eddie glanced at the screen and his eyes widened. Beneath the details of Eddie's bank account, a substantial dollar figure was highlighted, followed by a flashing TRANSFER NOW icon.

"The offer is real, Eddie. Considering your financial circumstances, I suggest you take it." Maxwell smiled to himself. He'd known Eddie would take the deal even before he walked into the restaurant.

The proposition was perfect—too perfect. Eddie couldn't put his finger on it, but he sensed something was wrong, that this man's outward appearance hid a darker self. The hastily stitched scar along his neck was recent. No amount of makeup could hide that rough ridge of torn skin. Eddie pushed these doubts to the back of his mind and considered the money he so desperately needed. "Who's your employer?" he asked.

As Maxwell stared into his tired eyes, Eddie started. Throughout their conversation, he had missed Maxwell's most striking feature. He suffered from heterochromia. His left eye was green and his right was blue. "Let's just say my employer wants to change the world," Maxwell said with a depraved grin.

1

Thanking the driver with a nod, Lincoln stepped from the bus—and into the storm.

Sunrise was still an hour away, and apart from the blurred motorbike headlight in the distance, the district was deserted. As the bus disappeared into the driving rain, Lincoln threw his Mil-Spec backpack over his shoulder and slipped on his black baseball cap. He made his way across Micro Beach Road to the flickering neon light of the all-night diner.

Although the diner was only a short walk from the bus stop, he entered dripping wet, his trekking boots, jeans, and hoody all soaked from the rain. He took off his cap and ruffled his short hair, then slipped into a booth near the back and scanned the menu.

A large, middle-aged Chamorro woman wearing a soiled apron emerged from the kitchen and lumbered around the counter. She smiled as she approached Lincoln's table.

"Well, I'll be damned! If it isn't Lincoln Monk, my favorite ex-employee. Well, come here sexy eyes. Give me some sugar."

Lincoln grinned and, with an exaggerated flash of his green eyes, gave her a big hug.

"Hello, Isa. It's good to see that you and the old diner are still here."

She folded her arms in mock defiance. "Always will be."

Lincoln glanced through the serving window at the empty kitchen beyond. "Where's Jonah?"

"I gave him the night off—again." She shook her head. "That man sure can complain."

"Husbands will do that."

"Now I haven't seen you in a long, long time. What have you been doing since you left the island?"

"A bit of this and a bit of that, mostly traveling." Lincoln eased himself back into the booth.

"I heard you worked for the government again, or something along those lines."

He shrugged. "Not anymore."

She waited for him to elaborate, but when she sensed that he didn't want to talk, she said, "You always were the quiet one. Well, good luck to ya, honey. As they say, a man's gotta do what a man's gotta do." Changing the subject, she asked, "What brings you back to the island?"

"Just catching up with an old friend."

"Mich?"

Lincoln nodded.

Isa pulled a pen and order pad from her apron. "So? What can I do ya for?"

"Bacon and eggs, sunny-side up."

"Coffee?"

"Thanks."

"Back in two shakes."

Lincoln stuck the menu between the catsup bottle and salt and pepper shakers, then leaned back against the booth's vinyl backrest. He loved the design of these nostalgic railcar diners: the row of booths that looked out through the main windows, the long counter opposite the booths, and the smell of good wholesome food and freshly-brewed coffee.

Soon the aroma of sizzling bacon wafted through the diner.

The monotonous overnight flight from Manilla combined with the arduous bus ride from the airport had made him lethargic. He could never sleep on planes, and the pot-holed motorway from the airport made resting on the bus impossible. He rubbed the sleep from his heavy eyes and glanced at his watch. Still too early for the local bus service.

His plans of trekking the world, working when he could find it while taking in the pleasures that life had to offer, would have to wait. He hadn't thought he'd return at all let alone so soon, but recent events had thrown an emotional spanner into the works.

He glanced at the television mounted behind the counter. An old Bogart movie was playing—*Key Largo*, one of Sienna's favorites. Lincoln allowed himself the luxury of reminiscing and smiled at the recollection of good times past. He gazed beyond the rivulets of rain streaming down the diner's window to the beachfront only a short walk away, where yachts, anchored to the shoreline, swayed in the stormy waters.

His smile faded as the purpose for his return flooded his mind. He slipped the flash drive from his pocket and re-examined it for the umpteenth time. Locked inside was a mystery—a mystery an old friend could help him solve. Lincoln preferred to let sleeping dogs lie, but he had no choice. He dropped the drive back into his pocket as Isa returned with the breakfast order.

Lincoln finished his eggs and had just started on the three strips of bacon when the diner's door flew open and slammed against a nearby table, causing the condiments to topple over and spill across the floor. Lincoln's tiredness disappeared as his instincts kicked in. *Be alert. Be prepared.*

Three of them stood in the doorway. Lincoln knew their type—gangster wannabees, eyes glazed over, reeking of whiskey. The Tall Guy with the shoulder-length hair and pockmarked face sweated profusely. Skinny One's body was covered with tattoos that snaked up around his neck. Several gold chains hung loosely around Fat Boy's neck. They were horsing around and laughing among themselves.

"What can I do for you boys?" Isa asked, eyeing them from behind the counter.

They ignored her and continued with their horseplay until Tall Guy spotted Lincoln at the back of the diner. He pointed him out to his boys. They talked among themselves for a moment before stumbling toward him.

With his swelled chest and cliché swagger, Tall Guy was clearly the alpha male of the group. He sat opposite Lincoln and slammed his fist down saying, "This here's our table, boy."

Lincoln continued to eat, trying to ignore the stench of cheap booze. Without raising his head he said, "I'm not looking for any trouble."

"You just found it, asshole." Tall Guy smiled, displaying a mouthful of gold and rotted teeth. He opened his jacket to reveal a knife. His boys glanced at each other and laughed.

"Say hello to my little pal," Tall Guy sneered.

"Oh, you're referring to the 1982 classic, *Scarface.*" Lincoln glanced at the knife. "However, in the film's climactic scene, the protagonist wields a machine gun, not a knife. And the line is 'Say hello to my little friend' not 'my little pal.'" Lincoln continued eating, adding, "Go away, you annoy me."

This wasn't the reaction Tall Guy or his boys expected. Rattled by Lincoln's response, and unsure of their next move, the boys turned to Tall Guy. To regain his machismo and reassure his control in front of his boys, Tall Guy pulled out the knife and stabbed it into the table.

Lincoln sighed and put down his fork. "It doesn't have to be this way."

Tall Guy yanked his knife from the table and stabbed it down again. "Yeah, it does."

His boys laughed.

Wherever you go, there's always an asshole. So be it.

Lincoln stood, unblinking, his gaze never leaving Tall Guy's eyes. "I'll finish my breakfast here in about twenty minutes. Then I'll probably order another cup of this delicious coffee. You know what? Make that half an hour. This coffee is really good. So in the meantime, Cinderella, why don't you and your ugly sisters go play somewhere else?"

Jaws dropped. The three looked at each other, speechless.

"What the fu—?" Tall Guy stammered, unable to comprehend the last remark.

Isa, watching from the counter, sensed that the confrontation would end badly. "Hey, guys, that table is clean and ready to go," she said, nodding toward the booth furthest from Lincoln.

"Shut the hell up, bitch!" Fat Boy shouted at her. He opened his jacket to reveal a gun tucked into his oversized pants.

Isa backed away, not taking her eyes off them.

Lincoln spoke to her in a calm and reassuring voice. "Babe, everything will be okay."

His endearing term surprised her, considering his reluctance for small talk earlier. Then she caught on. "Okay," she said, nodding.

Skinny One gave Lincoln a drugged-crazed, evil-eye stare. "We should end this piece of shit now," he said to Tall One.

Lincoln's gaze went from one thug to the other. He calculated their distance from him, their capabilities, disabilities, and reaction times—and made the judgment call.

His tone changed from somber indifference to light-hearted banter. "Speaking of great '80s films, did you guys ever see *Streets of Fire?* It's a really good flick. Very underrated, but very entertaining. You should all watch it someday. Anyway, at the beginning of the movie, our hero is confronted by a group of assailants—much like yourselves. Now the great thing about this movie is that he disarms them all—without ever using a weapon."

The three frowned and looked at each other, unsure where this was leading.

Lincoln grabbed Tall Guy's head and slammed it on the table, breaking his nose. Tall Guy screamed and crumpled to the floor, clutching his bloodied face.

Skinny One stepped up throwing a roundhouse punch that Lincoln easily deflected. Using Skinny One's forward momentum, Lincoln propelled him onto the table of a nearby booth. He crashed and landed heavily on the floor, gasping for breath.

"How about I mess you up?" Fat Boy sneered. He tried to steady his gun in Lincoln's direction, but his hand shook, his false bravado fast disappearing.

Lincoln's tone dropped to a menacing whisper, his good-natured humor gone. "How about you let me finish my breakfast, or I'll show you what pain really feels like?"

Fat Boy hesitated. From nowhere, the baseball bat cracked him across the back of the head. He collapsed, unconscious before he hit the floor. Isa stood behind him, bat in hand. "I really hate being called a bitch."

"I can see that," Lincoln said, eyeing Fat Boy's unconscious body. "What I meant was for you to pass *me* the baseball bat." He surveyed the broken furniture and bodies littering the floor. "But—this works, too."

"Those assholes have been coming in here for a long while causing all sorts of problems and scaring customers. High time someone showed 'em some manners. Thank you." She surveyed the groaning bodies. "The local cops are good guys. They'll understand. They know this bunch and won't ask many questions, but I still gotta call 'em. Just go. I'll clean up this mess."

"You sure?"

She smiled. "If they cause any more problems before the cops get here, I'm sure Babe and I can handle it." Lincoln kissed her cheek, grabbed the last piece of bacon, and threw his backpack over his shoulder. "Good luck, darlin'," she called.

Lincoln popped his head back through the door. "You're the best boss I ever worked for." He smiled and gave her a thumbs-up.

Isa turned back to the three thugs sprawled on the floor, tapping the bat lightly against her palm. Carved down the side of the bat was the word BABE.

2

When the storm hit, the young Japanese honeymooners took cover under an upturned dinghy. The quick-thinking husband erected a piece of rotted wood between the sand and the bow so that the craft rested on the gunwale. They were protected, yet they could still enjoy a magnificent view of what could be seen of the beach and the ocean through the darkness and rain.

Several hours later, the storm showed no signs of abating. Their hotel, a mile down the deserted beachfront, was a world away. Huddled in each other's arms, they enjoyed the drumming of the rain as it pummelled the boat's hull, embracing the adventure and their new life together.

From behind the boat, a large man in a white lab coat staggered toward them, moaning and swaying. The bride yelped as he collapsed to his knees on the white sand in front of them.

"Hey, guy," her annoyed husband said, "go get drunk somewhere else, okay?"

The man clutched his midriff and coughed up blood. The wife screamed and wrapped her arms around her new spouse. "Oh, shit," he gasped. The injured man was big, with broad shoulders. He fell over on the sand and gradually released the grip on his stomach.

The husband pulled the towel from beneath them. He placed it over the wounded area and applied pressure to stem the flow, but below the coat, blood continued to ooze. He turned to his bride. "Go back to the hotel and get the police." Shocked by the tragic event, she stared at the dying man, unable to move. "Now," he pleaded. He kissed her lightly on the cheek.

She snapped out of her stupor and nodded. Bending low, she crawled from under the boat and into the pouring rain. She stumbled on the wet sand but quickly regained her balance and ran down the beach toward the hotel.

The stranger convulsed violently, coughing blood over the husband's face. His back arched as he whimpered in pain, then slumped on the sand, eyes closed. "Come on, stay with me," the husband pleaded. "Help will be here soon." He recognized the sound of a motorbike roaring in the distance.

The wounded man whispered repeatedly as delirium took control. His bloodied coat flopped opened, revealing the nametag pinned to his shirt: *James Faraday.*

The husband leaned close, trying to decipher the dying man's last words. He couldn't be sure, but he thought he heard *Save La Palma.*

3

The bus shelter across the street did little to protect Lincoln from the downpour as he observed the police arrive at the diner a full hour after the incident. Isa gave her statement to the officer in charge as the second officer threw the handcuffed assailants into the back of the police wagon. The officer in charge cringed as Isa swung her bat in a mock display of defense. He chuckled inwardly and continued writing his report.

The storm abated, and the sun peaked over the horizon, its rays glittering through the falling rain. Lincoln reviewed the bus timetable. He still had an hour before the first bus arrived.

Saipan shop fronts were opening for business. Lincoln searched for a familiar sight and recognized the bookstore at the next intersection as one that catered to the morning crowd. He slung his backpack over his shoulder and picked up an old newspaper left on the bench. He covered his head with the paper and was about to leave when he spotted the graffiti. On the back of the bus shelter, across the plastic panelling, an unknown author had scrawled *Neptune when.* Lincoln pondered the author's intentions in writing such an odd phrase. He dismissed the distraction and headed in the rain toward the bookstore.

The sweet aroma of barrister-brewed coffee pervaded the café/bookstore. New and old books, trendy magazines, and assorted coffee products filled the shelves. Designer tables and chairs lined the store windows overlooking the main street. Lincoln was in heaven. He ordered a cappuccino and checked out the book selection.

A woman stood in front of the bookcase, phone in hand, engrossed in her personal affairs. Her bulky leather pants and jacket, the kind motorcyclists wear for protection, couldn't hide her trim and curvaceous figure.

"Excuse me," Lincoln said, indicating the book directly in front of her.

She glanced at him, then stepped back and continued tapping her phone.

Lincoln slid the book from the shelf and started reading. He hadn't read Nietzsche in years. He loved the quote: "Beware, when fighting monsters, that you yourself do not become a monster ... for when you gaze long into the abyss, the abyss gazes also into you."

The woman slid her phone into her jacket and talked into her earpiece as she headed toward the exit. From what Lincoln heard of her end of the conversation, the discussion was heated. Discreetly he watched through the window as she paused on the sidewalk, barking at the person on the other end of the line. The conversation became even more intense as she threw her arms in the air and stepped into the busy road.

Lincoln spotted the truck hurtling toward her. He sprinted out of the bookstore as the driver slammed on his brakes. Lincoln grabbed the woman's jacket and yanked her to safety while the truck skidded to a stop. Instinctively the woman's hands shot up in defense and she stood her ground, ready for action, not realizing how close she'd come to serious injury.

Lincoln understood her reaction and backed away, giving her space and time to assess the situation. He held his hands up in a friendly gesture, aware that some women were accustomed to violence. The driver leaped from the truck's cab and rushed toward them.

The woman realized what had happened. She lowered her hands and straightened her jacket. Embarrassed by her reaction, she tapped her earpiece. "Thank you," she said to Lincoln.

"No problem. You were distracted. Are you okay?"

"Thank you for your concern, but I'm fine."

"Maybe you should take a break. You know, steady yourself. Give your body time to rest."

Her tone switched to cold and emphatic. "Like I said, I'm okay. Thank you again." She strode away, tapping her earpiece.

"You think she's okay?" the driver asked.

Lincoln watched the woman cross the street and turned down an alley. The low rumble of a motorbike engine filled the morning air and merged with the noise of the traffic.

"Yeah. I think so," Lincoln replied, unsure of his answer.

4

Michio pinned Lincoln's arms behind his back and slammed his face against the bungalow wall. "I told you if you ever came back, I'd kill you." He clamped his hand behind Lincoln's head.

Lincoln's voice was calm and even. "You don't need to do this, Michio."

"I'll decide what I need to do." He flattened Lincoln's nose against the wall. "You got that?"

"Okay, you're the boss. I just came to talk."

"I was through talking to you a long time ago. I thought you, of all people, understood that."

"I did. I do. I didn't want to come here, but I had no choice."

"We always have choices—" Michio's voice rose an octave "—and you just made another really bad one."

"Don't get agitated," Lincoln said. "We can sort this out, this thing between—"

"Agitated?" Michio sneered. "That's what anger and rage does to a person. That's what happens when your best friend steals your girlfriend. You get a little *agitated.*"

"You know nothing happened between us. I'd never do that."

"Just shut up."

"I need your help," Lincoln said, hoping to change the subject.

"You really think I'm gonna help *you*—you piece of shit?" He clamped his hand tighter around Lincoln's neck.

Lincoln flinched. He had to tell him. "Sienna's dead," he rasped.

Michio paused, and Lincoln felt the pressure ease against his head. The silence was deafening.

• • •

Behind Middle Road, Michio's small bungalow overlooked the hillside and a creek. Coconut palms, banana, papaya, and mango trees grew wild in the surrounding forest. Birds and lizards moved among the vegetation, and an eagle soared above. Lincoln felt like he'd stepped into a sixties B-grade jungle movie.

They sat on the porch. The rain continued to beat down, running off the veranda's roof like a never-ending waterfall. Lincoln took a swig of cold beer while Michio stared into the green waters of the swollen creek, his loud Hawaiian short hanging loosely on his taut body.

He and Lincoln shared the same lean physique, and they were roughly the same height. Even their skin tones matched—tanned, but not overdone. Apart from Michio's Japanese heritage and longer hair, seen back to back they could have been brothers from different mothers. They'd been friends since grade school and more recently, constant traveling companions.

Lincoln always appreciated the phrase *Wherever you lay your hat, that's your home* because it seemed fitting for the lifestyle he had chosen. While traveling around the Pacific region, he and Michio had met Sienna, a fellow travel junkie. Michio and Sienna clicked. Their fondness for each other blossomed into a passionate romance. They chose to stay on the tropical island and make a life for themselves. Deciding it was best to give them time together, Lincoln kept away and took odd jobs as a day laborer, bodyguard, and fry cook at the diner. The steady work had paid his way, but when the holiday season ended so did the money.

Michio's work as a freelance computer consultant flourished, and with the proceeds he put down a deposit on the bungalow. Seeing Michio with Sienna at his side and his tech business booming, Lincoln understood that the time had come to step aside and allow his old friend space to live a successful life.

Sienna noticed Lincoln's reluctance and discomfort when she and Michio were together. After many walks along Saipan's pristine beaches and many late night discussions about love and relationships, she and Lincoln formed an unintentional bond. Michio was understandably jealous, and a rift tore his and Lincoln's lifelong friendship apart. Lincoln had never meant to hurt his old friend, but Sienna's love for life was intoxicating. Nevertheless, Michio and Sienna's relationship suffered until they decided to end it. Lincoln's bond with Sienna waned after the breakup, and he, too, drifted away from Sienna's allure.

When an old cop buddy living in Manilla called and offered Lincoln a job as a bodyguard, he jumped at the opportunity to give Michio space to deal with his emotions. That was six months ago. Lincoln hoped that the passing time had eroded some of the emotional pain. Even if his return wasn't welcomed by everyone, returning to the island and seeing old faces again was comforting.

"Nice place," Lincoln commented, admiring the view and the house. The scene would have been picture-perfect except for the entrance. In contrast with the bungalow's laidback ambiance, its five-inch thick double door of evergreen oak almost spoiled the mood of the relaxed setting. Clearly the oversized double door were out of place in the small cottage. Lincoln looked quizzically at Michio, indicating the door.

"A gift from my parents. A reminder of back home."

"Who do your parents hang out with—King Kong?"

Michio continued staring at the creek.

Lincoln tried again. "How's the freelance tech consulting going?"

"How's the hobo job going?" Michio countered with a tinge of sarcasm.

Silence. They glared at one another, neither wanting the other to know his true financial or mental status. Finally, Michio spoke. "How did it happen?"

"They say it was a boating accident."

"They say?"

"Sienna's mom. She emailed me a month ago, but I've been away, so I only got the message a few days ago."

Michio took a swig of beer. "Why do you think otherwise?"

"I checked my lockbox at the post office in Manilla and found this." He pulled out the USB drive and handed it to Michio. "It arrived four days after her official death. I figured she knew her life was in danger, and this drive was her insurance."

"So what's on it?"

"You tell me. It's encrypted."

Michio examined the drive. It looked like all the other flash drives on the market. Then a pattern caught his attention. He examined it more closely, but in the sheltered porch light, he couldn't distinguish the worn engraving. He disappeared inside and returned with his tablet. He slid the drive into a side port.

Lincoln took another drink, then pulled out a pack of cigarettes. He inhaled deeply before slowly exhaling. Michio glanced over with disdain.

"I know, I'm in the fifteen percent," Lincoln said, taking another puff. He noticed a newspaper sitting on the small table between them, the local rag, its date current. "Bit old-school for you, isn't it?"

"Spoken by the man who still wears a watch."

"Touché," Lincoln muttered. "So, what do you think? Can you crack the encryption?"

"Maybe. This is gonna take time." He tied his hair back Japanese-style in a traditional ponytail and went to work.

• • •

"How's it going over there?" Lincoln lit up his second cigarette that hour.

"Like I said, it takes time." Irritated by the interruptions, Michio added, "You have to get through three levels of encryption. If you mess with the fourth level, it corrupts the data and renders it useless. We're talking about 256-bit military grade encryption here. Do you know what that means?"

Lincoln shrugged.

"It means its not as simple as they make it sound in your idolized movies. So shut the hell up and let me work."

Lincoln waved his hands in mock surrender. "Fine." He disappeared into the kitchen and emerged moments later with a beer in each hand. He set one down by Michio and then took a gulp of his. Leaning against a veranda post and hypnotized by the rhythm of the beating rain on the tin roof, he again surveyed the lush greenery surrounding the bungalow. Part of him envied his longstanding friend. *Michio has made a home for himself. Good for him.* But mostly Lincoln respected his former, full-time traveling companion. While they hadn't agreed on much, and a lot of water had recently passed under the bridge, the bond of a lifetime friendship was hard to break.

"Done!" Michio declared. Lincoln swung around and knelt beside him as he struck a key and several files appeared on screen, "Let's see what's in box number one," Michio said, opening the first file. A series of mathematical equations filled the screen—actually, hundreds of pages filled with mathematical equations of the highest order, quantum computations that looked more like hieroglyphs than mathematics.

Michio opened another file. This time, pages of complicated images and diagrams appeared, all intricately linked in another form unknown to him. "This is top shelf tech, way beyond my pay grade." He was about to remove the drive then stopped. "Maybe ..." He found the application he had created that searches for anomalies in code and ran the data on the drive. He punched more keys, and lines of code appeared. A smaller window opened at the bottom of the screen and filled with individual code lines. He scrolled through them, scanning line after line. "Whoa," he said, staring in surprise.

"Whoa. What does 'whoa' mean?"

"I've already counted twelve zero days and I haven't even finished yet."

"Zero days? What's a zero day?"

"Basically, it means that the software is vulnerable to hacking."

"You mean, what we just did?"

"No. We hacked *how* the program was encrypted. A zero day is a fault in the program. This code has at least a dozen zero days. The code was meant to be accessed at a later date."

Lincoln frowned. "For what?"

"My guess would be to corrupt it."

"So let me get this straight. The guys who developed this software designed it to be—destroyed?"

Michio sat back and considered what Lincoln had just said. "Yeah," he said, nodding slowly.

"Destroyed by who?"

Michio turned up his hands in an *I don't know* gesture and shrugged.

"Okay, we'll figure that out later," Lincoln said. "How about the files you opened earlier? Do any of them make sense?"

Michio shook his head. "Like I said, those equations are way over my head. We're talking Stephen Hawking-level physics—but I know someone who might help us."

"Who's that?"

"My old applied physics professor, Dr. Marcus Enheim. He used to work for all of them—JPL, Lockheed, MIT."

"Used to?"

"Let's just say Professor Enheim was asked to leave these establishments. He's, ah, a little bit—odd."

"You mean he was fired?"

"He was considered by some, ah, to be a little too, ah, eccentric."

"Eccentric. You mean crazy?"

"Let's just say he's a little outside the box."

"Whatever. Where do we find him?"

"Right here. Saipan. On the other side of the island."

"What's a professor in applied physics doing here?"

"When you piss off all of your peers and colleagues, word gets around. Sometimes you've gotta go where nobody knows your name. He moved here last year and took a job at Mariana College. Married some Russian Olympic athlete, or something like that."

"All right. Time to visit the professor," Lincoln said. "Have you got his number?"

"Are you kidding? The storm knocked out the landline service yesterday. Even when it works, it's intermittent. Besides, cell phone coverage on this island is next to nil. On a good day, we're lucky to get dial-up."

"Great. So we take a fourteen-mile hike— Hey, you've still got the Triumph, right?"

Michio wanted to get to the bottom of Sienna's death as much as Lincoln. He handed Lincoln the flash drive, locked the front door, and disappeared behind the bungalow, cursing himself for not keeping in touch with Sienna and hating that he hadn't known about her passing until now.

A deep rumble erupted from behind the cottage, and Michio reappeared straddling a Triumph Bonneville T120 motorcycle. He pulled up in front of the porch and patted the passenger seat. "Just get one thing straight, Monk. It isn't over between us."

"I get it."

Michio revved the bike.

"You don't have to do this," Lincoln said. "I can find him on my own."

Michio paused. "I loved her, too. Remember?"

5

The bike wound its way up the treacherous mountain road with Michio driving and Lincoln seated behind. They followed the twists and turns of the unlit roadway despite the torrential rain that made the slippery blacktop almost undriveable. Several times they stopped to remove fallen branches that blocked the road, slowing their progress to a crawl.

When they made it to the top of the mountain, Michio turned the bike into a darkened side street and pulled up before a set of large metal-spiked gates. The intercom was mounted next to the gate. On either side of the locked entry, a ten-foot-tall security wall receded in both directions.

"So this is where Enheim lives," Lincoln commented, taking in the sheer size of the wall.

"I didn't know professors made this type of money," Michio said.

"They don't. This can't be the home of an applied physics professor. This is an estate restricted to movie stars and millionaires who want their private lives to be just that—private. Is it possible we took a wrong turn somewhere back down the mountain? The downpour washed away large sections of road, and a signpost could have wa—"

"Who the hell is that?" a male voice barked from the intercom. Instantly Michio recognized the cockney accent.

"Professor Marcus Enheim?" Lincoln asked.

"I know my friggin' name! Now, *who the hell are you?*"

"My name is Lincoln Monk, and my companion is Michio Lee. We'd like to have a word with you, please, if we could."

26

"I told you guys in town and I'll tell you again now. I'm an atheist, so piss off."

"We're not here to talk about God," Lincoln said.

"Good, so piss off."

"Please, just a few minutes of your time. We would have called, but we couldn't get through because the telephone lines are down."

"The lines are always down on this damned island. Shit, you're lucky to get dial-up in the best of circumstances."

Michio caught Lincoln's eye and gave him a *told you so* look.

"Please, Professor, just a few minutes. We've driven across the island in the storm to see you, and we're soaked to the bone."

"I'm busy right now!" Enheim snapped. "Come back some other time—preferably when I'm not here."

"We have some questions about quantum mechanics and real world applications," Michio piped up.

The intercom went silent.

"Michio, Michio Lee," Michio continued. "I had the privilege of attending several of your lectures at MIT before you—left."

"Left. That's an interesting way of putting it." The intercom went silent again.

Moments later, the gates parted. Lincoln and Michio took that as an invitation and started the Triumph.

At the end of the long winding drive, they pulled up to the stately, two-storied home. Relieved to get off the bike, Michio stretched his legs while Lincoln wrung out his shirt front.

Two solid mahogany doors opened to reveal a middle-aged man holding a black pug. Athletically built and with a clean-shaven head and steely-eyed glare, Marcus Enheim appeared more like a hoodlum than a professor of physics. He wore jeans, and his tucked-in white shirt featured a smiley face with a bleeding bullet hole in its head. From Enheim's accent, Lincoln concluded that the professor had grown up in a tough working-class neighbourhood in England.

Michio extended his hand. "Professor Enheim. I'm so glad you've allowed us this time to talk."

Unsure of their intentions, Enheim eyed his new arrivals as he guardedly shook Michio's hand. "Well, what can I say? You sparked my friggin' interest."

Michio took the USB drive from his shirt pocket. "Professor, I guarantee that this is gonna knock your socks off."

"It better. I'm missing my soap operas because of it."

Michio laughed at the professor's joke.

"What's so friggin' funny?" Enheim said with a blank look.

Michio froze. How could he have known that the genius professor enjoyed soap operas?

Enheim glared at him, his gaze burning into Michio's brain.

Hastily Lincoln extended his hand—not to the professor, but to the pug in his arms. Gently Lincoln rubbed under the dog's jaw, and the dog moaned in approval.

"What's his name?" Lincoln asked, not taking his eyes from the dog.

"Napoleon. Usually he's aggressive toward people he doesn't know, but for some reason, he seems to like you."

Lincoln stopped caressing Napoleon and extended his hand to Enheim. "Lincoln Monk, and this is Michio Lee."

Enheim accepted his handshake and stroked his jaw, as if contemplating his next move.

Then he smiled and spoke in baby talk to the dog cradled in his arm. "What does Napums think, boy? Should we let them in?"

The dog barked twice—obviously code for approval.

Enheim smothered the dog with kisses. "Daddy can't say no to Napums, can he?" When he looked up at Lincoln and Michio, his smile died. His gruffness, glaring eyes, and colourful language returned. "All right you two, inside the friggin' house."

6

The trio—and Napoleon—sat in Enheim's living room. A sliding glass wall divided the living room from the outdoor entertainment area. The drawn floor-to-ceiling satin drapes revealed an Olympic-sized pool just beyond the al fresco dining area. Strategically positioned mall floodlights illuminated the back of the mansion, casting a soft white light through the driving rain.

In the living room opposite the glass wall, a collection of antique clay figures and pots, each carefully positioned, filled a glass display case that spanned the width of the wall. Framed pictures, mostly of Enheim and Napoleon, were interspersed among the artefacts. A few of the pictures depicted a beautiful blonde standing on different sports podiums or skiing down snow-capped mountains—rifle in hand.

One frame caught Lincoln's eye. Half-hidden behind a large picture of Enheim kissing Napoleon was a smaller picture of a thin blond man in his thirties wearing thick black glasses and smiling at the camera. The elegant frame seemed out of place among the large, garish frames.

The biggest television screen Lincoln had ever seen took up the entire wall opposite the sofa. Sure enough, a soap opera was playing—in full HD. Napoleon climbed onto the sofa and relaxed on the backrest, but kept a vigilant eye on the living room.

With effort, Enheim turned his gaze from his beloved pug to the visitors seated before him. "Okay, you have my attention. What's this all about?"

Michio held up the USB drive. "Do you have a computer?"

"Do I have a computer? Of course I have a friggin' computer!"

Enheim took the USB stick and rummaged among the stack of books and scattered candy wrappers on the glass side table. After a few moments, he turned toward the staircase and shouted, "Katya!"

"What?" From above Katya's voice sounded bored and dismissive. Then a gorgeous woman wearing the smallest black bikini Lincoln had ever seen sashayed down the stairs and into the living room. Her straight blonde hair flowed to her thighs, complementing her curvaceous suntanned body. Katya was strikingly athletic with taut muscles in all the right places—but still feminine in every way. She appeared to be in her early twenties. When she saw Michio and Lincoln, she ogled them with interest. "Who are you?" she asked.

Enheim continued his rummaging. "They're Lincoln and Mitch."

"Michio, not Mitch," Michio corrected.

"Katya, where's my pad?"

"Where you left it," she snapped.

"I left it on the damned side table, and it's not here."

"You didn't leave it on the damned side table," she mocked in a Georgian accent. "You left it on this coffee table under your girly magazines."

"Bullshit!" Enheim stabbed the side table with his index finger. "I put that pad right here less than an hour ago."

Katya passed in front of Michio and Lincoln and bent over the coffee table, displaying her perfectly tanned, near-naked ass. She retrieved the tablet from under a stack of magazines and handed it to Enheim.

"Lucky guess," Enheim growled. He slid the USB drive into the pad, unconcerned that his female companion was flaunting her body in front of strangers.

Katya looked from Lincoln to Michio and said, "So, you two are—how you say—gay?"

Lincoln held back a chuckle at her directness. "No, we're just old friends."

Delighted with Lincoln's answer, she clapped her hands and nodded. "This is good. What do you think of my breasts?"

"Not the tits thing again." Enheim had heard this conversation before. He sighed, but stayed focused on finding the channel linked to his pad.

"Yes. The tits thing again." She spat in indignation. "I work hard to keep them beautiful. All day I train. My body is my temple. You must always respect the temple." She turned to Lincoln and Michio. "What do you think?" Hands on hips, she tossed her hair back, thrust out her chest, and posed like a model on a catwalk.

"They are nice, aren't they?" Enheim asked distractedly, still adjusting the channels.

"Oh, very," Michio stammered, nodding in total agreement and unable to turn away from the beautiful breasts before him.

Lincoln casually averted his eyes. He wasn't a prude, but he felt uncomfortable and a little embarrassed by the direct question. He rubbed Napoleon under the chin, knowing that Katya was waiting for a compliment. "Spectacular," he said in a matter-of-fact tone.

"Yes." Katya nodded. "Spectacular. *Spectacular* is the correct word to describe my breasts." She shook her head disapprovingly at Enheim. "Not—*nice*."

Enheim found the channel he needed. A menu with a list of files appeared on the television screen. "Nice, spectacular—it all means the same," Enheim said dismissively.

"You are ignorant like pig in farm. You don't appreciate me. Screw you!" Katya stormed out of the room and stomped back upstairs. A door slammed shut.

"Don't be like that," he called after her. "Damn it, now I have to go upstairs and explain why I'm *like pig in farm* and why I don't appreciate her the way I'm supposed to friggin' appreciate her."

Enheim pressed a key on the pad and the television went blank. He flung the pad onto the coffee table and stood. "Family comes first. We'll do this tomorrow. You two seem like okay guys. You didn't ogle Katya the way most guys do when they get a free eyeful of nice tits. I respect that."

He removed the USB stick from the pad and slipped it into his pocket. Michio was about to protest when he saw Lincoln discreetly shake his head.

"You can't go back to town tonight," Enheim continued, gesturing toward the driving rain and lightning in the distance. "The guesthouse is out past the pool. I'll see you both for breakfast tomorrow. Have a good friggin' night." He headed upstairs, leaving Lincoln and Michio to themselves. Napoleon hurried down from the backrest, crossed the living room, and trotted up the stairs.

"That's a break. Trying to get back to town tonight in this weather would be suicidal. Still, he's very trusting, allowing us to stay here for the night. He doesn't even know us," Michio said.

"We showed our trust by giving him the drive. This is his way of returning the favor. But he is one crazy bastard." Lincoln grinned. "Crazy and spectacular."

7

Lincoln woke to sounds of birds chirping outside the bedroom window. His good night's sleep had refreshed him and he was ready to go. He put on the clothes he had worn the previous day, which were now dry, and left the guesthouse.

Sporadic dark clouds from the previous day's storm still loomed in the sky, but the rain had stopped and the sun's rays warmed the morning air. Michio was already outside, sitting at a small table overlooking the pool. A glass pot of percolating coffee sat in the centre of the table with a tray with cups next to it.

Lincoln pulled up a chair and inhaled the sweet aroma of the freshly brewed coffee. "Smells good." He poured himself a cup and sipped with enthusiasm, savoring the rich flavor. "One item on my bucket list is to have a coffee in every country on earth." Michio didn't respond. "Earth to Michio," Lincoln joked.

Michio grunted slightly indicating that he had heard Lincoln, but he kept his eyes on the pool.

Lincoln heard a splash and followed Michio's gaze. Katya was doing laps in the pool. He hadn't seen her when he left the guesthouse, so apparently she'd been swimming underwater. She emerged from the pool completely naked, her perfectly tanned skin glistening. As she removed the elastic and pulled her hair back from her face again to catch the loose ends, she saw the two men watching and smiled. She took her towel from the deck chair and strolled over, totally at ease with her nakedness.

"Hello, Lincoln and Mitch-o," she said, drying herself. "Would you like more coffee?" she asked, trying to be a good hostess.

"Bloody love some." The gruff male voice came from behind them. Enheim closed the glass partition that separated the house from the pool and joined them. He grabbed Katya around the waist, pulled her gently towards him, and kissed her on the cheek.

"You beast," she said, smiling in playful mock-disgust.

"You love it." He rubbed his unshaven face against her smooth, flawless cheek.

She slapped him half-heartedly, as she'd slapped him many times before. Then she finished drying herself and wrapped the towel around her body. She picked up the empty coffee pot and disappeared into the house. Evidently the rift between them had been resolved.

"So," Enheim said, clasping his hands and nodding toward the house, "when you two are finished pretending not to stare at Katya's girly bits, we need to see what's on that friggin' drive."

8

The windows' exterior shutters closed, darkening the room, and the downlights dimmed for viewing. Jonathan Kane sat on the edge of his stately desk, arms folded, waiting for the advertising commercial to appear on the giant monitor mounted to the wall. Next to him was his chief of security and right-hand man Leon Maxwell who occasionally glanced at the screen while cleaning his fingernails. Sophia, Neptune's publicist, stood beside them, her petite figure sheathed in a tailored pencil skirt and collarless blazer. Her shoulder length blonde hair partially covered her face and her oversized black-rimmed glasses did little to complement her beautiful features. She carried a notebook and by her side was a briefcase.

The advertisement showed a three-year-old African child living in squalor. The image faded to the same child, now aged ten, wearing a clean school uniform, then dissolved to a boy carrying a book into a classroom. Another fade to the image of a smiling young Kane standing next to a young Maxwell, both wearing graduation caps. In the next image, Kane stood on the deck of a research vessel wearing a flight suit and helmet. Behind him was a tilt-rotor Osprey resting on a helipad. The image faded to Kane, laptop in hand, seated at the bow of a rusted fishing trawler with Maxwell behind him studying the screen. A picture of the two men scuba diving Australia's Great Barrier Reef filled the screen, followed by an underwater shot of the two standing before deep-sea construction equipment in the foreground and a flat stretch of seabed in the background. The image dissolved into dozens of divers and submersibles gliding over acres of kelp being harvested from the sea floor. The picture faded to a mature Kane, now in his late thirties, sitting behind an executive desk in a plush office, with Maxwell standing faithfully behind him. Another fade showed Kane in the Oval Office shaking hands with the president of the United States. The image split to one of Kane giving out computer notebooks to small children from all over the world, followed by an image of him addressing the United Nations. The picture reverted to Kane standing before a sprawling building complex the size of a small city. This image faded to an aerial view of the complex and its surrounding acres of farmland. Next a montage featured people of all nations and races seated around tables dining on and enjoying delicious cuisine created from the spoils of the ocean floor. The montage was replaced by a map of the Earth with several countries marked with red dots to indicate the global reach of the Neptune empire. Finally, a blue rectangle standing on end with an orange trident in the center—the Neptune logo—filled the screen. NEPTUNE was emblazoned across the base of the trident's prongs, and beneath the logo, THE OCEAN—THE FUTURE. The advertisement finished and the Neptune logo screen-saver reappeared.

Kane broke the silence. "This is it?" he asked Sophia, clearly disappointed.

Hearing his dissatisfaction, Sophia hesitated. "Y-Yes," she said, pulling a small clipboard from her briefcase. "This is the transcript for the narration." She passed him a sheet of paper and waited. "We'll be adding the Morgan Freeman voice-over in the next few days," added, "but this is the final edit, Mr Kane. What do you think?"

When Kane finished reading the script, he glanced at the monitor and winced. "A bit cheesy, don't you think?"

"Sir, we've had nothing but positive feedback from all the test groups. The public loves the idea of a poor orphaned kid who pulls himself out of hopeless despair to become a world leader. People just eat up an underdog story."

Kane sighed. "Very well." He signed off on the transcript and handed it back to her. "Thank you, Sophia. That will be all."

Sophia picked up her briefcase, nodded, and left the office.

As soon as Sophia had closed the door, Maxwell said, "We need to talk. Eddie's becoming a problem."

"Again? What do you mean—a problem?"

"He's having difficulty with cohesion. Says he can't break it down in the time we've given him."

"He's had two years to solve the equations, and now he says he can't do it?"

"He's not saying he *can't* do it. He's saying he doesn't have enough time."

Kane exhaled. "That man tests my patience." He rubbed his hand over his face in frustration. "I've given him everything he wanted, and this is how he repays my generosity." He shook his head, tapping his fingers on the desk. "Encourage him."

Maxwell smiled. He always looked forward to encouraging people. "How much encouragement would you like me to use?"

"Our chief engineer needs to be alive and capable. A couple of bruises, nothing else. Make sure you don't go overboard. Just—inspire him."

Maxwell nodded. "Something else. Big John got away again."

Kane responded tersely. "Find him and teach him a lesson."

"We have another issue to deal with," Maxwell said, his voice tentative.

"Which is?"

"Someone off-island has accessed the data security algorithm. The protocol's been breached."

"Faraday?"

"I doubt it. Faraday didn't have clearance."

"Who then?" Kane demanded.

"We don't know yet."

"How did they get it?"

"I don't know. It's next to impossible to access the data from the outside. We operate on a closed system." He hesitated. "It's possible the breech may have originated from here, on the island."

"If one of my employees did this, I want to know who. Do you understand? I want whoever is guilty brought to my office."

"I understand," Maxwell said. "We triangulated the receiving end of the data before it was identified and switched off. How would you like to proceed?"

Kane glanced at the Neptune logo screensaver on the television monitor. His eyes glazed over as he pondered the near future and smiled. "All this secrecy will soon be at an end. We are on the edge of a new world that beckons us. Nobody will stop what is our destiny." He turned to Maxwell. "Deal with it."

Maxwell straightened his Armani suit and prepared to leave, but Kane stopped him. "Don't use Christina. I have other duties for her."

Maxwell nodded. Leaving the office with his back to Kane, he grinned at the reference to Christina and other duties.

A female voice, Kane's secretary, came through his headphone earpiece. "Mr Kane, I have Senator Wilson on the line. He wants to talk to you right away. He sounds very upset."

Spineless politicians. Kane shook his head in disgust. "Give me a minute then put him through," he said.

"Yes, Mr Kane."

Kane tapped a key on his pad. A deep grinding noise emanated from the vista window before him, and slowly the outer shutters opened. Soft blue light flooded the room, reflecting across the tile floor and pastel walls. The light rolled over the contours of his dark skin as he stood, transfixed, by the beauty of the ocean—and all it had to offer. He pondered the future of the human race.

"Kane?" A rough male voice sounded from the desk speaker.

"Ah, Senator Wilson. It's good to hear from you again. And how is your beautiful wife?"

"Cut the shit, Kane. We need to talk."

Despite continuing to admire the vista before him, Kane recognized the uncertainty in the senator's voice. "Senator, we're not getting cold feet now, are we?"

9

9:24 a.m.

The trio was again assembled in Enheim's living room. With the curtains pulled back, the balmy heat of the morning sun filled the room. Sunrays streaming through the glass wall cast a faint orange glow across the living area, giving the room a warm feeling of welcome and relaxation.

Enheim and Michio sat on the sofa. Lincoln stood to the left of the television screen. Napoleon climbed onto the couch's backrest and plonked himself down, prepared for the long haul. The USB stick, slotted into the pad, synchronized with the television and provided the onscreen information.

The screen filled with multiple split images of mathematical equations, diagrams, graphs, and charts. Below the charts were pages of mathematical formulae that looked more like alphabetical disarray than numeric unity.

Enheim delved into the equations, transfixed by the numbers and figures before him. "This is very friggin' fascinating. The equations appear to circumvent the decoherence quandary. They remain partially unanswered, but they do hold up." He nodded absently. "Whoever came up with this formula was definitely thinking outside the box. I like it."

Lincoln, completely lost, frowned, trying to make sense of it all.

Michio caught Lincoln's confused expression. "Professor Enheim," he said, "could you explain to Lincoln what this is all about before his brain explodes?"

Enheim's tone transformed to that of a teacher addressing a student. "It is important that you understand a few of the basics of physics before we proceed. So, we will start with Einstien."

Michio sat back, put his hands behind his head, and grinned. This was going to be good.

"Einstein's laws govern everything we can see. His laws govern orbits—the orbits of the planets, the stars, the motions of galaxies—pretty much everything in the known friggin' universe. However, Einstein's equations don't work at a molecular level, the level of atoms and sub-atomic particles. It's like trying to squeeze a square peg into a round hole. No matter how hard you try, it just isn't going to bloody fit. So while Einstein was getting hand jobs from every physics groupie on the planet, a bunch of other physicists, led by Niels Bohr, were trying to figure out why Einstein's theories didn't hold up at the molecular level.

"They came up with some ground-breaking conclusions. In experiment after friggin' experiment, they proved that molecular level atoms don't act the way they're supposed to. Atoms at that level do things that are so counter intuitive to human nature—and to Einstein's laws—that a whole other approach has to be applied. Thus, quantum mechanics was born."

From the professor's animated gestures, Michio could tell that Enheim was enjoying his lecture. He enjoyed seeing his professor back doing what he did best. Even now, he still found Enheim's style—his use of traditional teaching and foul language—to be a startling combination and educational tool that most students and some adults thoroughly enjoyed.

"Quantum mechanics really is screwed up, but it works—one hundred per cent of the time. We owe today's technological breakthroughs to our understanding of quantum mechanics.

"Richard Feynman was right when he said that if you think you know quantum physics, then you don't know it at all. Our understanding of the subject is still in its infancy. To comprehend quantum physics means sometimes having to forego logic and common sense, which some of my ex-colleagues—complete wankers without an ounce of bloody vision—fail to do."

"What's a wanker?" Michio asked.

Lincoln, familiar with the word having heard it a hundred times from Aussies and Brits he'd met in his travels, said, "We say jerk off."

Michio nodded, smiling at Enheim's gibe, while Enheim glared, annoyed at the interruption. Michio help up his hands apologetically. "Sorry, Professor."

Enheim continued with his lecture. "It's only when you start getting deep into the equations that you realize that the world and universe we live in doesn't play by our rules."

"I'm confused," Lincoln said." How can something that works be so screwed up at the same time?"

"I'm glad you friggin' asked," Enheim replied. "It all boils down to the dual properties of atoms. They can be physical matter, measurable in any lab around the world, or they can be a probability wave. Thanks to the double-slit experiment conducted decades ago, we can confirm with absolute certainty that one atom can be in multiple locations seen by the interference pattern produced by a wave—that is, until detected. Once detected it becomes the particle we can identify.

"This understanding of the complexity of the atom and its numerous locations while in a wave state means we can use its nature of multiplicity. Think of a computer. It's binary. At its core, it thinks in ones and zeros. But if you use the properties of the wave function and in addition to one and zero you introduce everything in between, then the computer's power becomes exponential. At this very moment, labs around the world are trying to harness this multiplicity. Once they do, our world will change. We'll have processors the size of a grain of sand making computations a million times faster than our computers could ever hope to friggin' achieve. This quantum computer breakthrough will make our world unrecognizable once the idea is fully realized. We're just not there yet."

Lincoln frowned. Wave functions. Probability waves. "I barely made it through high school, Professor, and up until a few minutes ago, a quantum computer was something Kirk and Spock used. I don't have your intellect and never will, so you need to sell me on the idea."

Enheim's face lit up at the Star Trek reference. "Spock was my high school nickname. None of the other wankers could even come close to my grades." Enheim reached into his pocket and pulled out his wallet. He removed a two-by-three photograph and showed it to Lincoln and Michio. It depicted Enheim as a red-headed, acne-covered teenage wearing the blue Star Trek uniform made famous by Spock. "Second prize that night for best costume," he boasted, returning the picture to his wallet.

"Who won?" Lincoln asked.

"Some asshole who thought he was Indiana friggin' Jones."

Katya, now wearing tiny bicycle shorts and a tank top, entered the living room carrying a silver serving tray. "Sorry for the interruption, boys, but my husband must have his customary morning snacks." She smiled at Enheim and placed the tray, filled with sandwiches cut into quarters the way a mother would do for a young child, and a jug of iced-tea and glasses, on the coffee table.

Enheim studied the sandwiches on the tray. "Cucumber?"

"Of course."

"My favorite." Enheim grinned and winked at Katya. "You're the best."

Katya was studying the equations on the television screen. Her eyes lit up. "Is this the mathematics for the stringy things?"

"No, this isn't String Theory. This is something else." Enheim tried to steer Katya away from the living room, knowing where her inquiries were leading. "Thanks for the sandwiches, love."

"Do they know about the stringy things?"

"I know about String Theory." Michio beamed with pride.

"What's String Theory?" Lincoln asked. Enheim groaned. He knew what was coming next.

"Marcus, tell Lincoln here about the stringy things and how they are the energy of the universe." She smiled at the two on the Sofa. "It is wonderful the way Marcus explains it. It is so elegant and beautiful."

"He doesn't want to know about String Theory."

"Katya does make it sound interesting," Lincoln admitted.

Enheim frowned at Katya, his steely-gaze locking with her pale blue eyes. "You've heard this a dozen times."

"I want to hear it again," she demanded.

They stared each other down until Enheim gave in with a grin. "You know I can't say no to you or Napums. All right, String Theory it is."

Katya clapped her hands with glee and sat on the sofa's armrest, eagerly awaiting her husband's lecture.

Enheim cleared his throat. "So, like I mentioned earlier, on one hand you have Einstein and the Theory of Relativity—aka gravity, and on the other hand you have Niels Bohr and quantum mechanics—aka electromagnetism or the strong nucleic force and the weak nucleic force. Now, Einstein couldn't accept the fact that two completely different forms of mathematics describe the universe. It was messy. One theory should encompass everything. So, he spent the next thirty years searching for one theory, a theory that would unify the two. They called this Unification. Einstein died in 1956 without ever attainting that goal."

"The poor fuzzy-haired man," Katya said, nodding in sympathy.

"In the 1960s, a physicist accidently discovered mathematical papers written two hundred years earlier that seemed to describe one of the fundamental forces of physics. By 1984, after having overcome a few hurdles along the way coupled with the ground-breaking work of Leonard Susskind and other physicists, the mathematics was proved to be correct. The equations described quantum physics and gravity in one beautiful theory. Thus, the Theory of Everything was born, which later was called String Theory. Actually, it's known as M Theory. When everybody jumped on the bandwagon they discovered that there were five different versions of string theory. Then in 1995 Ed Witten, a renowned physicist who has been compared to a latter-day Einstein, shook the physics community by combining all five versions into one elegant theory. But I'll concede that most people know it as string theory.

"What they discovered was that all atoms—everything in the universe—is made up of tiny strands of energy, vibrating at different wavelengths. It's these wavelengths and variations in the vibrations that create the different atoms that we see. Think of the universe as a grand orchestra with these strings of energy playing the beautiful music of reality. We, too, are made of atoms, so that music of life is playing inside our very own existence. At our core, we humans are pure energy in the universe and are bound together as one."

Katya, her expression filled with delight, turned to Lincoln and Michio. "We are all energy. It's so spiritual and such a beautiful explanation of life."

Michio nodded while Lincoln grappled with Enheim's last statement. "Wow. And you say they can prove all this?"

"Well … " Enheim hesitated. "Yes and no. String theory can be proved mathematically, but it has two major flaws. First, for string theory to work there must be at least ten dimensions. We live in a world of three dimensions and time, so there are at least another six dimensions that we are unable to see or detect. And second, string theory can't be proven in a laboratory. Science is based on observation and experimentation, neither of which can be applied to string theory. The strings are literally billions of times smaller than any atom, so we may never know for sure. Until we overcome these two hurdles, we must concede that even though the math directs us toward string theory, reality doesn't. Therefore we must ask ourselves—is string theory science or is it philosophy?"

"I don't care what they say. I believe in the stringy things." Katya stood up. "Thank you, Marcus, for making science beautiful. If anybody needs anything, I'll be in our room. " She stroked Napoleon across the brow, blew a kiss to Enheim and disappeared up the stairs.

Glad that the distraction was over, Enheim chopped down on a sandwich. He recollected an image from the display and turned to the screen, searching for the drawing. He grabbed his pad and flicked through schematics as they flashed by on the television screen. He paused on one particular page and focused on the graphics display. The image appeared to be a device of some sort, but the diagram was incredibly complicated with measurements and equations. "Well, I'll be a monkey's uncle," Enheim whispered, still chewing on the sandwich.

"What is it?" Picking up on the professor's hushed tone, Lincoln peered at the screen and strained to make sense of the information.

"Forget what I said earlier about a fully functioning quantum computer being unrealized. It appears the problems with decoherence and isolation have been mostly rectified." Enheim rose, gazing at the screen, unable to believe what the diagram represented.

Lincoln finally spoke. "Okay, is someone going to tell me what we're looking at here?"

"What we're looking at," Enheim said, still entranced by the visuals, "are the schematics for a fully-functioning quantum computer."

"Whoa!" Michio gasped.

"No shit, whoa." Enheim tried to determine the size of the device pictured on the television screen, but nothing indicated scale. He was studying the algorithms displayed across the screen when music from upstairs filtered down to the ground floor. "Dancing Queen," the classic Abba tune, filled the living room. Katya was turning the volume up higher and the thumping beat reverberated around the men.

Enheim groaned. "For chrissake, Katya," he yelled to the upper level, "turn it down!"

The music continued. Annoyed, Enheim turned to Lincoln and Michio. "I love her. I really do. I'd die for her—but sometimes …" his voice trailed off as he made the strangle gesture with his hands. He took a slow deep breath and exhaled. "Katya, please, turn the friggin' music down!" he shouted to the upstairs again."

Still no reply as the music played on.

"Katya! We're trying to concentrate down here!" Sensing his master's sudden mood change, Napoleon ducked his head between his paws.

Katya began singing along with the song. Her accented voice mixed with the classic rhythm as the beat pulsed about the room. Unable to hold a tune, her untrained singing made the melody less than enjoyable.

Exasperated, Enheim wiped the perspiration from his face. "Damn it."

"How about if I go upstairs and ask Katya to turn the music down?" Lincoln offered, shouting above the blaring pop song.

Enheim shook his head and indicated the equations on the television. "No. I don't want anything else to break my train of thought. I'll sort this out from here." He snatched his cell phone from the coffee table, tapped the screen and waited for a reply.

Lincoln glanced at Michio as the seconds ticked by. They wondered what the outcome would be if Katya failed to pick up her phone.

"Katya!" Enheim shouted into his phone. "We're trying to work down here. Turn the friggin' music down … I know you have to train … I know you're training hard for the Olympics, but I'm asking you to turn the music down for just a little while … No, they don't want to hear Abba right now, and neither do I. We're all trying to friggin' concentrate, but we can't because you're playing the music too friggin' loud. Just turn it down, will you?"

The music's volume turned down a few notches, and Enheim sighed with satisfaction.

Lincoln and Michio couldn't hear Katya's end of the conversation, but they watched Enheim nodding to his cell phone. Reluctantly he turned to them, his voice strained. "Katya wants to know if you would like to listen to *Ace of Base*, *The Village People* or *The Beach Boys?*" he said, shaking his head *no* at them.

"*The Beach Boys* sounds good," Lincoln said, nodding in appreciation. Enheim's steely-eyed glare zeroed in on Lincoln alone. "But, maybe next time."

"Katya, our guests need to help me but thanks for asking … Yes, you're the perfect host." He cupped his hand around the phone and turned away from Lincoln and Michio. "You know I do," he whispered. "I don't have to say it … fine … Yes, I love you, too … goodbye … Napoleon loves you, too … By the way, great sandwiches. Okay, bye." He dropped the phone on the table and turned back to the screen. "Where was I?" he fumed, frustrated at the interruption.

"You were talking about a fully functional quantum computer," Lincoln recalled.

"That's right. Aside from the partial equation, what we have here is real-world quantum computing. The practical applications of this technology are mind-blowing. If this technology is introduced to the population, the world will change overnight. This is turning out to be one great friggin' day." Then it hit him like a ton of bricks. "The patent for this information is worth billions." Contemplating the implications of the technology, he placed the pad on the coffee table. "Where did you get this?"

"Our friend was murdered because of it," Lincoln said.

"Well, don't look at me," Enheim joked. "I've been in this house for the last month. Katya and her nice tits will vouch for that."

"We don't suspect you, Professor. We want to know if you recognize the work." Michio pointed to the equations on the television screen. "A name, perhaps?"

Enheim scrolled through the charts displayed on the screen, this time looking for telltale signs of peer-produced work.

A map of the eastern seaboard of the United States flashed past, with areas down the coastline highlighted in red. Beside the image was another map depicting what looked to be an island chain near the coast of Spain.

Lincoln's curiosity got the better of him. "What's this?"

Enheim's tone was sardonic as he continued to scroll through the pages. "I don't know. Maybe someone's opening a chain of seafood restaurants."

A combination of work written on paper and photographed, and work typed on the computer, appeared on the screen.

Enheim studied the image. Using his thumb and forefinger, he magnified the picture on his pad and scrolled down, settling on a small piece of writing at the bottom of the screen: Edward Ramirez, Chief Science Officer. "That'll be friggin' right." Enheim's tone was disapproving. "Looks like Ramirez whored himself out to the highest bidder. I should have known that asshole would have something to do with this."

"You know him?" Lincoln asked.

"Oh, I know him all right. Asshole owes me five hundred bucks."

"Let's go pay this Eddie Ramirez a visit, then." Lincoln stood, ready to go.

Enheim and Michio glanced at one another. "There's one problem," Michio said.

"What's that?" Lincoln asked.

"No one knows where he is. He disappeared from the face of the earth two years ago."

"I know where he is," Enheim said. "On a project of this magnitude you don't advertise that you've developed technology that might result in some heavy hitter losing his livelihood. Word gets out and you could find yourself stopping a bullet with your friggin' head. I've been involved with projects like this in the past, and—believe me when I say this—those running the operation will stop at nothing to keep their secrets. Lives depend on it, literally. This includes non-disclosure and secrecy contracts. The whole damned shebang."

"So how do you know where he is?"

Enheim scrolled back to a previous document. Partially visible at the bottom right corner of the document was a stamp with a trident logo.

Lincoln recognised the symbol instantly, as did anyone who hadn't been in a coma for the past year. "He works for Neptune? For billionaire Jonathan Kane? How can you be sure?"

"Of course," Michio said slowly, putting the pieces together. "That makes sense."

"What makes sense?"

Enheim aimed his gibe and pointed thumb at Lincoln, but spoke to Michio. "Not too bright, is he?"

"He just got back here on the island. He wouldn't know." Michio turned to Lincoln. "For the last two years, the Neptune Corporation has been secretly constructing something big over on Agrihan Island— so big, that according to the news reports and sound bites, it's going to blow everyone's mind. The buzz is extraordinary. Jonathan Kane is supposedly going to make some big revelation tonight on the Larry Jones Show."

"Any clues as to what he's building?" Lincoln asked.

"No one has any idea. You can't even get onto the island. Security is unbelievable. Rumor says there's a small army over there. The air space around the island is a no fly zone for three miles in all directions, and they've implemented an electronic communications blackout—no exceptions. Even Google Earth has the entire area blurred.

"A journalist from the New York Times decided to fly over the island—you know, to get a sneak peek. The guy was nearly blown out the sky. They found bullet holes in the plane's left wing. It was a miracle he survived. The hype was getting so crazy that even the White

House tried to get a private inspection for the president, but Kane told them politely to go screw themselves."

Enheim grinned. "I think I like this Kane guy."

"When they interviewed Kane later about the incident, Kane's response was 'The world will get to see this project as a community, as—'"

"Wait a minute," Lincoln said. "There's nothing on Agrihan Island. It's basically a dormant volcano surrounded by jungle."

"It's not called Agrihan Island anymore," Michio said. "Kane bought the island from the governing body of the Mariana Islands and renamed it."

"And they sold it, just like that?"

"Forbes' top-ten richest list. Money talks, and a man that rich could buy an entire country."

"All right, so what did he rename it?"

"The name sounds really cool," Michio said. "Neptune Island."

Napoleon's ears pricked up. He jumped to his feet and faced the glass wall, growling.

10

9:43 a.m.

They heard and felt the distant rhythmic thumping, followed by minor vibrations that made the house tremble. "Brickman, you bloody pervert!" Enheim cursed. He stood before the sliding glass wall, peering beyond the pool and guesthouse, searching for the cause of the thumping. "Brickman lives down near the bay, but he thinks he can fly over whenever he wants to look at Katya's tits."

The thumping was getting louder, and the growing vibrations shook the house to its foundations. A black Eurocopter EC120 materialized over the surrounding tree line like a coiled cobra raising its head to strike. The blast from the turbine rotary engine combined with the thrum of its rotating blades was deafening as the craft angled above the trees and maneuvered into position over the pool.

"Brickman, you asshole!" Enheim yelled, waving his fist at the helicopter. "There are no tits to see here today, so piss off!"

The helicopter hovered above the pool. The downdraft from its rotor blades sent a cloud of swirling vapor into the air. Pummelled by the gale force of the rotor blades, the table setting flew across the patio and shattered against the side of the house. The craft banked slightly, then angled its nose directly toward the glass wall.

Through the cloud of water engulfing the Eurocopter, Lincoln spotted an attachment mounted on its right landing skid—an M134 mini-gun. Its rotating six-barrelled titanium housing glistened through the haze.

Enheim stared at the gun. "Brickman?" he wondered aloud.

"That's not Brickman," Lincoln yelled over the din. "Everyone down!"

Knowing Lincoln's uncanny instinct for survival, Michio didn't hesitate. He grabbed Enheim and dove for cover.

Lincoln scooped up Napoleon from the couch and snatched Enheim's notebook from the table. He leaped over the sofa, using it as a barrier between them and the chopper. The mini-gun, capable of two thousand rounds a minute, opened fire. 7.62 millimeter tracer rounds tore into the side of the house.

The glass wall erupted into the living room, shattering into a thousand shards of lethal glass that covered the entire space. The men flattened themselves against the floor to avoid the bullets screaming overhead. Tracer rounds streaked through the room like short laser beams, striking the adjacent wall and shattering Enheim's collection of priceless antiques and photo frames. The glass shelving exploded as the tracer rounds obliterated everything in their path.

The helicopter rocked from side to side, performing a sweeping motion with the mini- gun. Hundreds of rounds swept across the wall-sized television shattering its LCD screen before it crashed to the bullet-riddled parquet floor. The matching glass side tables splintered as the hot metal rounds shot through them. The white leather sofa was ripped to shreds as fragments of upholstery, leather, and stuffing catapulted into the air before fluttering to the ground. The room looked like a scene from a Quentin Tarantino film—flying bullets, mass confusion, and above all, total destruction.

"Katya!" Enheim yelled to the top floor.

No answer.

Lincoln instinctively covered Napoleon's head as the bullets whistled by, inches away. With his other hand, he ripped the USB drive from the notebook and shoved it into his pocket. Michio dragged Enheim behind a large cabinet full of books, seconds before a wave of bullets tore paperbacks apart.

Then, the copter did something unexpected. Seemingly out of control, the chopper swung around on its axis—but kept on firing! As the chopper continued to spin, the backyard was bathed in bullets, annihilating everything in the chopper's path. To the right of the residence, the privacy wall took a full barrage of gunfire as the Gatlin continued its deadly strafing. A horizontal line of bullets ripped into the façade of the guesthouse, shattering it into thousands of pieces of brick and masonry. The chopper dipped slightly, but the gun sustained its unrelenting torrent of gunfire. Bullets tore into the garden's centrepiece, a grouping of perfectly trimmed rose bushes, and cut them to shreds. As the unremitting strafing continued, the garden became a churning mix of leaves, flowers, and dirt catapulted into the air. Without warning, the chopper's spiraling slowed, and the copter swung back a complete three-sixty to its original position facing the house.

Inside the chopper, the pilot clutched his blood-soaked shirt. "Shit," he blurted through his headset to the hooded passenger in the bay behind him. "I've been hit!"

The hooded gunner in the passenger cabin clipped on a safety harness and hooked it to a ring above the rear door. "Shut up and just keep it steady," he shouted into his headset over the roar of the engines. He flipped open the long metal case beside him.

The gunfire stopped.

Lincoln peeked over the sofa at the attacking Eurocopter now hovering above the pool. He noted five small holes perfectly grouped, in the helicopter's windscreen.

The chopper's side door slid open, and the masked gunman emerged. He maneuvered into position, and prepared to fire a grenade launcher.

"Oh, shit," Lincoln groaned. He surveyed the living area and spotted an adjoining room, its wall between them and the chopper. "Follow me," he shouted as he tucked Napoleon deeper into his chest. He crawled over to the next room, with Michio and Enheim close behind.

"Who the hell are these assholes?" Enheim yelled.

"It's the USB drive. The owners want it back."

The gunman raised the six-chambered ICS-190 grenade launcher to his shoulder, took aim, and fired. The living room erupted in a ball of flame and billowing smoke, destroying what was left of the interior design layout. The hooded gunman fired again. This time the kitchen wall, also facing the backyard, exploded outwards, showering the courtyard with shards of brick and debris.

Lincoln, Enheim, and Michio scrambled into the adjoining room behind the kitchen where a billiards table took center stage. A hallway leading to the stairs ran adjacent to the room. They scampered behind the table as the gunman launched another grenade. The wall exploded inward, spraying large chunks of concrete in all directions. A section of the wall collapsed onto the billiards table, crushing it beyond repair. Lincoln choked as acrid smoke and the smell of cordite filled the room.

Lincoln jerked his head in the direction of the staircase. Enheim and Michio darted upstairs with Lincoln following. As they ran into the nearest room, another explosion rocked the mansion.

The back garden and entertainment area looked like a war zone. The guesthouse was destroyed, the privacy walls resembled Swiss cheese, and what was left of the mansion looked more like a building still under construction than an established home. Black smoke billowed from the remains of the lower level, and small segments of the walls were starting to crumble.

The gunman, satisfied with his demolition of the ground level, reloaded the grenade launcher and turned his attention to the second story. Lincoln, Enheim, and Michio heard the window in the next room shatter as the gunman continued his relentless barrage. The dividing wall exploded onto them, showering them with plaster and brick. A lump of brick struck Lincoln in the face. Excruciating pain shot through him as blood seeped from his left cheek. He willed himself to ignore the hurt and search for an alternate escape. Another explosion left a gaping hole where the stairs had been, cutting off any possibility of retreat. Napoleon whimpered, and Lincoln held him tighter.

"Go to the next room!" Lincoln shouted. They made a dash for the master bedroom—and stopped cold. Katya stood feet apart, knees bent at the window, her Anschütz 9003 rim-fire rifle cradled in her arm, firing at the attacking helicopter.

Enheim saw Lincoln and Michio exchange quizzical glances. Over the din of another explosion he yelled, "Katya's in training for the Olympics. The Biathlon. You know—skiing and shooting!" He took shelter next to Katya.

Lincoln nodded. "Any more?" he yelled to Katya over the gunfire, indicating the rifle butted up against her shoulder.

She thumbed in the direction of her walk-in closet. "Behind the evening dresses," she said casually, continuing to return fire at the chopper.

Lincoln threw a Sig Sauer pistol to Michio and drove a magazine into a Beretta 265. He reached into his pocket and tossed the USB drive to Michio. "It's safer with you," he said, indicating his standard jeans' pockets. Michio nodded and dropped the drive into a small pouch in his cargo pants, then buttoned the flap.

Lincoln passed Napoleon to Enheim who stroked the pug's head reassuringly as the dog snuggled in his arms. Lincoln noted Enheim hadn't asked for a gun. "Can you shoot?" Lincoln shouted over the gunfire.

"I'm a lover, not a fighter," Enheim said, caressing Napoleon.

Katya rolled her eyes.

Lincoln cocked the Beretta. "Fine. Stay down."

"Don't have to tell me twice." Enheim crouched next to Katya. She paused to pat Napoleon's head before turning back to the shattered window. Lincoln and Michio joined Katya at the window and returned fire. They all knew they were running out of rooms to hide.

The men in the chopper were systematically eliminating their target room by room, destroying everything and leaving nothing to chance. The gunman launched the last of the grenades and threw the launcher to the floor. "Use the gun," he shouted to the pilot. The pilot nodded and readied the Gatlin.

The explosions ceased, only to be replaced by the deafening sound of hundreds of rounds hitting the exterior of the bedroom. The entire wall, facing the backyard, shuddered as the bullets ripped into it. As the glass window shattered, they all dove for cover.

Lincoln shouted to Enheim over the din of gunfire. "Do you have a car?"

"Of course I have a car. It's in the garage."

Katya glared at Enheim. "My car, not yours."

"Okay, fine. Your car."

54

Lincoln recalled the downstairs layout of the mansion. "That's below us, right?"

Enheim nodded.

"Is there another way to get to it without going down those stairs?"

Enheim thought for a moment then shook his head.

"Yes, yes!" Katya shouted over the bullets. She turned to Enheim and shook her head, yelling, "Do I have to do everything?"

Enheim held his hands palms up and shrugged in an *I don't know what you're talking* about gesture.

"The laundry slide," she blurted. "The opening is at the end of the hall and it goes straight down into the laundry next to the garage."

"Yeah, that's right." Enheim nodded. "Well done, Katya. Good thinking!"

"Someone in this family has to," she replied, firing back at the chopper.

Explosions tore into the rooms above as they scrambled out of the laundry.

"Wait!" Enheim grabbed a small harness from the laundry counter and fitted it to his chest. Carefully he placed Napoleon in the pouch and tightened the harness around him. Once he was certain that Napoleon was snug and secure, he gave the group a thumbs up.

As they followed Lincoln into the garage, the entire roof shook causing small wisps of dust to float down into the laundry. The four-car garage was ultra-stylish with framed pictures of Bugatti Veyrons, Aston Martins, Lamborghini Reventons, and other sleek sports cars mounted around the walls. However, only one car occupied the garage today. It was not sleek, and it certainly wasn't a sports car.

In the center of the garage was Katya's 70s style white Volkswagen Kombi van. Having clearly been in several accidents, the van had seen better days. In addition, the passenger door was dented, rust dotted the exterior, and the tires looked bald.

Lincoln was incredulous. He turned to Enheim and Katya. "Really?"

The garage door burst outward and the van tore through—in reverse.

Michio swung the van around and lined it up with the narrow driveway to the road. Enheim and Napoleon sat in the passenger seat while Katya and Lincoln took aim, guns ready, in the back seat.

Michio jammed the gear shift into drive. The tires screeched in disapproval as he gunned the van down the driveway. He smashed through the wrought iron security gates and skidded onto the main road.

The gunman in the chopper spotted the van as it raced down the storm-weathered street. He leaned over to the pilot and pointed at the escaping vehicle. The pilot nodded, still nursing his wound with a bloodied hand.

The chopper lifted up and over the mansion and took off after them. The throbbing vibration from the chopper's engines and the pulsating downdraft from the rotors was enough to destabilize the damaged house. The roof caved in, flattening the second story beneath it. Chunks of concrete fell from the portico and crushed Michio's Triumph, burying it under rubble and brickwork. Seconds later, the complete left hand side of the mansion collapsed, sending a black cloud of dust and dirt into the air.

11

9:50 a.m.

The van swerved around a clump of palm fronds lying across the road, courtesy of the previous night's storm. As the van slid off the blacktop and onto the shoulder, the front tires spun wildly on the sand. Michio corrected with a hard right, and the van bounced back onto the road again.

Enheim's mansion, like most of the expensive housing on the island, was located at the crest of the hillside, and visibility was good on the downward slope. Michio took advantage and drove as fast as he dared down the incline. Branches and small trees littered the road, preventing any chance of a quick getaway.

Without warning, a line of tracer bullets strafed the tarmac to their left and showered the van with chunks of road and dirt. Michio veered to the right, only to cop another strafing run seconds later. This time, the van's right side windows exploded, covering them with shards of glass.

"Everyone all right?" Lincoln asked, removing broken glass for his face and body.

Katya gave him a thumbs up as she picked small pieces of upholstery from her hair.

"Still here," Michio said.

Enheim made sure Napoleon was okay, then checked that his crotch was still in working order. "All accounted for."

The Volkswagen van veered down the winding road with the chopper in hot pursuit. Bullets ripped into the panel of the van's rear end and showered Lincoln and Katya with more glass. Trying to avoid the deadly onslaught, Michio swerved again, but a stray round struck the van's rear-mounted engine. Black smoke streamed from the engine cowling.

Lincoln and Katya fired back, but the swaying of the van made it impossible to aim, so most of their return fire missed its mark. On the right, the mountainside towered above them. On the left was a deadly drop into the ocean. Their only option was forward.

The chopper banked out over the cliff's edge and swung around. Its nose lined up directly with the side of the speeding van and opened fire again. As the strafing followed the van down the roadway, the mountain face behind the van erupted in a blast of rock and dirt.

The helicopter slowed, then swung back behind them and took aim. The pilot raised the chopper and lined the Gatling level with the back of the van. The whirring grew louder and louder as the barrels on the gun began rotating at 900 revolutions a minute.

"Everyone down!" Lincoln yelled, grabbing Katya and throwing her to the floor.

Enheim didn't need to be told twice. He bent, careful not to crush Napoleon. Michio ducked low.

The chopper edged closer, its nose just a few feet from the back of the van. With the blades rotating directly over the vehicle, the thumping was deafening. The backwash from the blades churned the air within the van into a maelstrom of mayhem as it pummelled the occupants. The wind whipped about them at tornado speeds, and Lincoln was momentarily blinded from flying debris.

The pilot held his bloodied hand to his blood-soaked shirt, smiled, and pulled the trigger.

Nothing.

The barrels on the Gatling rotated, but the gun did not fire.

Lincoln raised his head and peeked through the shattered back panel of the van. The chopper was still there, looming behind them like a giant black vulture ready to feed, but the gunfire never happened.

"Shit," the pilot muttered. He turned to the gunman behind him. "Empty," he yelled.

The gunman swore under his breath and pulled a Sig Sauer pistol from his shoulder holster.

Michio threw caution to the wind and gunned the van for all its torque. From this sudden abuse of power, the van fishtailed and skidded off the road into the runoff. Spinning around, the backend slid toward the cliff's edge where the soft ground caused the tires to lose traction. As the back end swung into nothingness, the rear wheels spun wildly in the air.

Eyes wide with terror, Enheim stared through his window at the abyss below.

The front tires gripped. The van turned sharply and veered back onto the roadway. "Sorry!" Michio yelled.

The van was barrelling down the blacktop, snaking in and out of fallen debris, when Michio spotted the chasm—a fifteen-foot wide gap spanning the roadway. "Lincoln! We got problems. The storm washed out a chunk of road."

Lincoln peered through the dirt-stained windshield at the gaping hole in the road. *No way around, can't go back. Shit! No, there's always a solution, always a way out. Think. This stretch of road is on the downward slope, so the other side of the chasm is lower than this side. This side could act as a crude ramp.*

"Hammer it!" Lincoln shouted.

Michio slammed his foot to the pedal and shoved the van into top gear. The back wheels spun on the slippery road, then the van took off at top speed.

Enheim stared in disbelief as the van bee-lined for the gaping hole. "You're friggin' kidding me," he muttered to no one in particular, covering Napoleon's eyes.

"Hang on," Michio yelled.

Lincoln and Katya braced themselves against the van's side panelling while Enheim jerked his seatbelt even tighter.

The van ploughed through a pile of palm fronds at the edge of the chasm and launched into the air, arcing over the yawning crevasse and landing to the screech of metal as the undercarriage scraped the asphalt. The back end of the muffler broke from its mounts and dropped, sending up a shower of sparks as the van sped away.

"Lucky bastards," the gunman yelled above the din of the chopper's turbine as he watched the van leap over the gap.

The pilot slowed the chopper as the van disappeared under a canopy of trees overhanging the roadway. Hidden by the foliage, the road snaked around and behind the mountainside, and the gunman and pilot lost sight of their quarry. The pilot yanked hard right. The chopper banked toward a visible section of highway a mile ahead. The rotor wash crushed the undergrowth as the helicopter roared low over the jungle flora, whipping up leaves and loose groundcover and leaving a swirling cloud in its wake.

A short distance down the mountain, the van emerged from its leafy cover. The only sounds were from the creaking of the van's cab and from its overworked four-cylinder motor. Lincoln peered through the shattered window and scanned the surroundings for any sign of the chopper. Despite the silence, he kept his pistol raised, ready for the next onslaught.

Without warning the helicopter loomed over the hillside behind them and roared overhead. The chopper continued for a hundred feet, then banked and hovered before them, blocking their escape like a giant black wasp targeting its prey.

The little van's engine spluttered. There was nowhere to go.

The gunman raised his pistol and smiled. Like shooting fish in a barrel, he thought, pleased at the turn of events.

Lincoln calculated the distance between the van and the chopper, taking into account the slippery road. "Remember Thailand?" he asked Michio, grinning.

"Oh, yeah," Michio grinned back.

"What about Thailand?" Enheim asked nervously.

Michio tightened his grip on the steering wheel. "Hang on, everyone. We're going for a ride!"

Enheim braced himself against the dashboard, eyes still wide with fear, while Lincoln and Katya steadied themselves in the back seat.

"When I say now," Lincoln said to Katya, "let it rip." She nodded and took aim.

Michio yanked the wheel hard right and slammed his foot on the brakes. The van lurched to the right. The back end swung around and Lincoln threw open the sliding door yelling, "Now!"

Lincoln and Katya opened fire with the van sliding sideways down the road.

The chopper's windshield spider-webbed with cracks and holes as a dozen bullets pierced it, peppering the pilot's already injured body. A bloody mist covered the windshield as he slumped over the stick—dead.

The van screeched to a stop, a short distance from the hovering chopper.

Now out-of-control, the chopper banked hard. With its nose down and backend swinging wildly, it began tilting on its axis until the right side angled toward the ground and the gunman lost his footing. He flailed about, grabbing for anything, but fell backwards through the open door, sheer terror on his face.

He landed with a sickening crack as his legs broke beneath him, twisting out at awkward angles. He screamed, oblivious to the out-of-control chopper overhead.

The chopper continued to fall until the spinning rotor blades ripped into the tarmac, sending sparks and chunks of asphalt into the air. The chopper's cabin crumpled, enveloping the gunman in a sea of twisted metal and spinning rotor blades that shredded his body in a spray of blood and bone. The fuel tank ruptured, and the chopper erupted into a ball of red-hot flame and billowing black smoke. As the collapsed mess of warped metal burned in front of them, they breathed a collective sigh of relief.

The van spluttered violently and jerked to a halt. Michio wiped the sweat from his eyes and focused on the dashboard gauges. He turned to the others. "Out of gas."

12

"Tell me again why we have to do this," Enheim said. They were pushing the van toward the cliff's edge.

"Whoever's chasing us may not know who we are yet," Lincoln said. "We have to cover our tracks."

Lincoln strained against the back of the van as the front wheels caught in the loose sand on the road's shoulder. He made his way to the front and turned the steering wheel back and forth. Eventually, the tires created a gap around themselves. After a few more tries, the van worked itself free from the boggy sand and rolled to a stop, inches from the cliff. They all gazed over the edge at the rolling waves below.

Katya took one last look at her trusty van, then nodded to Lincoln.

They watched the van disappear over the cliff and tumble, end over end, down the rocky face. The wreckage crashed into the waves, then slowly sank out of sight.

They made their way into the coverage of the hillside and headed for the township. Katya jogged out front while Enheim followed, still carrying Napoleon. Lincoln and Michio lagged behind. The palms and local flora offered a respectable cover from another airborne attack, so Lincoln was confident they had at least a few hours reprieve.

Under these high-stake circumstances, Lincoln knew that their trek on foot would help hide their movements, which was critical since their adversaries—people who didn't hesitate to order shooting up a residential home—could have easy-access to more sophisticated equipment like satellites. He recalled a magazine article that cited more than one thousand active satellites currently circling the globe and looking down on Mother Earth for all sorts of reasons: environmental, militaristic, logistic, intelligence, communication. In low Earth orbit six hundred kilometers up, Worldview Three, one of the most sophisticated cameras ever built, could take a clear picture of a golf ball—and identify the logo. Satellites could track heat signatures with ease, but, ironically, tracking four bodies hiking through a steaming tropical jungle at midday was next to impossible.

Michio turned to Enheim. "How's Katya holding up? She doesn't seem bothered, but she could be suffering from post-traumatic stress disorder or something similar."

"I'm okay, Mitch-o. Thank you." Katya glared at Enheim for not having asked first.

"Katya's fine," Enheim said. "She's Georgian, remember? Over there, people get shot every day. You walk down the street, and some wanker tries to shoot at you. It's no big deal."

"And you?"

"Are you kidding? I'm from East London. We invented tough."

"So, Lincoln, what happens now?" Michio asked.

"We don't want the police getting in—"

"Police?" Enheim interrupted. "On this island? Are you serious?"

Lincoln shrugged.

"Out here, real law doesn't exist. Justice depends on the size of the bribe, and believe me, nobody out here will say shit—or more accurately, no one out here gives a shit. Everyone keeps to himself and that's how we like it. That's why we're on this island in the first place—privacy."

Reluctantly, Michio agreed.

"We could call in the Feds," Lincoln said. "The Northern Mariana Islands is a commonwealth of the United States."

"Are you kidding?" Enheim said. "Do you really think the feds are gonna care about a few bullets in the side of a house? They have bigger fish to fry in the Middle East. Which means we're on our own."

"My brother Roland could help," Katya said.

At the mention of Roland, Enheim glared, not even trying to hide his disapproval.

Lincoln and Michio noted the animosity the mere mention of this relative provoked, but Lincoln decided to let it go. "So we're at loose ends," he concluded. "This means, they'll be back—and soon. Looks like we're all in it up to our eyeballs, whether we like it or not."

"Good! I want to find the asshole that gave the order to fire that friggin' Gatling at Napoleon, Katya, and me—and stick one up his bloody arse." Enheim turned to Napoleon "Daddy will find that bad man and stick it up his arse, won't he, Napums?" Napoleon licked Enheim's face and barked.

"That's right," Katya said, petting Napoleon. "Nobody shoots at our baby and gets away with it."

"Michio, we go back to your bungalow. I need you to weave your computer magic and get me an exact departure location for that chopper."

Michio nodded. "Might take a few minutes, but I can do it."

Lincoln lit up a cigarette.

"Really?" Enheim shook his head at the cigarette. "You do realize this is the twenty-first century?"

Lincoln understood but ignored his protestation.

"So, darlink, what happens now?" Katya asked Lincoln.

"We get proof of who registered the helicopter, and then we get some answers."

13

Deep within the Neptune Island complex was an unused meat locker that had been converted into a small interrogation room. The walls and ceiling were concrete. The room's only illumination was from a ceiling-mounted fluorescent tube. Two cameras in opposite corners were angled down toward the room's only furniture, two chairs and a metal table with a clean ashtray in the center.

Eddie Ramirez, exhausted, bruised, and beaten, sat in one of the chairs, his hands bound with zip ties and his head bowed. Blood seeped from an open wound above his eye. His dishevelled lab coat was stained with dirt and blood.

A grating noise sounded as the locking bolt slid aside. Leon Maxwell, in his usual two-piece suit, stepped into the room, strapping a Glock nine at his waist. He positioned himself behind Eddie and waited. Eddie did not raise his head.

Moments later, Jonathan Kane entered the room. He sat opposite the battered physicist.

He glanced at Maxwell and indicated the zip tied hands. "Please?"

Maxwell pulled out a long blade and cut the tie. Eddie rubbed his aching wrists, trying to soothe the bruised skin.

Kane reached into his pocket and pulled out a pack of cigarettes. He took one from the pack, produced a lighter, and lit it. He inhaled deeply, then slowly exhaled through his nose. The smoke hung over the table, creating a thin haze between them. "We all have our weaknesses, don't we?" he said sheepishly, never taking his eyes from Ramirez. He inhaled again. As if it were an after-thought, he offered Eddie a cigarette. "I apologize. Where are my manners?"

Eddie lifted his shaking hands and accepted the cigarette. He put it in his mouth and Kane leaned over and lit it for him.

Kane took another puff of his cigarette and shook his head. "Torture does not work. Certainly under extreme pressure, all men will succumb to the will of their interrogator—all men, no exception. I once heard of a man, a few years ago, not much older than thirty years of age, admitting to the assassination of John Kennedy. 'I was the shooter on the grassy knoll' he confessed." Kane chuckled. "The man wasn't even born at the time of the Kennedy assassination, yet he admitted to it. Remarkable, don't you think? At the time, a car battery was connected to his testicles, and he had been deprived of sleep for three days, so he was in a frame of mind to give his interrogators any information they wanted. And herein lies the problem. To stop the pain, a man will say anything, but any information isn't always the right information."

He took another puff of the cigarette and exhaled. The smoke haze above the table had become a thick cloud.

"No, torture does not work. To get information from a man, what you need is persuasion—encouragement—a pressure point. Men have different values, different life styles, and therefore their needs will differ. Some will break at the thought of an imminent death. Others will be turned by the prospect of financial gain."

Kane frowned, his eyes fixed on the obese man before him. "We gave you everything your disgusting heart desired, Eddie. We gave you money. We gave you women … We gave you dignity again. But most of all, we gave you purpose. You could hold your head up knowing that you were working on a project that would change the world. My scientists were excited when you came on board. They could see years of hard work finally paying off." He sighed, then nodded to Maxwell.

Maxwell drew the pistol from his holster and placed the barrel against Eddie's temple.

Eddie eyes widened with fear. "M-Mr Kane, I-I just need more time to work on the decoherence problem. It-it's more complicated that I thought it would be."

"Eddie. You've had nearly two years to solve the equations. You told me you could do this."

"I can, Mr Kane. I can do it. I just need a little more time."

"We don't have time, Eddie. You know that." He glanced at Maxwell.

Maxwell cocked the gun. He grabbed Eddie's right hand and fired at its pudgie pinkie. The 9mm round tore into the flesh, separating the finger from his hand. Ramirez screamed, then stared in horror at the bloodied finger on the table. In agony he cradled his hand as blood flowed from the gaping wound. He moaned and sobbed, terrified at what would follow.

Kane watched, detached. "I didn't want to do this, Eddie. You gave me no choice." He took one last puff of his cigarette and ground the stub out in the ashtray. He stood, ready to leave, but paused for dramatic effect. "Make it happen, Eddie."

"Hypocrite," Eddie mumbled.

Kane glanced at Eddie. "What was that?"

Eddie clutched his bleeding four-fingered hand. "Yes, Mr Kane."

"Good. Now go see Dr Mallory. He'll treat the wound, put that hand on ice, and give you some pain killers."

Kane watched as Maxwell helped Eddie from the chair and escorted him from the room. Then he inspected the severed finger lying on the table. "All you have to do is find that pressure point."

Sophia entered the room, notebook in hand. "There you are, Mr Kane," she said. "Mr Maxwell said you'd be down here. You need to sign off on these release forms for the Larry Jones interview. They've already set up the cameras in your office, but the producer needs you for lighting and final adjustments."

"It never ends," he said with a smile.

She smiled back politely and gave him the notebook. While Kane perused the documents, she glanced around. The room reeked of cigarette smoke and another odor she didn't recog— She gasped. A finger lay in a pool of blood on the table. Horrified, she jumped backward, repulsed at the sight before her.

"Don't let that bother you," Kane said nonchalantly, continuing to scroll through the documents in the notebook. Sophia continued to stare at the bloody table until Kane signed the release form and indicated the door. "Shall we?" Sophia turned her gaze from the grisly sight as Kane ushered her from the room.

"One more thing, Sophia. Mr Maxwell is busy right now, so please remind the boys in security and IT to disable the electronic scrambler for the period of the interview. We can't keep Mr Jones waiting now, can I?"

14

The storm had wreaked havoc in Michio's yard. The four picked their way among the palm fronds littering the long path to his bungalow.

"I can run an algorithm that uses all current and relevant aviation data recorded in the last twenty-four hours," Michio said, kicking debris out of the way. "As long as I don't get greedy and keep the parameters to within a few hundred miles, I should be able to track the flight back to its place of origin."

Lincoln frowned. "Greedy? What do you mean?"

"It's not my algorithm. I'll just borrow it for a few minutes—so we have to be quick."

Lincoln and Enheim groaned.

"Relax," Michio said.

They had reached the porch. They crowded around Michio waiting for him to open the doors. He picked up another palm frond and flung it into the yard. The frond swirled through the humid air before landing on a pile of yard debris.

"Ah, home sweet home!" Michio sighed and inserted the key into the—

The windows shattered outward while beneath them, the porch lifted then buckled. The explosion blew the doors off their hinges and picked them all up, throwing them backwards through the air into the storm-ravaged yard. A fireball tore through the roof sending hundreds of burning wood, metal, and glass shards in all directions. The force of the blast vaporised the walls, turning the bungalow into a fiery pile of kindling.

Together, they managed to lift the heavy doors off themselves and shove them aside. "Is everyone all right?" Michio asked, removing an entangled palm frond from his hair.

Dazed but intact, they brushed off the fragments.

"Nothing a warm bath won't fix, darlink." Katya pulled her dishevelled hair back from her face.

"Is my baby Napums good?" Enheim and Katya inspected Napoleon for injuries. The little dog licked their faces in appreciation.

"Looks like these doors of yours saved us from the blast and flames." Lincoln kicked one of the charred smoking door. "Thank God for bad décor."

Michio gave him a sideways smirk before approaching the burned-out bungalow. Stepping carefully over smouldering palm fronds and what used to be his front porch, he entered the charred remnants of the cottage. Small strands of smoke streamed from the rear of his laptop. A USB stick had welded itself to an input port, and several keys had fallen off. He turned the computer over and peeled away a five-by-nine photo taped to the back. Except for a small burn mark on the top left corner, the photo was intact. He removed the charged battery and threw the laptop on the floor. Still holding the photo, Michio knelt in the center of the living room and tugged on a floorboard.

From a hidden compartment beneath the board, Michio removed another laptop. He replaced the dead battery with the charged one, then turned the computer on. The screen illuminated. "Good," he said aloud. "I should have … the info … in … just a moment …" He sat back. "Just as soon as I hack this program so we can triangulate the helicopter's flight plan, we'll have the proof we need." While he waited, Michio's thoughts wandered to the events of the day, to what might have caused the violence. Minutes later, Lincoln's backpack in hand, Michio returned to the waiting group.

Michio tossed the burnt backpack to Lincoln. "Okay, everyone. I'll give you three guesses as to where the chopper originated—but you only need one."

They nodded. Neptune Island.

Michio followed Katya's gaze to the picture in his hand. He shrugged. "Something I needed to have." The picture showed Sienna and Michio on a beach posing in exaggerated modeling stances and smiling for the camera. Each time Michio saw this photo of Sienna with her short dark hair and sparkling grey eyes, he imagined what might have been.

"She is beautiful," Katya said, admiring the photo of the two ex-lovers on the beach.

Lincoln glanced at the picture, then turned what was left of his backpack upside down. The charred contents spilled out. No clothes, no toiletries, no books—nothing.

Michio eyed Lincoln before folding and slipping the picture in his back pocket. "Yes," he said softly. "She was beautiful."

"Oh, I am sorry. I did not know she passed away." Katya glared at Enheim for not having told her. Enheim shrugged, palms up.

Michio produced a small necklace from his pocket and handed it to Katya. She inspected the chain and admired the heart-shaped locket's unusual design. "It's beautiful," she said, giving him a curious look.

"It's a reminder from the past that I don't want to lose. Would you do me a favor and keep the necklace safe with Napoleon? I know he'll be well looked after."

"Of course, Mitch-o darlink," Katya assured him, still mispronouncing his name. She placed the necklace around Napoleon's neck and fastened it.

Lincoln threw his charred bag back into the bungalow and then surveyed the surrounding area for suspicious characters. "We can't stay here."

Enheim cleared his throat. "I have a question. "How the hell did they know about my house and Michio's place?"

Lincoln considered all the possible answers, then shrugged. "The USB drive must have a tracking code embedded in it."

"That makes sense," Michio said. "Only why didn't they come for us yesterday when we first decrypted it?"

"You said it yourself— bad weather." Lincoln turned to the group. "Trackers work online. Your Internet connection only worked intermittently yesterday because of the storm. More than likely, the trackers couldn't lock onto the weak signal. The tracker must have activated when we plugged the USB drive into the professor's TV set. Most TVs are Internet connected now."

"True," Enheim said, nodding. "I get my soap operas streamed live off the net."

"We have to drop off the radar now." Lincoln was insistent.

"Okay, I call Roland." Katya reached for her cell phone.

Enheim's face darkened. "No, you don't call Roland."

"I call Roland. He owes me."

"Roland is an asshole," Enheim said.

"Who's Roland?" Lincoln asked.

"Roland is my half-brother," Katya announced, beaming with pride.

Enheim struggled to keep his temper in check. "Roland's a fence."

"Do not call him fence." Katya glared at Enheim. "My brother is businessman."

Enheim turned to Lincoln and Michio. "Her brother gets things for people and takes a ten percent commission. That's what I call a fence."

"What kinds of things?" Lincoln asked.

"Anything you want—legal or otherwise."

Katya conceded. "Yes, my baby brother is entrepreneur—but he also runs successful tourism business here on the island."

"Entrepreneur?" Enheim laughed. "That's a good one."

"If I am not mistaken," Katya countered, "Roland has not tried to get us killed today—twice."

His temper fraying, Enheim pleaded with Katya. "Why can't you agree with me? Just once. Please. Why does everything have to be a big friggin' debate with you?"

Her hands on her hips, Katya stood her ground. "Look at Napoleon. He's trembling." Napoleon was indeed quaking.

"Of course he's trembling!" Enheim shouted. "He's been in two house explosions on the same bloody day—as have I!"

"Can Roland get us to Neptune Island?" Lincoln asked.

Enheim glared at Lincoln. "Don't encourage her."

"He can take us wherever we want to go," Katya said. "My asshole husband and Roland do not get along," she added.

"I wonder why." Lincoln's tone dripped with sarcasm.

"We don't get along," Enheim said, "because he's an asshole, not me."

"You two are like little boys in playground. You fight over nothing."

"Where is Roland?" Michio asked. "Is he close by?"

Enheim could see it was three to one. He sighed, rubbing his forehead in resignation. "Oh, he's close, all right. Too bloody close."

Michio sensed movement behind him and spun around.

Standing there with a pink sun visor perched on her head was an elderly woman wearing leggings and a loose-fitting pole shirt. She had stopped walking her dog in front of Michio's smouldering house to scrutinize the fire-damaged bungalow and the people arguing in front of it.

"Mrs. Sweeney. How are you?" Michio asked, hoping to distract his nosey neighbor from the smouldering ruin. "And how's Little Leroy?"

An enormous pit bull with drool running down the side of his mouth snarled at Michio. The identification tag dangling from his spiked collar read: Little Leroy - I BITE.

Little Leroy snarled again, while Mrs. Sweeney stared at the burning bungalow.

"Faulty gas bottle," Michio lied.

"Uh-huh," Mrs Sweeney nodded, unconvinced. "Must have been a big gas bottle."

Little Leroy turned his gaze from Michio to the burning bungalow, then back to Michio. He barked once, then continued snarling.

Even the dog knew his story was bullshit.

15

4:00 p.m.

Kane sat behind his desk reviewing the paperwork. Sophia stood next to him, ready to assist. "You have the Larry Jones interview at five o'clock, sir." She unclipped several sheets from her folder and passed them to him. "He'll be asking you these questions. His people would like a rough draft of your answers. And you have the book signing on Friday morning."

"Fine," Kane answered. He browsed through the papers, highlighting certain questions and jotting down notes.

A female voice sounded on his desk intercom. "Mr. Kane, Christina is here to see you."

Kane smiled and straightened the sheets into a pile. "Send her in." He turned to Sophia. "Thank you. I'll get these back to you with the answers."

Sophia took her folder and nodded a polite hello to Christina, who gave her a prudent nod in return. Sophia was aware that Christina's gaze never left her as she passed. The publicist admired Christina's athletic build, her fashion sense, her auburn hair flowing down to the small of her back, but her feline features—her watchful eyes, her defensive demeanour— gave Sophia the uneasy sense that danger and caution surrounded her.

As Sophia closed the door behind her, Christina strode around Kane's desk and draped her arms around his shoulders. She kissed him on the cheek, as old lovers would. He continued reading the manuscript.

"Distractions," Kane smiled. "They can be dangerous. You lose focus. Your mind becomes clouded. But beautiful distractions? Well, they're a different story," he said, putting the papers down. He swivelled his chair around and patted his thigh, welcoming her. "A beautiful distraction is like a muse. It inspires. It is the source of knowledge. It can excite creativity. It can benefit one's mind in so many ways."

She straddled Kane and wrapped her arms around his neck in a loving embrace. They kissed the way lovers kiss, with an eager, all-consuming passion.

He pulled away to admire her physique, her delicate features. He gazed at her soft flawless skin, her deep brown eyes—yet he struggled to understand her mind. "So passionate … yet so distant." He tapped her gently on the forehead. "One day I would like to get inside there, to understand how you think."

"Maybe one day," she replied impassively, but without conviction. Nevertheless, she felt her guarded ways beginning to unravel as she tentatively contemplated his words and actions. Yes … maybe one day. She smiled and leaned forward to kiss him again.

The desk phone beeped.

Kane sighed. He withdrew from Christina's full lips and tapped the screen, not turning from her gaze. Irritated he asked, "Yes?" then kissed her lightly on the neck as Maxwell's voice came through on the phone.

"Jonathan. We've lost contact with our team."

Kane scowled. "Leon, I pay you to employ the best people available. In turn, I want results, not excuses. What happened?"

"I don't know. That information isn't available yet, but as soon as it becomes clear and we know who is responsible, I will let you know."

Kane turned to Christina. "If only all my employees were as professional as you."

She kissed him slowly on the neck, and made her way to his ear. He moaned with satisfaction and kissed her on the mouth.

Maxwell's voice continued. "Jonathan, I'll send another team. This time there won't be any mistakes. I personally guarantee it. I'll go along with the new team and—"

"Don't bother," Kane interrupted, pulling away from the warmth of Christina's mouth. "I'll get it done."

"Jonathan, you don't need to send that red-headed bi —"

Kane tapped the screen and ended the call.

"He's a liability to you and this company," Christina said matter-of-factly.

Kane repeatedly tapped his fingertips together, deciding on a course of action.

"He cannot command men," Christina added. "He has little respect for women, and he's a sadistic bastard."

"We go way back, and he is my loyal friend. We shall leave it at that." He admired her for all the right reasons—and the wrong ones. "Find out what happened and fix the problem. You know what to do. Get the details from Maxwell. And keep me informed."

Christina smiled.

16

"Enheim, you asshole." The droll German accent belonged to Katya's half-brother Roland.

Enheim was about to reply to the snide remark when Katya scowled at him. He didn't need to weigh his options. He decided to keep his snappy retort to himself.

Roland was thin and wiry and slightly shorter than Katya. He wore skinny jeans with a black turtleneck sweater. His short blond hair was brushed back, and his thick black-framed glasses sat perfectly on his clean-shaven face. He greeted Katya with a firm brotherly hug and air-kissed both her cheeks. "Ah, new tits," he commented.

"Thank you. It's nice to see some family notices these things."

Enheim rolled his eyes.

"And who do ve have here?" Roland inquired, turning to Lincoln and Michio.

"Roland, this is Lincoln and Mitch-o," Katya said as Roland shook Lincoln's hand.

"Firm. Masculine. I like that." He nodded to Lincoln in appreciation.

"You're siblings, yet your accent is German and Katya's is eastern European?"

"Ja. Same mother, different fathers." Roland smiled. "As you Americans vould say, she ..."—he searched for the phrase—"... got around. You know."

Roland's eyebrow raised in surprise as he and Michio shook hands. "Vonderful, vonderful. Such soft hands, beautiful to touch." He stared into Michio's eyes.

"Thanks," Michio said, unsure how to take the comment. He tried to withdraw his hand, but Roland held it a few moments longer before releasing it with a wink.

Roland turned to Enheim and lifted Napoleon from the harness around Enheim's chest. He hugged the little dog and in turn, Napoleon licked his face and gave a friendly bark. "Napoleon, my cute little friend, how are you?"

"He's been through a lot of stress lately," Katya said.

Roland continued to stroke Napoleon under the snout while looking Enheim in the eye. "No doubt he has," Roland said in his trademark monotone. "That's vat assholes do, you know. They create stress."

Enheim understood if he wanted Roland's help and resources, he would have to shut up and endure his insults.

Roland carefully placed Napoleon back in the harness, then sat down at his desk. "Please, everyone, sit down," he said, indicating the chairs.

Roland's ultra-modern office featured a right-angled sheet of glass for a desk with a laptop perfectly placed in the exact center. A meticulously trimmed bonsai sat next to the laptop. Behind the desk, a floor to ceiling glass wall spanned the entire length of the office offering a picturesque view of the hinterland. The other walls were bare except for a large wall painting opposite the desk. Depicted on the black canvas using white brush strokes was a full frontal naked man, hands on hips, his head turned to the side gazing upwards. The three men sat on a beautifully reproduced Coco Chanel sofa opposite the desk, while Katya sat nearer on a sleek ergonomically-designed office chair.

"So," Roland began, "vould anyone like a beverage? We have a vonderful barista on staff who can make anything you vant— cappuccino, latte, anything. You should try his triple espresso." Roland raised a playful eyebrow toward Michio. "It vill keep you up all night—if you know vat I mean."

"N-no, thank you," Michio stammered, his face flushed.

Lincoln's grin caught Roland's attention. "Vat about you, big boy?"

"Hacienda La Esmeralda?" Lincoln asked, knowing the answer would be no.

"Of course."

Lincoln stared. "Wow! The most expensive coffee in the world next to Kopi-Luwak? You're a man with refined tastes."

"Thank you. I, too, prefer the Hacienda. The vay they treat those Civet cats is just too deplorable."

Lincoln nodded. To the others he said, "Kopi-Luwak coffee is made from the excrement of Civet cats after they've eaten the coffee beans. Unfortunately, the cats are treated quite poorly."

"Cat-shit coffee?" Enheim looked away in disgust.

"I tip my hat to you, Lincoln—to a man who knows coffee. Ja. Hacienda La Esmeralda is a good choice. I order for everyone." Roland tapped a key on his laptop and spoke into a small microphone attached to the screen. "Sasha, call Rolf. Five Hacienda La Esmeraldas." He tapped the keyboard again, ending the conversation.

Enheim drummed his fingers on the sofa's armrest . "Enough with the coffee bullshit," he muttered.

"I have known your friends for less than a minute," Roland said, gazing at Enheim, "and already I like them more than I like you. I can have a more fulfilling conversation vith Napoleon than I can vith you. Vy do you think that is?"

Katya glared at Enheim, who understood that they needed Roland's help if they were to find the perpetrators responsible for the destruction of his home. His only choice was to shut up and bear it.

"You know vy I cannot have a conversation vith you?" Roland continued. "Because you are a Philistine—a brute—a Neanderthal man. You may know physics and mathematics, but you have no social skills vatsoever. You … are an asshole, you know."

"Roland, my dear brother, my husband is indeed all of these things—and more. You forgot to mention, idiot, uncouth, irritating, and obnoxious. But he can also be a wonderful and caring man. Napoleon is treated like a king. My husband will stand in the pouring rain, holding an umbrella over Napoleon while he does his doggy business. My husband would die for Napoleon and me, rather than see us come to harm. Yes, he is all those things you said—but inside, he is a good man."

"So, how can I help my little sister today?" Roland asked, ignoring Katya's kind remarks about Enheim. He took a small water dropper from his pocket and began drip-feeding the Bonsai tree.

Katya was about to speak when Roland looked up. "Oh, I forgot to ask. How is my beautiful holiday home? You are not forgetting to clean the glass vall to the garden, are you? The people who installed it insisted it be cleaned once a week, you know. They were adamant about that. And have you been watering my roses twice a day as I asked?"

"About your home ..." She was at a loss for words.

Detecting her hesitation, Roland's voice filled with concern. "The flowers are delicate, you know. They must be watered every day."

"Yes, I know."

Alarmed, Roland pressed on. "Yet you hesitated ven asked about them, you know. This tells me something has gone wrong with my roses. Is this correct?"

Katya was searching for the words to tell her brother the bad news when Lincoln spoke up. "With Enheim's help, Michio and I have been investigating the murder of our good friend. Whoever is responsible for her murder learned of our involvement. They found our location and tried to kill us. In the process they destroyed your home. I'm sorry about that, but we need your help. Katya tells us you're a resourceful man who can get things done, uh, quietly." The water dropper produced one more droplet of water that hung for a moment before dripping on the Bonsai tree.

"Destroyed my home? Vat do you mean—" Roland began softly, anger building in his voice, "—destroyed my home?"

Enheim was unable to contain himself any longer. "The right side of the house is fine," he said. "The left side—not so good. About a thousand bullet holes strafed the wall that overlooks the pool, the glass partition to the garden was shattered into a million pieces, and most of the rooms are completely destroyed as a result of multiple hand-grenade explosions."

"Is that all?" Roland asked sarcastically. Sighing, he clasped his hands and rubbed his cheek. "And the roses?"

"Torn to shreds."

Speechless, Roland glared at the group.

"If it's any consolation, my house was blown up too," Michio offered.

"Roland, my dear brother, they tried to kill us—and Napoleon."

Napoleon barked for emphasis.

Roland snapped out of his daze. "Lucky for me, everyone survived," he said derisively, gazing in Enheim's direction.

Enheim gave him a wry smile.

"I do not know how to respond to this information. I do not have vords to describe my feelings." Anger rose in Roland's voice. "Vat do you think I should do vith you all? I trusted you, Katya, to look after my beautiful home, you know, and now I learn that it has been—"

Sasha entered carrying a tray with coffee cups. As she placed the tray on the table in front of the sofa, Lincoln couldn't help admiring her curvaceous form and natural beauty. She gave him a quick glance, apparently liked what she saw, and smiled.

Roland waited until Sasha closed the door behind her before resuming his tirade. "I cannot believe this! I trusted you vith my home—and my roses." He got up from his desk and came around to face the group, hands on hips. "You assured me everything vould be fine. But everything is not fine, is it?"

"Relax, sister," Enheim said to Roland.

Roland, infuriated at Enheim's dismissive attitude, felt his face turn crimson.

Enheim extended his palm to Lincoln and Michio. "The drive."

"Vat is this?" Roland fumed.

Enheim dangled the stick in front of Roland's face, glorying in his opportunity to take the lead and trump him. "This, my asshole brother-in-law, is your retirement plan."

"Vat are you talking about?" Roland demanded, but his anger was toned down a notch, his business sense tweaked.

"What's on that stick got my friend killed," Lincoln said.

"What's on this stick is going to make you a lot of money." Enheim enjoyed enticing Roland, knowing that he wouldn't be able to resist.

Roland's demeanor transformed from rage to curiosity, his entre-preneurial instincts piqued. "Vat do you mean?" he asked, reaching for the stick, but Enheim handed it to Michio.

"Brother," Katya pleaded. "We need your help. Do you still have *The Stingray?*"

Roland's right eyebrow lifted in curiosity.

17

The television producer adjusted the image on the monitor. The split screen showed the network's leading journalist, Larry Jones, on the left and Jonathan Kane on the right. The studio booth buzzed with assistants, producers, and station personnel all eager to hear what Jonathan Kane had to say. The build-up to this broadcast was unprecedented in the network's history. Every hour on the hour for the last twenty-four hours, the station had gloried in presenting the scoop of the decade.

Looking beyond the control room to the studio, the producer spoke through his headset. "Everything all right, Mr Jones?"

Larry Jones turned to the monitor closest to him and gave a thumbs-up.

"Mr Kane, how are you doing?"

Kane's voice sounded through his mouthpiece. "Fine."

"Okay, on five—four—three—two—one—"

Larry read from his notes. "Tonight, we have a special guest who needs no introduction. You all know him as a mega-wealthy man who, for the past decade, has been among the top five on Forbes World's Billionaires list. Now he has a secret he wants to reveal to the world. Jonathan Kane, thank you for being here tonight— even if it is via satellite."

"Thank you, Larry. My business needs me right now, so I couldn't make it into the studio. However, I would certainly have loved to be there with you in person."

"Okay. So let's get started. You're the world's most famous orphan who made it good. You became a marine biologist and made billions harvesting food from the ocean depths and bringing it to our dinner tables at a reasonable price. Now, if that—"

"Larry, excuse my interruption, but I don't believe our audience wants to hear about my past experiences. You know, I know—and the world knows—why we're here today."

The producer nodded, along with everyone else in the control room. "You got that right," he said to himself.

Larry laughed. "Okay." He moved his interview sheets aside while Kane flashed the camera a mischievous grin. "Okay. So, let's talk first about the island—Neptune Island. You've chosen to operate your billion-dollar business on a remote island in the middle of the Pacific Ocean. Why?"

"As almost everyone knows now, Neptune Island was formerly Agrihan Island. For those who may not be aware of its position on the world map, Neptune is located in the Northern Mariana Islands chain, approximately 1500 miles off the east coast of the Philippines."

A world map appeared on the monitors behind Larry. The camera zoomed in on a chain of islands in the western Pacific above Australia and below Japan.

"Why the Northern Mariana Islands?"

"Forgive my amending a common phrase, but we were able 'to kill three birds with one stone.' First—privacy. The remote location guaranteed a place where my eco-friendly company could build a project without the prying eyes of the media or those of competing businesses. Recently the media and the competition have become an issue, but we've managed to protect our little project.

"Second—the location is ideal for deep sea exploration and marine research. Your viewers may not be aware that the island chain is famous for the Mariana Trench, a ridge of underwater mountain ranges approximately two and a half thousand kilometers long, sixty-nine kilometres wide and at some locations, as deep as eleven kilometers. The marine life around that entire area is extraordinary. Marine biologists are making remarkable finds on a daily basis.

"Third—the islands themselves. Saipan Island, the chain's capital, has a sad history of military involvement over the first part of the twentieth century. During the Battle of Saipan in 1944, more than twenty-five thousand men, women, and children lost their lives—three thousand of them United States soldiers. It's a tragic reminder of the brutality of war. Yet, ask almost anybody about Saipan, and most people have never heard of it. I thought it was time for the world to remember, to bring the issue to center stage.

"I don't know whether you're aware, Larry, but the Marianas were incredibly important in the final days of World War II. The Enola Gay, the B-29 Superfortress bomber, was launched from the United States Air Force base on Tinian on July 6th, 1945. She carried the world's first deployable atomic bomb that, as we all know, was dropped on Hiroshima.

"Pagan Island has a dramatic story to tell as well, yet few know it. Although the war ended in 1945, a Japanese soldier was found still living on the island in 1954. He believed the war still raged on. It took some convincing, but eventually he was swayed and left the island.

"Many other islands in the chain have rich histories, yet much of their past has been forgotten. I've made it my duty to society to remind us all of the fragile—yet violent—nature of humanity."

"Okay. That's very humanitarian of you, Mr. Kane. Now, if you don't mind, let's go back to what you said earlier—that you 'had issues'. Do these issues involve the incident with the President of the United States or the journalist who was shot down?"

"Both. The journalist had no authority to fly over my land—over my private property. The specific terms of the no-fly zone were established in full accordance with local aviation laws. I make no apologies to those who choose not to follow those laws."

"So the journalist was shot down over your airspace. Don't you think that was taking your privacy just a little too far?"

"No, I don't. How many times have the media buzzed your private home for the chance to—to catch Larry out? Catch Larry with his pants down? Would you like to have the law on your side regarding the decision you'd make? Well, I did."

"The Cessna had bullet holes in the wing."

"Granted, in hindsight, my security personnel could have handled the situation with more finesse. But given the circumstances of the flight's low altitude, my people had no other options. From their point of view, the intruders could have been terrorists or eco-terrorists. We didn't know their intentions, and we weren't going to take any chances. I'm sorry if some find this too direct, but this is how I run my billion-dollar business—with efficiency and total trust in my staff and their abilities. Without that trust, a person has nothing."

"You refused the President of the United States access to the island. Tell us about that."

"Not much to tell. His office demanded a tour of the island's facilities, and I declined."

"Why?"

"As I've said many times, the refusal was nothing personal. I don't care which party is in power, Republican or Democrat or—the other ones. I just don't care. Politicians think they are better than everyone else because they hold office and wield power. They think they deserve more than you or I or the average man. They think they're special. They're not."

Inside the control booth, the station crew cheered and whooped in appreciation.

"The island," Kane continued, "will be available to everyone who makes the effort."

"What do you mean by makes the effort?"

"Well, if you want to see what Neptune Corporation has developed for the past two years, then you will have to get up from your chair and go to Neptune Island. Just think: If you go, you—and all who are determined to participate—will witness firsthand an unforgettable moment in world history. If you get to Neptune Island, you will be part of history in the making. Now I know the events will be televised, but to be there in person when history is being made is a chance of a lifetime. This exciting opportunity is there for the taking."

"Okay. So, the moment of truth—the secret of Neptune Island. When will it be revealed?"

Kane stared long and hard at Larry Jones, milking the pause for every televised second it was worth. The air thickened with anticipation as the seconds ticked by.

"Say it," the producer said to himself.

"Tomorrow morning, 10:00 a.m. That's 10:00 a.m., here in the Marianas. All will be revealed," Kane promised.

"10:00 a.m.? That's short notice. You haven't given the world much time."

"Like I said, Larry, if you make the effort, the reward will follow."

"Any tips as to which end of the island we should be gunning for?"

Kane grinned. "The no-go zone has been reduced to one mile, so if I were John Q. Public, I'd head for the south end of the island."

"Jonathan Kane, thank you for your time."

"It's been my pleasure, Larry."

The producer lowered his earphones and exhaled in relief. "Whoa, that was intense," he said to no one in particular. He turned to the associate producer behind him, but the room was empty. Through the jammed open door, he could hear the sounds of running footsteps up the stairwell to the helicopter pad on the roof.

• • •

Washington DC- Georgetown

Senator Theodore Wilson sat behind the polished oak desk in his home office and tapped the key on the remote. The television flickered off. He felt the bile rising at the sight of Kane grinning and talking excitedly about his alleged creation for the citizens of Earth. The burden of knowledge pressed hard against his conscience, making him sick to his stomach. Knowing that the outcome of the next few days would ultimately bring sadness and ruin to him and his family, he decided on the only course of action available to him. He pulled a bottle of fifteen-year-old scotch from his desk drawer and poured a double into a glass. With shaking hands he gulped down the smooth whiskey and poured another. He could no longer be a part of Kane's plan for world change.

Wilson scanned the books arranged in neat rows on the bookshelves lining the walls: books on literature, the arts, national histories, and dozens of books on the United States and her turbulent past and uncertain future. History was clear in the books, but few citizens nowadays took the time to comprehend let alone value the country's unmistakable presence on the Earth. Numerous wars had been fought to defend her way of life, and many men and women had lost their lives defending her values. Soon it would all be gone.

When Jonathon Kane first approached him with his vision of a new world order, he politely dismissed the billionaire's ideas as the ravings of a man with too much money and too little real-world experience. However, Kane's persistence and meticulously detailed plan eventually won him over: infiltration at the highest levels, financial management, legalities of transfer of power—even moral dilemmas faced by the new regime. The man had thought of every minor detail right down to specifying who the new governing body and its representatives would be. The prospect of having influential status, of being able to make real change for the country he loved, was irresistible. Wilson chose not to think about the possible undesirable consequences of his actions, and focused instead on the possibilities for bettering the country that would be available to him after the event.

The United States had been morally and financially bankrupt from years of corrupt practices and poor management. The national debt was now twenty trillion dollars. Misguided attempts at imposing its will upon other nations for financial gain and regional control had created an understandable mistrust and hatred toward the United States. Unemployment was spiralling out of control and the very people the Constitution was created to protect were now considered second-class citizens when compared with those of other nations. Its policies had failed inside and outside its borders. It was only a matter of time before another nation without the burden of institutionalized corruption would become the world leader.

Wilson had witnessed the country he loved deteriorate before his eyes. Rich politicians found loopholes in the political process to further their own agendas, promoting vile corporations that violated the Earth and twisted the laws of the nation for financial gain. The time for change—for a new vision, a better life—was overdue. Wilson decided that Kane was the man to bring about that change.

Kane's rhetoric was mesmerising. The allure of a new start from the ashes of the old world was a gift for the taking. Government officials hogtied by bureaucracy relished the idea of a new beginning. Their influence stretched like a spider's web around the globe and soon, not just politicians, but many business-minded individuals were caught in

Kane's web of seduction. In exchange for a piece of the new pie and a ringside seat to govern, all Kane requested was absolute obedience.

When reports filtered down to his office about guilt-ridden colleagues and their families meeting accidental deaths or alleged random murders from home invasions, Wilson understood Kane's new world would be much like the old world. He was certain that Kane truly believed in his plan for a new beginning, but his method for achieving control and silence—murder—was less than inspiring. The price was too high, the burden too heavy. To risk exposing Kane for what he truly represented meant a death sentence for him and his loved ones.

Wilson could think of only one course of action to ensure that his family was spared after his departure. From his briefcase, he retrieved the note explaining that while he loved his wife Janine and their baby girl Melissa with all his heart, it was best this way. He was sorry, but his financial status guaranteed a comfortable life for them and they would live without need. He had intentionally omitted any mention of Neptune or of anything that could link him to Kane or any of Kane's business dealings. Wilson read the note again, then slipped it into the envelope. He sealed the envelope and placed it on the corner of his desk.

He opened his briefcase and pulled out his great grandfather's Smith & Wesson six-shooter. Wilson made sure the gun was loaded, then flipped the revolving chamber into place. He put his thumb on the hammer and pulled it back when a thought crossed his mind. He quickly scribbled on a sheet of paper on the desktop. Then, consumed with utter sadness at the realization that he would never seeing his wife and daughter again, he placed the barrel inside his mouth, closed his teary eyes, and fired.

Blood sprayed across the wall behind him, spattering the family portrait. Wilson's body lurched backwards on the office chair, his limbs sprawling out and his head hanging at an awkward angle. His lifeless eyes stared at the ceiling as the back of his head spilled to the floor. The body movement had created a breeze that caused the sheet of paper to fall to the carpeted floor. It read—*Sorry about the mess.*

18

The black minivan pulled into the small complex at the east end of the Saipan airport and drove into one of the many aircraft hangars situated along the narrow runway. The hangar was in a state of slow decline. Its corrugated walls were rusted, and small horizontal shafts of daylight shone through various holes around the building. Sections of the ceiling, a combination of light-weight aluminium and corrugated plastic sheeting, had been torn off by high winds, leaving gaps scattered about the roof. Fruit doves flew in and out to a bird's nest located high in the corner girder. Cracks and cavities filled with dirt and weeds spider-webbed across the concrete floor, giving it an old and unused appearance.

"What's with the abandoned look?" Lincoln asked Roland.

"Keeps away prying eyes, you know."

Scattered around the hangar were several aircraft: a sleek, G-5 Lear jet that took center stage, and behind it, an older-style plane in camouflage colours. Lincoln's eyes lit up. Resting on two pontoons mounted to the under carriage sat a Dakota C-47.

Lincoln rolled down the van's passenger window to glory in the plane's charm and magic. He couldn't wait to share details about the classic plane he'd loved since childhood. "Beginning with World War II, the plane's two wing-mounted Pratt & Whitney engines and her sturdy practical design have made the C-47 the most reliable plane ever built," he informed the group. "The American military even used the C-47 in the '70s during the Vietnam War." He smiled at Roland who was nodding in appreciation. "Most people think it's a DC-3, but the DC-3 was the airline's version that was converted to a C-47."

"You do know your classic planes," Roland said, impressed with Lincoln's knowledge of older aircraft. "I fly tourists over the islands, adventure-seekers vanting that Indiana Jones old-vorld charm."

"Just this one," Lincoln replied, transfixed by the C-47. "A grand old dame of the sky."

Roland turned in his seat to face the plane. "Say hello to Eva."

Lincoln considered the unusual name Roland had given the plane. Then it hit him. Eva Braun—Adolf Hitler's partner. "She'll follow you anywhere," Lincoln said, grinning at Roland.

"Thanks for the info dump," Enheim added from the front seat, unimpressed.

Lincoln continued to admire the brown and green camouflage that added that extra feel of authenticity and adventure. Many of his favorite movies had C-47s in them— *Outbreak, Congo, Indiana Jones and the Last Crusade, Quantum of Solace.* The list was too long to remember. He couldn't stop smiling as he took in the beauty of this classic old friend.

A long trailer with a black fifty-foot cabin cruiser cradled in her mounts sat next to the two planes. *The Stingray* was stencilled in white down the side of the bow. Behind *The Stingray* a smaller vehicle lay hidden from sight under a dusty tarpaulin.

A young man in grease-covered overalls and with several engine parts stacked beside him was working on the back deck of the cruiser. As the minivan pulled up, he finished his mechanical repairs and stood wiping his hands on a clean rag.

Roland stepped out and headed toward the cruiser. The others climbed out to stretch their legs.

"Michel," Roland called to the young man, waving his hand at the pile of engine parts. "Vat is this?" he demanded.

Michel continued wiping his hands. "Bonjour, Mr Pom. How are you going today?" Michel was a contradiction of terms—a friendly Frenchman.

"Fine, Michel. But vat has happened to my magnificent boat?"

Michel looked from Roland to the group near the minivan. "We had a visit from the harbor people again. They say The Stingray is not seaworthy." He nodded toward the group, careful not to reveal too much in front of strangers.

Roland nodded. He understood the coded language with its emphasis on the word harbor.

"They said that under Section 39 of the Maritime Insurance Act of 1906, the modifications do not comply with the national standards and that the lines must be uninstalled. They made me remove the customised fuel lines, Mr Pom. That is what I am doing now. I am sorry. They said they wish to talk to you about payment alternatives—you understand?"

Roland's jaw set. "Yes, I understand," he sneered. "How much do they vant this time, the *harbor* people?"

Michel glanced over at the group again, unsure whether to talk openly in front of outsiders. "It is okay, you know," Roland assured him. "Just tell me."

"They said an extra five percent will cover the maintenance fees and administrative costs."

"More assholes to deal with," Roland said, shaking his head.

Michel removed the work order from the clipboard and passed it down to Roland.

Roland flipped through the pages that said the craft was unsuitable for ocean travel and the list of mechanical repairs that must be completed, inspected, and signed for before the craft could leave the hangar. "I tell you, this day is turning out to be one real pain in the ass—and not in a good vay, you know." He finished reading the work order and passed the clipboard back to Michel. "Michel, I need a boat. Now."

Michel pondered the request, then smiled. "Mr Pom. What about Ducky?"

Roland grabbed the dusty tarpaulin and threw it aside.

Again Lincoln's eyes lit up in pleasant surprise. He walked around the boat, mesmerised by the craft before him. "I didn't know they still existed. I never thought I'd actually see one of these things."

"What is this—this thing?" Michio was not impressed.

Roland was about to answer when Lincoln cut him off. "You live in Northern Mariana Islands and you don't know about the history of Saipan and Tinian?"

Michio shrugged. "Enlighten us."

Enheim whispered to Katya, "Here we go again—another history lesson."

"Shush," she scolded. "Listen to Lincoln. Maybe you learn something more than just your crazy mathematics."

Enheim busied himself with stroking Napoleon under the chin.

Lincoln continued to walk around the boat, admiring its functional and classic design from an era long past. "Imagine it. 1944, World War II. The Japanese forces, forever expanding into the Pacific, controlled this island. Needing a Pacific stronghold to counter Japanese military might, the Allies invaded and occupied Saipan—*this island*—giving us the edge we needed. Now the Allies were within striking distance of mainland Japan. The Seabees, a construction battalion of the US Navy, pretty much leveled the island and built everything you see around us now—the roads and docks, the runways, the infrastructure—everything needed to run the island. They even shipped over a couple of railroad diners so the sailors could feel more at home. When they declared the war over, it was cheaper to leave a lot of the old boats and vehicles here rather than ship them back to the States. But I never thought I'd see one operational." Lincoln stood back and admired the boat's boxy yet timeless design. "Ducky here is a rebuilt, fully-renovated World War II DUKW 353."

The Ducks, as they were nicknamed, were two and a half ton trucks simply converted into amphibious vehicles. Huge tires sprouted from the beam that supported the boat's bulky, dinghy-style frame. Ducky was thirty feet long and had a canopy mounted over the entire deck, refitted to fit several passengers in the stern.

"Vell done!" Roland gave Lincoln a golf clap. "You know your history, Mr Monk. Bravo."

Lincoln shrugged off the compliment. "Not so much. Well, maybe some." He managed to tear his eyes away from the latest classic craft to address Roland. "I really like your toys. Is she ready?"

Roland glanced at Michel.

"Just give me time to prime the lines," Michel said.

"Yes. " Roland nodded. "Ducky's totally refitted and ready to go, and licensed for road use as well—which brings me to my next question. Where are we going?"

19

The bike roared up the hill, swerving around fallen fronds and tree branches left from the previous night's storm.

Christina could have taken the main road into the hilltop community to save time, but she took the back road to keep away from prying eyes. The journey was longer, coming from the other side of the island, but she had guessed—correctly—that the road would be deserted.

She pulled her bike up outside the smouldering remains of Enheim's mansion. The wreckage of the garage door lay in a heap on the gravel driveway. The door had been crushed from the inside. Someone had left in a hurry.

Christina throttled down, kicked out the stand, and switched off the ignition. She withdrew her phone and tapped the keys. From the details Maxwell had grudgingly given her, this was the last location from which the helicopter pilot had reported before they lost contact. She entered the residential address into her phone. Seconds later, the information she needed appeared on the screen. She tapped more keys for relatives and associates here on the island. The list was small.

An image of Marcus Enheim appeared on her screen, along with his background information. He rarely socialised with islanders. Apart from his duties at the college, he kept his engagements with colleagues to a minimum, and he had no known relatives in the Northern Mariana Islands. She tapped more keys, and an image of Katya replaced Enheim's.

Christina read Katya's bio, scanned the information, and tapped more keys. A picture of Roland appeared on her screen—a half-brother, from her father's side, here on Saipan. Christina checked for his address and memorized it.

She stowed her phone and was about to gun the motor when, off in the distance, down the mountainside, she spotted a thin trail of smoke rising in the air. The foliage from the surrounding trees obstructed her view, but she could see that the smoke emanated from the bottom of the main road.

Fifteen minutes later, Christina hammered around a bend and skidded to a stop, just inches from a deep crevasse dividing the road. Beyond the chasm, she had a clear line of sight. The road meandered around the mountainside and disappeared behind a bend way off in the distance, before coming back into view again, but she didn't need to go any further.

Half way down the mountain, lying across the road, was the smoldering wreckage of the helicopter, a burning hulk of twisted metal blackened beyond recognition. Past the chopper, she could make out a few cars, parked on the side of the road, their occupants gawking at the sight in front of them.

She turned the bike around and roared off the way she had come.

After circumnavigating the eastern side of the island, Christina pulled into Roland's hangar at the end of the airport. His apartment was unoccupied, and this was the address listed in the local business guide.

Michel peered over the gunwale of the cabin cruiser and watched Christina dismount and approach the craft. He wiped his hands on a rag and climbed down to ground level to meet her, his hand extended. "Hello, miss. Can I help you?"

Christina shook his hand and scrutinized the hangar and its contents. "I'm looking for Roland Pom." She slipped a switchblade from her back pocket and held it hidden at the small of her back.

"He's taken tourists out to one of the islands," Michel said.

"Which island?"

"I'm sorry, miss, but he didn't tell me."

She toyed with the knife. "When will he be back?"

Michel shrugged. "Unfortunately, I don't know."

Christina glared at him. She positioned the switchblade for a better grip and flicked it open.

"I do the mechanical repairs for Mr Pom," Michel added. "He doesn't tell me about the business side of things."

Christina assessed Michel's friendly face for signs of deception. He was telling the truth. She didn't need the name of the island. She knew they were going to Neptune. But why, why go to the lion's den? Because with the electronic and communications blackout over the island, the only way to contact Kane was to physically go back and personally inform him of the new development.

Michel recollected the speech Mr Pom had given him for a five percent commission for all new customers. "We do have several brochures that may interest you. And for a very reasonable price, we can give you the ultimate tour of the Northern Mariana Islands." He flashed his best smile.

She rotated the switchblade in the palm of her hand as she decided what to do with the Frenchman standing before her.

20

1:12 a.m.

In one of the many control rooms inside the Neptune complex, a bored computer-console operator stared at the monitors surrounding him. The screen directly in front showed a topographical map of Neptune Island and the surrounding ocean. Above the map, highlighted in different colours, was an ever-changing image of swirls and patterns, all merging into one large picture of the local weather conditions over the island. He tapped a key, and the image changed to a radar screen with Neptune Island dead center. The classic white radar line passed clockwise around the green screen, continuously scanning the area for return signals.

Nothing.

His tired eyes and mind succumbed to the job's tedious monotony. He was rubbing his face, trying to wipe away the sleep creeping in, when the radar program emitted a beep. A return signal flashed just outside the island's perimeter. The signal showed for a second then disappeared.

"Damned ocean swells," he muttered, irritated at yet another false reading, the third that night. "I told those idiots twice to adjust the scan for the height of the swell, but no one listens. To make matters worse, I'm talking to myself. Great." He brought up his email and typed another strongly-worded message to the tech department.

The operator sent the email and yawned. He took another gulp of his energy drink and threw the empty can into the overflowing waste bin below his desk. Again the white return signal flashed and disappeared. He shook his head in frustration. He took another can from the mini-fridge and peeled back the lid. It was going to be a long night.

21

1:15 a.m.

The storm from the previous day had swung around full force. The Pacific's starry sky hid behind blackened clouds that churned ominously from horizon to horizon, and the ocean's once tranquil surface was now dark and threatening, transformed into twenty-foot rolling swells.

Since Roland and his guests set off from the island hours ago, the pounding rain had continued non-stop, hammering the small boat as it rolled with the waves. Fitted with a new Evinrude engine and all-new mechanical and fuel system upgrades, the Duck was ready to take on whatever came her way. Nevertheless, her paint was peeling, small spots of rust dotted her hull, and several hairline cracks spread across the windshield. Unlike other boats on the island, the Duck had been through countless storms in past eras and endured them all.

The driving rain pelted the small craft. The canopy over the open wheelhouse gave Roland little protection as he captained the vessel, and even less shelter to his passengers. Designed for shallow waters and not for ocean travel, the boat creaked and groaned through the rough swells. The thirty-foot Duck was out of its league as the lashing rain, wind and waves pounded its aluminium hull.

The yellow foul-weather jackets that Roland had given them did little to stop the onslaught. They felt the water making its way down the inside of their collars, spreading throughout their shivering bodies and chilling them to the bone. The undulating swell rolled the boat, nearly capsizing the small craft, and then regained its composure— only to roll back again moments later.

Michio had never been seasick in his life, but as he felt the bile rise in his throat, he thought this might be his first time. Moments later, he was heaving over the side of the Duck. With the gale force wind behind him, the contents of his breakfast scattered in the storm.

Roland glanced at Michio then at Lincoln. He nodded at the carry-bag filled with guns and bottled water next to his feet. "What's with all the water?" Lincoln asked.

"Always come prepared, you know," Roland said.

Lincoln nodded. Dehydration from the stifling humidity in certain regions of the Pacific was known to cause the occasional death. Better to be safe than sorry.

Lincoln pulled a small packet from the carry-bag and handed it to Michio. "Here, these will help," he shouted.

Michio, his face a pale shade of green, quickly swallowed the two tablets.

Enheim and Katya sat opposite, watching. At the sight of the vomit, Enheim turned away and began dry-retching. "Oh shit," he mumbled, clinging to the handrail that ran the length of the Duck. Napoleon, strapped in his harness around Enheim's chest, ducked his head back into the foul-weather jacket. In a comforting and reassuring gesture, Katya patted Enheim on the back, then continued eating a muesli bar, unfazed by the rolling seas.

Twenty minutes later, the Duck continued through the waves as the storm eased and the swells subsided to half their original height. Gradually, the cliff wall forming the west side of Neptune Island appeared through the darkness. With the rock wall towering above, the Duck seemed like a small toy on the rolling swells. The ocean thundered into the rocks at the base of the cliff, sending a frothy white spray high into the night sky. In the dark, the roiling water formed an almost uninterrupted glowing white line that spanned the entire base of the rock wall. The crashing waves were deafening as the group observed the deadly spectacle from the relative safety of the small craft.

"With all the security they have on this island, they'll pick up our boat for sure," Michio yelled.

"They von't," Roland said in his droll monotone. "The height of the swell hides the Duck. We are invisible to them, you know."

Lincoln nodded.

Enheim had regained his composure. "So, how do we get on the island?" he shouted over the beating rain and thundering ocean. Lincoln pointed in the direction of the cliff face.

They all stared at the rain swept black wall of rock towering three hundred feet above them.

"That's insane," Enheim shouted over the storm. "I ain't no mountain climber, and this ain't *The Guns of bloody Navarone.* How the hell do we get up that?"

Lincoln smiled. "We don't."

22

"Look," Lincoln shouted over the ocean's roar, indicating the base of the cliff. They all peered through the rain, focusing on the churning white water. The foam spanned the length of the cliff—except for a small gap directly in front of them.

Michio was feeling better and in good spirits. The seasickness had passed thanks to the medication. Despite the rain streaming down his face and into his eyes, he tried to focus on the vision ahead of him. "What are we looking at?"

"See where there's no white water? That's an alcove at water level," Lincoln explained. They all squinted at the frothy water, trying to spot the black gap.

The alcove was a natural niche in the rock face, carved over eons from the ocean swell. The battering water had found a weakness in the density of the granite and created a cavity in the rock. The alcove receded around a jagged bend and disappeared into the shadows behind the cliff face.

Lincoln turned to Roland. "Think you can you get us in there?"

Roland concentrated on the dark gap in the rock wall.

"You're bloody kidding me, right?" Enheim yelled in disbelief.

Lincoln ignored him. "I've done this before, Roland, many years go. If we time it right, we can ride the bottom of the swell into the alcove. It might get rough, but it can be done."

Clenching the helm, Roland assessed the alcove again.

Lincoln understood his hesitancy. "Katya told me some stories about you. It takes balls to land a plane without landing gear—and walk away. She says you inverted a helicopter—twice. Now that takes real balls."

Reluctantly Roland agreed.

"But the toughest thing a man could ever do," Lincoln said, nodding towards Enheim and grinning, "is have that guy for a brother-in-law."

Roland laughed, relaxed by talk of his past feats and the Enheim joke.

Lincoln leaned closer. "Just follow my lead and do what I say. We can do this, but I need a helmsman."

"Okay," Roland nodded. "Let's do this, you know."

The Duck edged nearer to the rock face. She drifted low within a deep swell as the base of the cliff came closer and closer. Roland tightened his grip on the helm in anticipation, waiting for word from Lincoln. Lincoln calculated the length and timing of the swell, waiting for the ideal moment to make their move.

A huge wave crashed against the cliff, sending a wall of foam high into the air. Before the thunderous crashing wave could settle, Lincoln slammed his hand down next to Roland. "Now!"

Roland throttled up, and the Duck shot off toward the small alcove in the wall. The swell behind them was gathering momentum, causing their little boat to rise with the water, her stern lifting higher than her bow. They all gripped the gunwales, prepared for the worst. Enheim hugged Katya as together, they tried to shield Napoleon.

At a forty-five-degree angle, the Duck rushed toward the alcove, riding the ocean swell beneath the hull. The gap in the rock face loomed in front of them, growing wider by the second. Lincoln clutched the side, his eyes fixed on the rock wall just a few feet ahead.

The Duck rode the crest, surging past the rock wall and into the alcove. The jagged rock face at the rear of the opening raced to meet them. "That way!" Lincoln shouted, pointing to a dark recess on the left of the alcove.

Roland swung the helm hard port. The Duck turned into the recess and rode the rough water into a small pool, sheltered from the swell. The boat drifted around, then smashed into an outcrop of rock jutting from an internal wall. As the boat dragged along the rock, the starboard hull screeched with the sound of tormented metal. Roland fought the helm as the swell caught the boat, pulling it back toward the opening stern-first.

Lincoln grabbed the anchor and threw it at some ragged rocks jutting up from a ledge. The anchor arced through the air, landed on a smooth rock, and with the movement of the boat, slid into the water. Hand over hand Lincoln pulled the anchor up and tossed it again. The anchor landed with a thud beside a small nook in the rock and again slipped into the water. Lincoln was hauling the line back in when the Duck swung around, caught in the receding swell. The boat picked up speed as the receding current dragged it toward the heaving water at the entrance to the alcove.

Oh, shit. Out of time.

Lincoln took aim at a rocky outcrop, swung the anchor once around his head, and let go. The anchor flew through the air and wedged itself around the crag. The line went taut. The Duck shuddered to a halt a boat's length from the alcove's deadly entrance.

Lincoln and Michio pulled on the anchor line until the boat was a safe distance from the swell. Lincoln leaped off the boat onto the rock ledge and secured the anchor to the outcrop. He scanned the surroundings. Despite the dark, he could make out a small hollow behind the rock pool. He stopped. What was that faint clicking? Before he could hear it again, the roar of the ocean crashing into the alcove swallowed the sound, and he dismissed it as echoes from the rock face.

Lincoln helped the others off the boat. They huddled in the dark shelter of the cave, a natural formation from eons of erosion that offered perfect protection from the rain.

Relieved, Lincoln said, "Now that was close." He patted Roland on the back. "Well done."

Roland answered in his usual monotone, without a trace of ego. "I did okay, you know." Smiling with the pride of a job well done, he reached into his carry-bag and passed each of them a Wolf Eye tactical flashlight. Flipping the bag over his shoulder, he switched the flashlight on, adjusted the brightness, and scanned the Duck for any signs of serious damage or waterline leaks.

Nearby, Enheim stood frowning while Napoleon's head protruded from his wet weather coat. "I could have sworn I heard a tapping sound earlier."

Roland reached into the bag and handed Enheim a Glock 19 handgun. "For Napoleon's sake— the safety's on the trigger. All you have to do is shoot."

"I don't know how to use one, but under the circumstances ..." Enheim could see the advantages of having the gun. He turn the pistol over, familiarizing himself with the weapon.

Michio flipped his flashlight on and turned to Lincoln. "How did you know about this place?"

"Before Jonathan Kane took control of the island and made it a no-go zone, tour boats operated here all the time. That's how I found out about the alcove. When the water would get a bit rough, they'd take refuge in this cave." Lincoln pointed toward a dark niche in the rock. "There's even a ladder mounted to the wall back there that leads up to ground level."

Enheim flipped on his flashlight and shone it at the far wall, illuminating the rickety ladder. "Well, I'll be damned." He nudged Katya to take a look.

But Katya's stare was fixed on Lincoln and Michio. She reached into her bag and produced her Rimfire rifle.

Lincoln was stunned to see the gun trained on him. He poked Michio who protested until he saw Katya cradling the rifle, taking careful aim at their heads.

23

Katya fixed her gaze on the cave wall behind them. "Lincoln and Mitch-o darlinks, could you make your way over here, please—slowly?"

Lincoln and Michio glanced at one another. They that Katya wasn't the problem—something behind them was the problem. A serious problem.

With danger close by, Lincoln's survival instincts kicked in. Katya slipped the safety to off and lined up the target sights on the barrel. Lincoln turned slightly and followed her line of sight. Michio did the same.

Lincoln gulped.

Michio's eyes widened in disbelief.

Katya's finger lightly eased on the gun's trigger.

Oblivious to the others, Enheim turned his flashlight from the ladder to scan the walls behind Lincoln and Michio. He froze.

Hundreds of crab-like creatures crawled about at the rear of the cave. They climbed the walls and ceiling and scuttled across the floor. As they snapped at one another, their brightly colored red and black exoskeletons sparkled in the flashlight's beam. Some fought, entwined in battle to the death, while others cannibalized the dead, feeding on the broken shells and raw flesh. Hundreds of broken exoskeletons littered the cave floor. Some were covered in mold and excrement indicating age, while others, the freshly killed, were being gorged on by the surviving creatures. Some of the creatures were as small as shoeboxes. Others had six-foot claw spans. The sight was unsettling—a nightmarish vision straight from Dante's *Inferno*.

"Are they friendly towards humans?" Michio whispered, not wanting to disturb any of the creatures of attract their attention.

Sensing their presence, a king-sized creature spun around to face them. Its stalked eyes shifted from side to side as it extended its claws, six feet from tip to tip. It reared up, showing its might, and snapped its claws menacingly as it edged toward them.

"Never mind," Michio answered his own question.

Lincoln recognized the creatures—Birgus latro, the largest land-living decapods in the world. Found only in the Pacific, a mature specimen could weigh ten pounds and have a claw span of three feet. These were unusually large for their species, and Lincoln had never seen them this aggressive before. "The locals call them *ayuyu* or palm thieves," Lincoln said, keeping his eyes on the creature directly ahead.

"I know. I had one for lunch last week," Enheim joked.

Lincoln surveyed the ground and surrounding rocks. Near the Duck, a few of the larger crab-creatures, the females, rested on the rocks at the water level. "They're spawning," Lincoln deduced. "This whole island is surrounded by a three-hundred-foot cliff, and they can't get to the water easily, so they migrate across the island to this shaft. More than likely they've been doing it for generations. It's in they're genes." He indicated the ladder disappearing up the shaft. "They climb down or they fall down—who knows? They find their way here and release their young into the ocean. They can't get back up the shaft, so they feed off each other or starve or die."

Lincoln recalled his short time on Christmas Island. Millions of crabs would migrate across the island only to be crushed under cars and trucks as they made their way across roads and highways toward the ocean. Recently, the local authorities had made provisions for the migration, but thousands still died ever year.

"So, what do we know?" Michio asked, not taking his eyes from the king-sized one.

"We do what Katya says. We back up slowly," Lincoln said, carefully stepping backwards. Michio followed.

With his back to the darkened ladder, Enheim didn't detect the glint of light from the small movement behind the rungs, but Napoleon poked his head out from Enheim's foul weather jacket and growled. As Enheim stroked Napoleon under the chin to soothe him, from the corner of his eye he spotted a gleam of light behind the rung. A red and black striped claw, its pincers furiously opening and closing, lunged out of the darkness just inches from his face.

Enheim stumbled backward and fell into Katya who, still focused on the king crab in front of her, inadvertently pulled the trigger. The shot sounded throughout the cavern as the round struck the creature, shattering its shell. The giant crab jolted sideways but quickly regained its footing, snapping its claws in retaliation. The sound of the serrated edges rapidly sliding together echoed throughout the cavern as the crab reared up again. This time, he fully exposed his colored underbelly, indicating a battle to the death.

Lincoln gasped. "Oh, shit," he said, backing up further. Michio followed.

Katya regained her line of sight and took aim. The sound of the gunshot distracted the other creatures from their feeding. They turned toward the group, their claws snapping in unison. The cacophony was deafening as hundreds of starving crabs snapped to attention, their focus on their next meal. They edged their way forward, wary of the intruders.

Lincoln nodded at Katya. "Knock yourself out."

Katya needed no encouragement. She took aim and fired at anything close by.

Roland was securing the Duck to a jagged rock when he heard the gunshot. He turned to see hundreds of creatures crawling around the cave, eerily lit by flashlight beams. He hurried to fasten the line as best he could, then inched his way around the pool toward the others.

Michio open fire at a creature just a few feet away. The force of the impact flung the crab backward through the air where it landed on top of others who then cannibalized the injured crab. After effortlessly devouring the crab, they focused their attention on the group. As Michio and Katya continued to fire, the cavern reverberated with gunfire and snapping claws. Nevertheless, the mass of creatures crawled closer to the pool, unperturbed by the gunfire. The smaller ones swarmed over the injured and hungrily consumed the carcasses, while the larger ones edged closer.

Enheim picked himself off the floor and checked Napoleon for injuries. He kept an eye on the creatures as he secured Napoleon in his harness. Napoleon retreated into his coat, trembling from the clatter of hundreds of claws snapping at once.

The creature behind the ladder rungs flayed about wildly before dropping to the floor, dead. Its back half showed where huge chunks had been eaten away. Behind the ladder, dozens of creatures swarmed from the fissure in the rock. Some fell to the ground while others gripped the rock and ladder, covering the cave in a sea of scuttling legs and snapping claws.

Hundreds of creatures moved forward *en masse*, closer and closer, becoming more daring, snapping at their targets. Only a few feet separated the creatures from the group that had backed up as far as it could, with the water's edge upon them.

Lincoln looked to the Duck for a getaway route. A dozen creatures had crawled onto the boat and were climbing into its every opening. He stepped back and nearly lost his footing on the slippery rock, but steadied himself in time to see the fin emerge from the water and circle the rock pool. Just below the surface, the shadowy outline of a ten-foot shark glided through the green water.

You've got to be kidding me, Lincoln said to himself. *Think. Think fast.*

The creatures were overrunning the Duck. Even if they could get the crabs out of the boat, they would still have to face the pounding ocean. If the thunderous waves didn't smash them to pieces on the rocks, then the shark would finish them off since their guns would be no match for the shark's tough, leathery skin. Escape via the ocean was next to impossible.

The ladder swarmed with more creatures every second. Lincoln craned his neck to look into the ascending shaft. Although the ladder's bottom rungs teamed with the creatures, the rungs further up and into the shaft looked clear.

Out of options.

The chance of escape was small, but the shaft provided that chance. Lincoln took off his foul weather jacket and wrapped it around his arm. He indicated to Michio to pass him his jacket, which he wrapped around his other arm. "When I say *now*," Lincoln said to the group, "climb that ladder and don't look back."

Michio appraised Lincoln's flimsy body armour. "What are you gonna do?"

Lincoln braced himself and took a deep breath. "This."

He charged into the creatures at the base of the ladder, flailing around and slashing at the crabs to knock them off the rungs. The closest creature snapped at him. He grabbed its shell and hurled it across the cavern where it slammed into the rock wall and dropped onto the mound of crabs below.

Lincoln continued to clear the rungs, and more creatures charged him. He swept them aside, smashing and crushing them with his boots. Several dropped onto him from the wall of the shaft. He brushed them off with his makeshift armor and resumed clearing the ladder.

Meanwhile, Michio kept firing at the onslaught of creatures. He assisted Lincoln when he could, kicking and crunching underfoot any that came at him, but the shear mass of creatures was overwhelming.

With her perfect aim, every shot Katya got off found its target. When one of the larger creatures prepared to strike, she fired—but the bullet ricocheted off the shell, hitting a smaller creature that stumbled and was quickly consumed by others hungry for easy prey. Katya continued firing, with the creatures gaining more ground on their march toward the pool.

Roland fired methodically, and one by one the closest crabs exploded, their body parts flying into the air. A king creature scurried toward him and snapped its claws, missing his thigh by inches. Roland swung his leg back and kicked the crustacean with all his might.

The crab sailed through the air before splashing down into the rock pool where it floated for a moment, preparing to swim back to the water's edge. The water darkened and the crab jerked backwards as the shark bit down and crushed its exoskeleton, tearing it in two. The crab flailed about in its final death throes before disappearing into the roiling water. Roland smiled, then turned to face the next onslaught.

With one arm across his chest protecting Napoleon and the other firing the Glock, Enheim shot at anything that threatened his dog's life. When a creature ventured too close and snapped its claws at Enheim's midriff, he pulled back fast. As the claw missed, he fired directly into the crab's head and watched the creature explode into a hundred pieces. Inside his coat, Napoleon whimpered.

'Don't you worry, Napums. Daddy's gonna keep you safe." Enheim whirled and fired at a creature coming up on his left. He spun around and took aim at another clamber behind him. He shot both at point-blank, straight through the head. "I think I'm getting the hang of this," he bragged.

Lincoln cleared the last of the creatures from the ladder and peered up. Dim natural light from the night sky penetrated down the shaft, allowing Lincoln to make out shadows moving high up the ladder.

Better than staying here.

"*Now!*" Lincoln shouted, motioning them to the creature-free ladder.

Katya fired her last round at a king creature snapping at her legs. She backed up and grasped the rungs first, then disappeared into the darkness above the ladder.

Out of ammunition, Roland threw his gun at the nearest crustaceans and followed Katya, with Enheim close behind.

Michio fired a few more rounds into creatures close to his legs. As they exploded into hundreds of pieces, a dozen others took their place.

A small fissure in the rock at the back of the cave exploded, causing fragments to crumble to the floor. Hundreds of creatures flooded in, filling the cave with a seething mound of crawling, snapping crabs clambering over or eating one another. The mound grew higher until it spilled into the pool. Creatures caught in the rushing current smashed against the rock walls of the alcove. The shark went into a feeding frenzy, twisting from side-to-side, jaws wide, crunching down on the hapless creatures caught in the swirling water. Piles of creatures nestled into the Duck. Their sheer weight lowered her deck almost to water level, causing most of the crabs to spill overboard into the churning water.

"Michio! Come on!" Lincoln kicked a crab across the cavern and grabbed the ladder, ready to climb.

Michio fired at a large creature almost at his feet. He watched the bullet ricochet off the crab's thick shell as the slide locked opened—the gun was empty. The creature reared up. Its claw shot out and clamped around Michio's thigh. He buckled, screaming in pain. The other claw swung in. Michio raised his arm in self defense as the serrated edge of the pincer locked onto his arm. Blood gushed from his leg and arm.

Lincoln fired his final round into the creature—with no effect. The crab climbed onto Michio, pinning him down, its mandibles gaping to reveal a black mouth. As its head closed in, Michio screamed in terror.

A yellow foul weather jacket fell over the creature's head. Startled and sightless, the crab released Michio, its claws fumbling at the coat. Lincoln dragged Michio away. "You okay?" he asked.

Blood ran down Michio's arm and stained cargo pants. "Could be better," he grunted.

Lincoln assessed the wounds: a deep slash across the arm, same across the leg. Large amount of blood loss. May go into shock.

The crab creature, with the jacket still draped over its head, staggered around, swiping away smaller creatures it stumbled upon.

Lincoln tore off a piece of Michio's pants and wrapped it around the leg above the wound. As he tightened the tourniquet, Michio grimaced. He tore off another piece and did the same for his arm while Michio struggling to keep from passing out. Lincoln supported Michio until he could put pressure on his wounded leg.

Michio winced. "I can do this," he said, bracing himself for the painful journey up the ladder.

The fissure at the back of the cave shattered outwards, and a giant claw emerged from the darkness. A second claw appeared, attached to the body of the largest creature yet. It climbed onto the hundreds of smaller crabs, crushing them under its weight, and headed for the pool.

Lincoln stared. "What the—?"

The creature's body was the shape of the local *ayuyu* but the size of an emperor Japanese spider crab. Though large and dangerous, the *ayuyu* lumbered about seldom bothering humans unless provoked. This creature was leaner and more agile—clearly a predator. Its legs spanned fifteen feet. Small barbs ran vertically along its outer shell. Its head turned freely from its abdomen, and its giant claws sliced through the air, constantly swaying, searching. Its body, the size of a dining table, was multi-colored with yellow and black stripes running down the shell. To Lincoln, the stripes gave it the fearsome and deadly appearance of a hybrid genus—two Crustacea species bred into one.

The emperor crab sensed Lincoln and Michio. It turned toward them and reared up, claws high in the air scraping the rock ceiling, ready to defend its territory against intruders.

From the breach in the fissure behind the giant creature, the stench of garbage, excrement, and death wafted through the cavern. Not even the gusts of ocean air, swirling and ebbing about the alcove, could hide the rancid smell.

Lincoln shoved Michio up the ladder and took one last look at the cavern and the Duck. The emperor crab stood dead center in the cavern, claws outstretched, king of its kind.

"Ray Harryhousen, eat your heart out." Lincoln gripped the ladder and climbed.

24

The storm continued to rage. Rain poured into the shaft, flowing down the rock wall. Water glistening in the dim overhead light kept the metal rungs wet and slippery. The shaft, an ancient lava tube, spanned six feet in diameter. Warm air, drawn down from above, wafted over the group, welcomed by all after the rancid stench from the cavern below.

Katya made good time as she led the way up the ladder. She felt her leg muscles tighten with every step, her biceps stretch taut. Her body welcomed the physical challenge as well as her determination and strength. She paused to peer into the hole of light still a hundred feet above, then continued climbing.

Roland struggled with every step. His breathing came in gasps, and he stopped regularly to catch his breath.

"Hurry up!" Enheim scowled from behind. Napoleon, still secured inside the foul weather jacket, poked his head out for Enheim to stroke his head. "Onkel Roland shouldn't smoke, should he? He's going to get us all killed."

Roland nodded as he paused again. "Maybe it is time to stop smoking, you know."

Lincoln brought up the rear behind Michio, keeping an eye on the emperor crab at the bottom of the shaft. The creature was still uncomfortably close. *Roland's smoking won't kill us; that thing will.*

Its bulky frame too large to fit into the narrow shaft, the creature writhed and thrashed furiously, hammering its giant claws into the rock wall in an attempt to reach the escaping intruders. Chunks of rock splintered off, spraying in all directions.

Lincoln could deal with the creature, but the crustacean wasn't his only problem. They had climbed a good two hundred feet up the shaft now, so the bottom was becoming increasingly distant. The creature was no longer the problem. Lincoln couldn't deal with the height.

Don't look down.

Look at the ladder.

Look up. Look at the top of the shaft.

Just don't look down.

Lincoln tightened his grip on the rung and rested his head for a moment.

Think of Sienna. You have to find her killers. You don't give up. You never give up. Do what's right. Relax.

The crashing and cracking of the claws as they smashed into the rock echoed and reverberated up the shaft. Michio peered beyond Lincoln to the creature below. "It looks really pissed."

Napoleon trembled, his eyes wide with fear.

"Enheim. How's the little guy doing?" Lincoln asked, trying to distract himself from the height of the shaft.

Enheim beamed and patted Napoleon's head hanging out of his coat. "He's tough, just like his old man."

Enheim's words resonated with Lincoln. He's a tough dog. Lincoln took a deep breath and wiped the sweat from his brow. He forced his vertigo to the back of his mind and climbed.

Intermittently, a smaller crustacean would emerge from the shadows of the shaft, but a quick backhand from Katya or Roland would send them falling to the cavern below. The rain was beginning to abate. Soon humid air from the jungle above wafted down with the intensity of the tropical climate.

25

They climbed from out from the top of the shaft and emerged into the bowl-shaped cauldron of Agrihan Island's long dormant volcano. The sides rose up, surrounding them with a thick ground cover of vines, bushes, and palm trees that comprised the bulk of the island's topography. Although the dark night and ominous clouds offered little illumination, they could still perceive the jungle around them. Trees and local flora reached high to form a partial canopy over the center of the cauldron, offering some shelter from the light rain. The occasional crab would scuttle past, but it appeared that the worst of the cavern nightmare was behind them.

They rested near but far enough away from the shaft entrance to be able to prepare for any surprises. The stifling humidity clung to them like heat from a sauna despite the continuous cooling rain. They removed their foul weather gear and placed the jackets in a neat pile.

Lincoln, on a hunch, searched the immediate area with his flashlight.

"What are you looking for?" Michio asked, cradling his injured arm.

Lincoln examined the ground nearby. "That stench back in the cavern wasn't just dead crabs. It smelled of human garbage, too." He pulled back a gathering of palm leaves. Beyond the clump, more fronds and vines obstructed his view. He circled the area and checked out the adjacent jungle. Through the dim light of the night sky, beyond a cluster of palms to his right, Lincoln glimpsed a small clearing. He made his way over and found what he was looking for.

The flashlight illuminated a dirt track, almost hidden on either side by undergrowth. He followed the track to the north but it disappeared into the night. The fronds and small shrubs that littered the path were untouched, fresh ground vegetation or newly fallen from the trees. Lincoln changed direction and lit up the trail that curved around a hillock to the south. Crushed and broken foliage lay scattered across the track. He followed the trail around the rise and directed his flashlight at an object shimmering in the dull light ahead.

On the ground was a circular metallic lid, ten feet in diameter, resting upside down. The metal cover was dented and battered. Next to the lid, another ancient lava tube disappeared into the depths of the earth, its craggy sides covered with slime and refuse.

Lincoln peered cautiously over the tube's rim. Even from this distance, he could hear the faint clacking of claws from below. A reflection on the tube's wall caught his attention. Several feet below the rim, a torn plastic bag hung from a ragged outcrop of rock. Most of the contents had vanished into the dark hole but a few items remained. A dull red glow that flashed intermittently radiated from the bag's interior.

Lincoln pulled a vine from a nearby palm and knotted it around the tree. He tied the other end around his waist and slowly backed up toward the void, checking to ensure that the vine had the tensile strength to hold his weight.

A hand grabbed his shoulder. Startled, he spun around.

"Vat is it?" Roland asked.

Lincoln took a deep breath. "Don't do that."

Roland removed his hand from Lincoln's shoulder. "Sorry," he said sheepishly. "So, vat is it?"

Lincoln lowered himself over the rim. "I'm about to find out. Do me a favour, Roland. Make sure the vine stays secured to the tree." Roland nodded and pulled the vine tight as Lincoln disappeared below the rim.

The odor of rotten garbage drifted from below, consuming Lincoln's olfactory sense with disgusting smells he hadn't known existed. His eyes watered from the stench as he released more vine and warily inched his way down.

Within arm's reach of the bag, he pulled a small tag from the torn opening. Lincoln recognized the hexagonal badge as a dosimeter, a device commonly used around the world for radiation detection. He had seen them worn by doctors and hospital technicians while spending long nights waiting in ERs for medical results from gunshot wounds after he had broken up fights. Another badge caught his attention, this one with a glowing red LED orb. He reached into the bag and retrieved the credit-card-sized label. The label featured a small readout display and keypad. Lincoln suspected this electronic label was an updated version of the older badge-style dosimeter. Inside the bag, Lincoln identified other types of radiation safety paraphernalia: wristbands, finger rings, and more body badges.

What the hell would Kane want with radiation badges?

Days of relentless rain had softened the vine's sinewy fibres, and rubbing across the lava tube's rough rim weakened the strands further. The vine snapped.

Arms outstretched, Roland lunged forward to grab the loose vine, but the vine shot over the edge and disappeared into the gaping black hole. Roland's heart skipped a beat. He froze, horrified.

Lincoln's hand appeared over the rim, groping for a hold. Roland gripped his hand and helped him over the edge. Lincoln rolled to the ground and sighed.

"I-I vas vatching vhere the wine was tied around the tree. The rough edge of the rim must have cut through the wine. I'm-I'm sorry. I didn't s-see it in the dark, you know." Roland stammered his apology.

Lincoln flashed him a thumbs up. "It's okay," he said, gasping in a lungful of air.

"Find anything interesting down there?" Roland asked, clumsily trying to change the subject.

Lincoln pulled himself up from the wet ground cover and wiped away the clinging leaves and dirt. "Yeah, radiation badges."

Roland frowned. "Vy vould Kane need radiation badges?"

Lincoln considered the info: revolutionary technology, mercenaries shooting journalists from the sky, an island fortress, the death of Sienna in a so-called boating accident, a full frontal attack on a residential home, and now the discovery of radiation monitoring equipment. All of this for a tourist attraction? The island hid a darker, deadlier mystery, a secret to unravel.

"That's what I'm going to find out." Lincoln re-examined the broken leaves and foliage across the track. He directed his flashlight beam over the palm stems. Picking up one of the stems, he studied the tread marks across the frond and then those on the track as it curved away into the dark jungle.

• • •

"Group meeting, everyone," Lincoln announced when he and Roland rejoined the others. "There's a trail just beyond that small hill that will, if I'm right, lead straight to Kane. Apparently, even billionaires still prefer the cheaper option of waste disposal. He's dumping his trash down a shaft next to the one we came up."

Katya shook her head in disgust. "Typical rich jerk. Thinks he can do whatever he wants," she said, unwinding the blood-soaked cloth from Michio's arm.

Enheim nodded and stroked Napoleon under the chin. "Daddy's going to punch Kane in the face, isn't he?"

When he saw the fresh blood dripping from the makeshift bandage wrapped around Michio's arm, Lincoln focused his attention on Michio, concerned that the humidity was preventing clotting. He watched as Katya rinsed as much as she could from the torn cloth and redressed his arm.

Michio winced as Katya tightened the bandage. "I'll be fine," he said unconvincingly.

Roland dug out a vial of tablets from his pocket and handed two to Michio. "They'll help with the pain, you know."

Michio swallowed the pills and rested back against a palm trunk.

Roland discreetly jerked his head at Lincoln indicating that he should follow him. When they were out of earshot of the others, Roland spoke quietly. "I have seen this before, you know. Ve don't have long before your friend becomes anemic."

Lincoln nodded. Michio needed medical attention—and soon. The constant loss of blood would weaken him further. It was only a matter of time before his body shut down.

The rain subsided to a light drizzle, and the leaves and branches glistened in the dim night light. Lincoln started. The crunch of distant leaves had caught his attention. He listened, but the sound disappeared into the night.

He addressed the group. "That old sixties song got it wrong. Time is not on our side, people. Let's go."

26

Katya led the group, followed by Enheim and Roland, with Lincoln supporting Michio at the rear. The humidity bore down on them like an open furnace as they followed the track linking the island's north end with the south.

Katya excelled in this type of physical activity. She power-walked along the track, oblivious to the all-encompassing heat. She had tied her hair back and still wore her high-cut bicycle shorts and tank top, so the men behind were pleasantly distracted from the overbearing humidity. She, too, dripped with perspiration, and the glistening moisture made her athletic body even more alluring.

Enheim sweated profusely. He constantly fed Napoleon water from a custom-made sports drink bottle with a nozzle attached. Although water trickled into Napoleon's mouth, he continued to pant.

The humidity caused Roland to wheeze as he walked. He took in several puffs of his inhaler, but they did little to help with the moisture-laden air.

Lincoln labored to keep up as the humidity fought to overpower him. He didn't mind walking, and actually enjoyed it most times, but not in this soul-crushing heat. He slowed his pace to allow Michio to keep up. Beside him, Michio struggled to maintain speed with his injured leg.

"Sienna— would have—enjoyed this," Michio said, breathing heavily.

"What do you mean?" Lincoln asked.

"Trekking." Michio paused to catch his breath. "She'd go for long walks by herself. Said it cleared her head. She used to take walks all the time when we were together. Sometimes I wouldn't see her for days, although she'd call and let me know where she was. She always said she needed the solitude. I'd get jealous and think she was with someone else. It used to drive me crazy."

"Yeah, she did the same thing with me," Lincoln said. He wiped the sweat from his eyes as they continued on the trail. "When she got that job promoting the rock band, she'd just disappear and show up a few days later. I never could figure her out. And going from one job to another didn't help. I think deep down maybe she did need to be alone. Sort out her life."

"She always seemed distracted, like her mind was occupied with other things."

"You mean, ditzy?"

"No, not ditzy. Just … distant."

"Yeah, you're right there." Lincoln's thoughts drifted back to his days with Sienna and the fun times they'd had together. "Did you ever watch Star Trek with her?"

"She'd only watch the original series," Michio said, laughing.

Lincoln chuckled. "Oh, yeah. She always said the others captains paled in comparison to Kirk."

"And she was right," Enheim piped up. "Kirk was the best captain. He didn't take shit from anyone." His tone became serious. "Plus, he had Spock."

"And Kirk had Uhura," Lincoln added, smiling.

"Oh, yeah … got that right." Enheim nodded in approval.

Roland decided it was his turn to contribute to the conversation. "Captain Picard from *The Next Generation* vill always be the best captain. He vas an intelligent and sensitive man and thoughtful to those around him. He understood art; he understood human emotion. He vas a Renaissance man, you know."

Lincoln nodded. "Picard was a good man. I respect that."

"Picard was definitely the coolest of the captains. He was the sort of guy you could sit down with, talk philosophy, and enjoy a glass of wine," Michio said.

"Bahhh," Enheim said dismissively. "Did Picard ever punch a Gorn in the face? No. Did Picard ever have sex with a green alien chick? No. And you know why? Because he was a wimp. He captained by committee. Now Kirk, he captained by his balls, by his gut instinct. A true leader."

"I always thought Archer from *Enterprise* was the best captain," Lincoln said. "He was a combination of Kirk and Picard."

"Enterprise? Wasn't that the one with the female Vulcan first officer?" Michio asked.

Lincoln smiled. "Yeah, her name's T'Pol."

"Yeah, that's right," Michio and Enheim said together. Silence followed as the men recalled her curvaceous body and alluring looks.

"Loved those … ears," Lincoln muttered.

"You men are all pigs," Katya called from the front. "The best captain was Kathryn Janeway from *Star Trek Voyager*. She was smart, resourceful woman."

"Okay, honey." Enheim turned to the men and rolled his eyes. He never saw Katya raise her hand but the slap across the back of his head was unmistakeable.

Notwithstanding, the Star Trek debate continued. After an hour of strenuous walking and heated discussion over the preferred captain, Lincoln called a five-minute rest. Only Katya protested. The men collapsed to the ground, heaving and panting.

Katya remained standing. With her hands on her hips, she addressed them like a coach challenging athletes. "You are all little girls. Back in Georgia, we would train in sauna for hours—then run for hours, and go back to sauna again. What about poor Mitch-o here?"

Michio coughed, but gave a thumbs-up. "I'll live."

"Well …" Enheim paused, wiping the sweat from his eyes. "Napoleon needed a nap." Napoleon had stopped panting and was almost asleep, his head resting on the harness.

"He looks fine to me," Katya said, unconvinced.

"Looks can be deceiving." Enheim gulped in oxygen. "Napums needed a rest, didn't you, my little man?" Napoleon barked once. Enheim turned to Katya. "See?"

"The dog is fine. You are all piss weak." She turned her back on Enheim and began jogging on the spot, as if this was all some training exercise.

The winded men sat, breathing heavily or drinking their water with gusto, finishing off their bottles in seconds. All they could do was watch, shamefully, as Katya continued her exercises.

Back on the track, Katya again took the lead, followed by Enheim and Roland, with Lincoln and Michio bringing up the rear. The sound of the jungle was not as Lincoln remembered it from his CDs. The fauna had disappeared when the storm hit, but now the life of the tropical rain forest had returned. He owned the complete musical collection of *Sounds of the Rainforest* and loved listening to the calming, almost hypnotic resonance on balmy nights. The real sounds, however, were far from soothing. Birds screeched continuously, squawking at each other as they fought for territory, and the constant chirping of a thousand insects coupled with the incessant chatter of jungle life made the journey unbearable.

"When we get back to civilization, Michio, remind me to burn all my rainforest CDs." Lincoln laughed as he wiped the sweat from his forehead.

Limping alongside, Michio nodded. "I'll bring the matches." He gulped from his second bottle of water and looked up. "At least the rain stopped."

A drop of water hit Lincoln's face. Instinctively he peered up into the rainforest canopy as a second and third drop hit. Michio, too, scanned the overhead foliage. Far above them branches and leaves swayed, as if some unknown force weighed on them. Lincoln sighed and gave Michio a deadpan look.

At first, the rain was light and refreshing. The water hitting their bodies cooled them down after the heat and humidity of the tropical climate. Then the moisture turned into a shower, and moments later a torrential downpour.

Soaked to the skin, they edged their way along the side of the trail, their foul weather gear long ago discarded. The deluge came in thick sheets, wave after stinging wave burning their skin. Michio slipped and fell heavily on the rocky ground. Lincoln helped him up and propped against his side. *What more could possibly go wrong?*

Without warning, the foliage tore apart, spraying fronds and small ground cover in all directions. Startled, they beheld the giant emperor creature towering from the jungle growth, its yellow and black shell glimmering in the rain, its pincers snapping as its outstretched claws swayed from side to side.

Without guns or defensive tools, Lincoln did the only thing he could to protect them from the menacing creature. He broke off a bamboo stalk and stood his ground, brandishing the stalk like a weapon. "Run!" he shouted to the others as he jabbed at the creature. It backed up a short distance.

Katya lifted Michio from the danger zone, but Roland and Enheim ignored Lincoln's order. They cracked their own bamboo stalks and positioned themselves on either side of Lincoln. Napoleon ducked back into the harness.

"If we get out of this alive, we're going to have a serious discussion about what I'm seeing here," Enheim said, not taking his eyes off the creature.

Not wanting to draw the creature's attention, Roland nodded slightly. "I didn't think I'd ever say this," he whispered to Lincoln, "but for the first time in my life, I have to agree with my brother-in-law."

"When I find out I'll let you know," Lincoln said. He swung his makeshift staff through the air to distract the creature from the others. The creature edged forward, after revenge from his experience at their hands in the cavern.

Lincoln tightened his grip on the stick and gazed directly into the black eyes of the horrifying monster before him. *Here we go.*

The creature reared-up, prepared to strike.

27

A hailstorm of bullets ripped into the creature. The force of the impacts threw the giant emperor backwards. It staggered, but regained its footing and stood defiantly, ready for more blows. Dozens of rounds peppered its thick shell. Another burst of gunfire tore into the creature's now cracked and fragmented shell. The injured beast backed up. One of its ten legs, severed by the hail of bullets, lay on the groundcover, jerking spasmodically. In a final show of territorial right, the creature stretched its claws wide and slammed them into the ground. The earth shook as the claws hit the hard rock below the underbrush.

Two men in foul-weather jackets over black tactical garb and wearing pistols at their sides appeared beside the creature. Each carried a length of heavy-duty steel line. They swung the cords above their heads, waited for the right moment, then hurled them at the giant beast. The creature reared up again and lashed out with its claws, slashing at the steel cables. It managed to sever one of the lines in mid-air but missed the other. The second cable lassoed the creature around its smaller back legs. The second man yanked on the line, and the creature stumbled and fell. The first man threw another cable, lassoed the front legs, and yanked hard. The creature's head smashed to the ground, its claws waving in fury. The figures retreated into the darkness.

Two spotlights lit up the surrounding area. Lincoln flinched and covered his eyes from the glare. The others did the same. Their eyes had become accustomed to the dim night light and it would take a moment to adjust to daylight level.

The spotlights were installed on a six-wheeled flatbed truck with a CLH 135 fully-automatic machine gun mounted to the rear deck. A third man armed the gun, his sight set on the thrashing creature behind them. A large trailer was hitched behind the flatbed. With his vision returning, Lincoln could see beyond the light to the original two men who were hunched over a large winch attached to the front of the flatbed.

Leon Maxwell, Kane's chief of security, stepped out of the truck. He assessed the bedraggled group in the harsh glow of the spotlight, keeping his pistol leveled at them while indicating to the guard in the cab to check them for weapons.

The guard climbed out weapon-ready and approached the group. One by one, he relieved them of their empty handguns and Roland's backpack. He took great pleasure in relieving Katya of her rifle while ogling her slim form. He turned and held the booty in the light for Maxwell to see.

Maxwell evaluated the five intruders. They had firearms, but many islands in the Pacific were havens to those who lived outside the law, so some locals discreetly carried protection. Civilians, Maxwell reckoned, judging by their clothing and total lack of preparedness. More than likely activists, or just stupid tourists wanting front row seats to the big event. With all the excitement following Kane's recent announcement, it was only a matter of time before an incident like this occurred.

"I see you've all met Big John," Maxwell said. "You're all very lucky. Usually those who encounter Big John don't come away unharmed." He paused, sliding his finger down the ragged scar on his neck. Then he reached into the back seat of the flatbed, retrieved a box-shaped gun, and strode over to Big John. He flicked a switch on the handle and an electric current buzzed and glowed at the end of the barrel. He took aim and fired. Two strands of thin cord shot from the gun and lodged in the creature's shell. Big John writhed about, shaking violently from the hi-voltage charge. Maxwell fired again and again, until the creature finally collapsed, unable to move.

Maxwell looked up and grinned. "Have to show 'em who's boss."

A long-wheelbase SUV with extra seating pulled up behind the flatbed. Maxwell slid the side door aside and directed them toward the open door.

He slammed the sliding door shut behind them, then clicked a small control device that automatically locked all the doors. He climbed into the front passenger seat and nodded to the driver. Peering through the wire mesh that separated the back of the SUV from the front he said, "All right people. You have a lot of explaining to do."

The driver maneuvered the SUV one hundred and eighty degrees, pressed down on the gas, and took off down the track, leaving the flatbed and trailer behind. The downpour continued as the SUV bounced down the jungle track, swerving to avoid the storm's fallen foliage. Above the tree line, the sky brightened with the approach of dawn's early light.

The SUV passed through a small clearing in the rain forest. The open stretch of grassland ended at a cliff-face, revealing the ocean beyond. Their jaws dropped at the spectacle before them.

They gazed through the side windows, mesmerized, unable to comprehend the sight beyond the cliff's edge. From horizon to horizon, hundreds of vessels— million dollar yachts, small runabouts, boats of all kinds—battled the heaving swells of the Pacific as they converged on the island. The clearing ended, and the SUV thundered back into the jungle again.

Welcome to the party.

28

6:55 a.m.

At the end of the trail, the SUV pulled up to two large security gates bordered by jungle on either side. A guard carrying a hi-powered rifle stepped from a pillbox to inspect the SUV. He spoke to Maxwell, the gates opened, and he waved them into the compound.

The compound was the size of a football field and surrounded on three sides by a ten-foot barbed-wire fence. The fourth side faced south and ended at a cliff overlooking the ocean. Void of handrails or safety fencing, the southern end of the compound disappeared into the morning sun, with a sheer three-hundred-foot drop to the Pacific Ocean below. Lincoln spotted a concrete borehole at the cliff's edge with a rusted ladder attached to its inner wall descending into the darkness.

Manned with armed security personal, the three-story sentry towers occupied all four corners of the compound. Several maintenance buildings were scattered about the complex, and to the left of the SUV, two helicopters sat idle on landing platforms. A third helicopter pad was empty. Behind the helipads, and facing the two loading docks, a large awning provided shade for the light commercial trucks parked beneath it. Behind the awning, dozens of rusted shipping containers were stacked two-high along the fence line. Two raised landing platforms dominated the right side of the compound, each the size of a house. Beside the platform closest to the northern fence, several guards were removing a large cover from a darkened pit.

At the end of the thoroughfare into the compound sat two loadings docks opposite each other. The SUV skidded to a stop beside the second dock where a concrete ramp descended one level down into the bedrock. The towering metal doors at the base of the ramp were closed.

Maxwell and two armed guards ushered the group out of the SUV and down the ramp. Lincoln helped Michio along the gradient, his condition worsening by the hour. Maxwell swiped his security card over a digital pad, and the metal doors groaned open.

"He needs medical attention now," Lincoln called to Maxwell.

Maxwell glanced at Michio's bloodied bandages and noted his limp. "Soon," he said without conviction. He escorted the group inside, and the doors closed behind them with a loud metallic clang.

Fluorescent lights lit the way as they marched through a maze of service corridors. The air conditioning was a cool relief from the heat and humidity outside. Maxwell stopped next to an innocuous-looking room labeled "Stores." He ushered Katya, Enheim, and Roland inside, then locked the door behind them.

A short walk down the hallway, he steered Lincoln and Michio into a similar room. He spoke into his headset for a few moments, then slammed the door. The bang of the metal door reverberated down the hallway, a clear signal from Maxwell that this was the end of the line for the uninvited guests.

29

Lincoln propped himself up in a corner to rest and enjoy the cool air, while Michio sat at the metal table unwrapping the blood soaked bandage around his still-bleeding arm. Clutching his arm and groaning, he inspected the wound. The gash was still open and fresh.

Lincoln hauled himself up from the corner and sat beside Michio. He squeezed the excess blood from the bandage and began redressing the wound.

Michio winced. "Thanks."

Lincoln noted Michio's pale skin. If he didn't get help soon, his condition would become life-threatening. He needed to get Michio off this island.

"I can see why Sienna left you," Michio commented without emotion.

"Oh? Why did she leave me?" Lincoln's tone had a touch of sarcasm.

"Well, you're not exactly Mister Reliable."

"What do you mean by that?"

"Isn't it obvious?"

"Not to me."

"You're a wanderer. You can't hold down a job—"

"—because I like to travel," Lincoln countered.

"It's because you can't settle down. And, you have trust issues."

Lincoln raised his eyebrows in disbelief. "Trust issues?"

"Yeah, you said so yourself. You couldn't trust Sienna. You didn't know where she went or what she was doing, and that got to you."

"It would get to anyone. It got to you."

"It got to me because I couldn't understand her way of thinking. It got to you because you and she were too much alike."

Lincoln finished dressing Michio's wound and walked around to the end of the table, unconsciously creating distance between them. "You couldn't be more wrong. We were different people with different ways of doing things. That's why we broke up."

"Bullshit. Do you know why she left me?" Michio asked.

"Enlighten me." This time Lincoln's tone was laced with sarcasm.

"She left me because I wasn't a project. I was already established. I knew what I wanted from life and I went after it."

"Really."

"Yes, really. Women love projects. They need men they can mold. Men they can manipulate to their idea of a perfect partner. They see a damaged man and they can't resist wanting to repair him. They buy his clothes. They tell him want to think, what to do. They look after him. It's in a woman's nature. You were a project she could work on, a major project."

"Hey, no one ever bought me clothes. I buy my own clothes."

Michio glanced at Lincoln's cheap jeans and discount store hoody. "You thought you needed to tell me that?"

"Look who's talking, Mr JET Q Style magazine. I'm sure cargo pants and Hawaiian shirts are all the rage in Paris this year."

"You were a project to her, whether you like it or not."

"What a load of crap," Lincoln snorted. "Do you really wanna know why it didn't work out between us?"

"I know why. You screwed up," Michio said matter-of-factly.

"I did screw up, big time," Lincoln snapped. "It didn't work ... because of you." "What?" Michio whispered, stunned by Lincoln's answer.

"Yeah. I was jealous she might go back to you if I didn't meet her expectations. I'm a traveler. I work when I need money and I enjoy that lifestyle. I wouldn't want it any other way. I could never give Sienna the finer things in life. She deserved better than that. You, on the other hand, owned your own house and earned good money and your income was steady. I didn't want to drag her down with me, and I was jealous that at any moment she would see her mistake and go back to you anyway. So ... I left. I thought it best for both of us."

Michio shook his head in bewilderment. "You left a great relationship because of your petty insecurities?"

"I left a relationship that was doomed from the start. I knew it, she knew it."

Michio's voice raised an octave. "Here I was thinking this whole time that she left me because I screwed up, but she left me because you were a hopeless case and she had to fix you. I can see that now."

"No one tried to fix me because I don't need fixing. This is who I am."

"And who are you?"

Lincoln paused, unable to find the words to respond to Michio's question.

"Yes, Lincoln Monk, who are you?" the male voice from the doorway asked.

Lincoln and Michio swung around. Maxwell leaned against the doorframe, arms crossed, smirking. He closed the door with his foot and sat at the end of the table. "I am Leon Maxwell. It's my job as chief of security to gather and attain all information possible on anyone I deem a threat or risk to this company. I have profiles on you," he nodded to Michio, "and the rest of your group—Marcus Enheim, Katya Enheim, and Roland Pom—very informative profiles indeed. You have all lead interesting lives, to say the least. You, on the other hand," Maxwell said, turning to Lincoln with a curious stare, "I know nothing about. Several years ago, you resigned from the Palo Alto Police Department for reasons unspecified. Then you dropped off the face of the earth. No bank account, no credit card, no fixed address, nothing. Why?"

"My friend needs a doctor, and we want to see Jonathan Kane," Lincoln said, ignoring Maxwell's probing.

"Yes, of course you do. So does half the world. Did you think you could just show up and get his autograph?" Maxwell waved his hand dismissively.

"My friend needs a doctor now," Lincoln repeated.

Maxwell glanced at Michio's wounds. "In good time." He shrugged nonchalantly, then leaned back to appraise the muddied and grimy men before him. "Who are you—Green Peace? Friends of the Earth? Some other hippie group hell-bent on saving this planet? Or are you just a bunch of assholes wanting front row seats for the big show?"

Lincoln and Michio gave each other sideways glances, unsure of Maxwell's intentions.

"You and your pals down the hall managed to get on this island undetected—well done, by the way. Let me guess: the height of the swell hid your craft from the radar?"

Lincoln and Michio subtly turned away from Maxwell, their unintentional body language a giveaway to the trained eye.

"Yes, using the swell is an old trick that occasionally still works. You were lucky this time. The Pacific can be unforgiving." Maxwell nodded, pleased with himself. "So, what do you think of Big John, the creature you met in the jungle? Awesome, isn't he? We've had several encounters with him ourselves, and he's caused many of my men injuries, but we can't bring ourselves to kill him. He is becoming an increasing problem, though. We have to keep him isolated from the other, uh … marine life. We've attached a GPS tracker to him and try to keep him here on the compound, but somehow he keeps escaping. He's getting more daring by the day."

"Good for him," Lincoln said with undisguised sarcasm. So Maxwell's people were tracking Big John when they discovered his group. They'd found them by accident.

Maxwell ignored Lincoln's comment. "My point is: You managed to get past our radar and our island security."

"Aren't we special," Lincoln sneered.

"Yes, you are. Normally, I'd offer both of you employment for being so resourceful. I always need men who … how do I say this … men who can do things others can't."

"No, thanks," Lincoln said. "Our friend was killed by someone in this company, and we want to know why."

"Your friend?"

Michio slid a photo across the table to Maxwell.

"Her name is Sienna," Lincoln said.

Maxwell studied the photo. The woman in the picture had darker hair, but her features were unmistakable. He laughed. "Yes. I know her."

Lincoln's hands clenched. "How do you know her?"

Maxwell's sadistic streak took over. The time had come to play games with them, to have some fun while teaching these hippies a lesson. With a big smile he said, "I killed her. So what are you gonna do about it?" He waited, eager for a reaction.

30

Lincoln lunged at Maxwell.

Maxwell whipped a pistol from his jacket and took aim at Lincoln's head. As Lincoln backed off, hands up, Maxwell snapped his fingers. Two guards in full black military garb stormed into the room. The cell door closed automatically behind them as they threw Lincoln to the concrete floor.

"Check him," Maxwell commanded.

The first guard held Lincoln with his hands behind his back, while the second guard searched for concealed weapons. He turned to Maxwell. "Nothing."

Maxwell waved his gun toward Michio who sat at the end of the table. The second guard slammed Michio's head on the table, pulled his arms back, and frisked him. Michio flinched, groaning in agony. The guard pulled the USB drive from Michio's pocket and tossed it to Maxwell.

Maxwell turned the drive over in his hand and glimpsed the worn image engraved on the stick. He angled the stick toward the light and squinted. The engraving had worn flush with the surface of the plastic. He brought the drive up to eye level and instantly recognized the trident design. Neptune's trident.

"Your friend Sienna gave you this." He dropped the gun to his side. "All this time we've been chasing you, and all we had to do was wait. You came to us." His laughter echoed throughout the room. The guards exchanged sidelong glances, uncertain as to how to proceed.

Michio, stricken with anger and despair, drew the last ounce of energy from his body and threw himself onto the guards, grabbing a holstered pistol as they stumbled. He fired at Maxwell. The round caught Maxwell in the upper-chest. He fell to the floor, unconscious.

Lincoln spun around and gave the first guard a powerful uppercut to the chin. The guard's head snapped back before he, too, crumpled to the ground, out cold. As the second guard scrambled for his sidearm, Lincoln elbowed him across the face, breaking his nose. After a swift jab to the solar plexus, the guard collapsed against the wall, gasping for air.

Lincoln grabbed Maxwell's weapon and the USB drive. He pocketed the security-card and knelt beside the winded guard. Lincoln relieved him of his firearm, saying, "You're alive because we have no beef with you, but if you ring the alarm, we'll come back and finish the job. Understand?" The guard nodded, still panting for breath.

Michio lay on the floor moaning in agony as pain pulsed through his weakened body. Lincoln lifted Michio gently and helped him to the door. As they passed Maxwell lying in a growing pool of his own blood, Lincoln lifted his gun and took aim.

"Do it." Michio watched for his moment of vengeance, but Lincoln considered the consequences. Past hasty decisions still haunted him and would for the rest of his life.

"I've done a lot of shitty things in my life, things I'm not proud of," Lincoln said, lowering the gun. "But I'm not a cold-blooded killer."

Michio understood Lincoln's reluctance. The past always had a way of catching up. He snatched the gun from Lincoln's hand and placed the barrel against Maxwell's forehead before Lincoln could react. Maxwell stirred but remained unconscious. With pure hatred etched across his face, Michio pressed the gun deeper into Maxwell's brow.

"Mich," Lincoln said calmly.

Michio sneered at Maxwell, "You killed Sienna, you asshole."

"We're not like him—" Lincoln spoke quietly, trying to ease Michio's anger, "—and we never will be."

Michio coughed, and the pain shot through his body again. Slowly, he lowered the gun.

"Good choice." Lincoln grabbed the gun from Michio and propped him against the wall. He removed the unconscious guard's shoes, then undid his belt and began pulling his pants down.

"What you do in your private life is your business, but right now we don't have time for that." Michio chuckled, appreciating the distraction after the intensity of the last few moments.

"Very funny."

Exhausted and drained, Michio nevertheless watched with curiosity. "What the hell are you doing?"

The pants finally released their grip on the guard's stocky frame and jerked free. "I'm getting us off this stinking island, and you're going home."

31

"We'll get cancer and die before we get out of here," Enheim complained as Roland lit another cigarette.

Roland inhaled. "It relaxes me, you know. Ve need to relax and stay calm, in case you've forgotten vere ve are."

Enheim swiped away the acrid smoke drifting toward Napoleon. "Oh, I know exactly where we are. We're one step closer to getting bloody cancer."

"Ve're locked in a cell on an island in the middle of the Pacific Ocean." Roland took another drag of the cigarette. "I deal vith people like this all the time, you know. Ven they vant information, they opt for the tried-and-true method—torture. Most likely," he said, his hand shaking as he took another puff of his cigarette, "they vill torture me first."

Enheim took the bait. "Yeah? Enlighten me. Why?"

"Logic," Roland said, relishing having the floor. "They vill save Katya for last. She vill be their trophy. You? You have a thick skull. They know a brute like you will be tough to break, so you vill be second on their list. I, on the other hand, have a low tolerance for pain. I have delicate features, you know." He waved his manicured hands. "They vill see I am refined and highly educated. I vill break easily, you know."

"So you'll fold like a cheap suit." Enheim shook his head in disgust.

"Stop talking like this," Katya protested, cupping her hands around Napoleon's ears. "You're scaring the baby."

Napoleon, still in the harness around Enheim's chest, lolled his head and yawned.

"Uncle Roland is a big asshole, isn't he?" Enheim spoke in his baby voice as he drop fed Napoleon some water. "But we're tough. He doesn't scare us, does he, Napums."

They stiffened. Outside the room a scuffle sounded. Roland's talk of torture had them on edge. The shuffling ceased.

Enheim's eyes lit up. "I've got a plan!

"Vat is it?" Roland asked, without conviction.

"Okay. Katya stands next to the door. When the guard comes in, I distract him, and she hits him as hard as she can."

"Me hit him? Why not you hit him?"

"I can't. I've gotta protect—" he indicated Napoleon, "—you know who."

"Why can't Roland hit him?"

Roland shrugged apologetically. "Like I said, I haf delicate features. These hands—" he gazed at them admiringly, "—vere not made for hurting people. Furthermore, I don't vork out every day. You do, you know."

Katya had to admit that he'd made a good point. She crossed to the door and readied herself flat against the wall and waited. Roland inhaled one more time and butted the cigarette. The door opened.

As the guard stepped into the cell, Katya swung with all her might. With lightning speed, the guard blocked her fist inches from his nose. Katya stared. "Lincoln!" she cried, throwing her arms around him.

"It's good to see you guys, too," he gasped as Katya hugged him tightly.

Dressed in the guard's black military uniform, Lincoln stepped through the door with Michio propped under his arm. The stocky guard's clothes hung loosely over Lincoln's lean frame. Even the guard's black cap, with the Neptune logo emblazoned across the brim, was a loose fit. Roland and Enheim helped with Michio.

"All right, who's the strongest here?" Lincoln asked.

Roland and Enheim looked at Katya.

Grudgingly Lincoln agreed. "Okay, everybody, this is the plan."

32

9:40 a.m.

Lincoln inserted the security card and the outer doors slid open. The group emerged from the underground complex and marched up the ramp. The storm had subsided, and the warm orange glow of the mid-morning sun washed over the compound. Roland and Enheim, their hands on their heads in the classic surrender posture, led the group, followed by Katya supporting Michio under her arm. Behind them, pistol in hand, Lincoln brought up the rear. They marched across the complex toward the southern boundary.

The guard operating the closest sentry tower a hundred feet away observed them as they crossed the compound. Ex-military and a body-builder, the guard's muscles bulged through his uniform. A snake tattoo starting on his hand appeared to run under his black military garb and up his arm, and ended at the back of his shaved head. Resting his M-16 on his shoulder, he followed their progress around the maintenance building near the cliff's edge.

Lincoln noted the tower guard in his peripheral vision. He gave him a friendly nod and, without arousing suspicion, casually lowered his baseball cap to hide his features. To add to the illusion, Lincoln whispered, "Sorry, guys. Have to make it look real," and shoved Katya in the back with his nightstick. She and Michio stumbled but regained their footing.

"Bastard!" Katya yelled, rubbing her back with her free hand. In a whisper she added, "Understood." The tower guard waved back to Lincoln, giving him a thumbs-up.

Although Lincoln knew he had to make the situation appear as realistic as possible, he cringed as he shoved Michio across the shoulders. Michio let out an agonizing groan and collapsed to the ground.

Curious, the tower guard picked up his walkie-talkie as he continued to watch the show. The radio at Lincoln's side came to life. "Where are you taking them?" he asked.

Think fast. Lincoln glanced around the compound. Dozens of men in security uniforms or safety coveralls were going about their business. The chance of the guard recognizing Lincoln from his downward vantage from the tower was slim. The odds of the guard being able to identify everyone's voice on the island was also a long shot.

Lincoln raised the receiver to his mouth and lowered his voice to give it a universal male tone. "Maxwell said to feed them to the sharks." He signalled the guard by drawing a finger across his neck. "He wants them out of the way."

"Shame," the tower guard's voice sounded over the two-way radio.

Lincoln followed the guard's line of sight to Katya's athletic body bent over Michio as she helped him to his feet. His cap still low, Lincoln turned back to the tower guard and gave him the universal *what can I do* gesture.

"What a waste. We could've had some real fun with her," the guard said, his tone lecherous.

Lincoln mock fired his gun at the men in the group, then grabbed his crotch and thrust it toward Katya. "No one said anything about getting rid of them right away."

After a pause, the guard answered, "If you get bored, let me know."

I'll let you know all right, with a bullet to the head. Lincoln waved a goodbye salute to the tower guard and continued across the compound.

They arrived at the concrete shaft. Lincoln waved them down onto the ladder. One by one, they descended into the bedrock of the cliff, and disappeared from watchful eyes above.

Lincoln brought up the rear, this time heading down into the shaft. "Well done, everyone," he said, congratulating the group.

Michio's hands and feet repeatedly slipped from the metal rungs as his condition worsened. Katya kept an eye on him from above, and Roland, directly beneath him, kept watch from below.

Lincoln climbed to the other side of the ladder and pulled up next to Michio. He grabbed Michio's arms and slung them around his shoulders saying, "Hold on."

Michio, his pale complexion evident even in the shadows of the shaft, groaned. "Always the friggin' hero."

With Michio hanging from him piggyback style, Lincoln edged down the ladder to the ocean below. Just a little further. Lincoln paused and took a deep breath. Sweat trickled into his eyes, and his hands were clammy with perspiration. His pulse rate soared as his heart pounded in his chest, not from the added weight on his back or the responsibility of getting his injured friend to safety—Lincoln could deal with that—but from what he couldn't deal with: the sight below.

Far below.

Don't look down.

Focus on the rungs.

Focus on getting Michio out of here.

Focus on getting everyone out of this mess.

Whatever you do, don't look down.

Michio needs you.

Don't let your old friend down.

The idea of his old friend dying outweighed his psychological issues and allowed him to will his acrophobia to the back of his mind. He made his way down the ladder, slowly but steadily, the anxiety locked away.

The shaft's concrete walls disappeared, exposing them to the elements. A metal safety guard, mounted to the rock flank, surrounded the ladder and continued all the way down the cliff to a landing at sea level. Lincoln flinched at the open sky above and the ocean waves far below.

Oh, shit.

Don't panic.

Focus.

Lincoln cleared his head and climbed down the ladder one step at a time, his gaze fixed on the rusted metal rungs.

33

The concrete landing at the base of cliff face was covered with barnacles and guano. An outcrop of rock, head high, partially surrounded the landing and sheltered it from the ocean swell.

Lincoln rested Michio against a mooring post. He stood trembling from the ordeal and wiping the sweat from his eyes. *Made it.* Lincoln took slow, deep breaths and began to relax. His heart rate eased and the adrenaline racing through his bloodstream subsided, but Lincoln had no time to congratulate himself on overcoming his personal fears. Michio needed medical attention.

Michio lapsed in and out of consciousness. The wound had re-opened. Blood trickled down his arm and dripped from his fingers to the concrete floor. Lincoln checked his pulse. His blood pressure continued to drop at a steady rate.

Lincoln unwrapped the bandage and examined Big John's laceration. The cut had widened. Lincoln squeezed the excess blood from the bandage and finished redressing the wound.

Roland tapped him on the shoulder and pointed toward the ocean. Thousands of sea-faring vessels were scattered across the waters from horizon to horizon. Dozens of circling helicopters buzzed the morning sky. With the reduced exclusion zone, the flotilla of boats and aircraft surrounded the south end of the island, one mile from the shoreline.

Hidden from view, a twenty-foot runabout anchored in a rocky alcove a few hundred feet from the landing. The name Big Richard adorned the bow.

Lincoln caught Katya's attention and indicated the small boat. "Katya, I need you to do me a favour." He averted his gaze from her, embarrassed by what he was about to ask.

"Yes, darlink?"

"I—I need you to get the boat owner's attention," he stammered.

She shrugged. "Okay. How?"

"I need you to—" he coughed "—to attract him over here." He hoped she would understand.

Katya's brow furrowed, unsure what he was asking.

"You know ... show him want you've got."

She frowned, still not comprehending.

Enheim stepped in. "He wants you to flash your tits at that guy in the boat."

"Oh! Okay. Why didn't you say so?" She turned to the small boat in the alcove and waved at the male behind the wheel.

The boating enthusiast, a balding playboy wearing a tan and white classic Henley and khaki cargo pants, was adjusting the settings on his camera when he spotted the gorgeous blonde waving in his direction.

Katya lifted her tank top, and beckoned him over.

His eyes widened. Grinning from ear to ear, his male instincts took control. He slicked back his thinning hair and tucked his loose-fitting shirt into his pants. He forgot about his expensive camera and threw it into the passenger seat next to him. Eagerly he gunned the motor and headed toward the blonde.

The runabout pulled up next to the landing. The boat owner tossed a rope around the nearest mooring post and stared at the ragtag group watching him. The blonde had covered herself, and one member of the group lay on the concrete, his right arm covered in blood.

Lincoln hurried over to the boat owner. "He needs urgent medical attention," he implored, pointing to Michio lying on the concrete.

The boat owner shrugged. "Call the authorities."

"There's no time. He'll die before they get here. I'll give you a thousand dollars to take him back to Saipan."

"I'm sorry about your friend, but I'm here to see the show." He glanced at Katya.

"The show?" Lincoln asked. "What show?"

"Kane's big unveiling. It's today."

Lincoln didn't care about the grand unveiling. "Look, if my friend doesn't get to a doctor soon, he's gonna die."

"I'm sorry about your friend, but he's not my problem," the boat owner replied.

"I'll give you ten thousand dollars," Lincoln urged. "Please!"

"Have you got the cash on you?"

"No. You'll have to trust me," Lincoln pleaded.

The boat owner looked away, indifferent to the empty promise. "Sure, heard that one before."

"What do I have to do to get you out of here and back to Saipan?"

He ogled Katya's perfect body, nodding in approval. "One date with her."

"Over my dead body," Enheim fumed.

Lincoln shook the boat owner's hand. "Deal."

"What?" Enheim bellowed.

"We'll take care of this later," Lincoln said. He turned to Roland, and together they lifted Michio from the concrete landing and carried him over to the edge of the quay. Gently, they rested him in the back of the runabout. Lincoln placed a deck cushion behind Michio's head.

"Back in the cell, you asked me who I was." Lincoln paused. "Well ... this is it."

Michio fought back unconsciousness and opened his heavy eyes. He reached up, grabbed Lincoln around the head and gave him a man-hug. They shared the moment, their bond of friendship unbroken. "Still the bloody hero." Michio managed a small laugh, coughed, and collapsed back onto the deck. Within moments, he was unconscious again.

The boat owner turned to Lincoln. "One date with her," he repeated, nodding at Katya. "That's the deal."

"You have my word," Lincoln replied. He turned to the others. "Nothing has gone according to plan, so if anyone wants to go now, I'll understand."

Enheim, Katya, and Roland glanced at one another. "I can't speak for these two," Roland said, indicating Enheim and Katya, "but I'm here for the information on that drive. I stay, you know."

Katya stood next to Enheim, rubbing Napoleon under the chin to calm him. "Lincoln," Enheim said, "that asshole in the Armani suit you shot in the cell back there. Was he the guy who ordered the hit on us?"

For a moment, Lincoln flashed back to his days as a police officer. "No. Lieutenants and foot soldiers don't make those kinds of decisions. An order like that comes from the man at the top. In this case, that man is still here on the island, and I intend to find him."

Enheim turned to Katya. "Go with Michio. Make sure that runabout asshole gets him to Saipan General."

"What about you and Napoleon?" she protested.

"We're staying here. Napoleon never leaves my side. I still have a date with the asshole who gave the order to kill us and destroy our home."

"My home," Roland interjected.

Enheim ignored Roland. "And that's a date I intend to keep." He pulled Katya to him and kissed her passionately on the mouth.

She weakened a little in his arms as she always did and smiled. "What a man."

"Family comes first," Enheim said proudly.

Katya kissed Lincoln on the cheek. "You are a good friend to Mitch-o here. It's my turn to look after him now. Mitch-o will be fine." She climbed aboard the runabout and sat next to Michio.

The boat owner gawked one last time at Katya. He winked at her then throttled up. He pushed forward on the throttle and roared away. The runabout disappeared among the thousands of other crafts lining the horizon.

Roland, standing next to Enheim, glimpsed movement in the water to the left of them. The ocean churned, swirled, and became a frothing maelstrom of white bubbles. The landing shuddered as a shockwave resonated from the ocean and surged through the rock face.

"What now?" Lincoln groaned.

34

10:00 a.m.

The ocean turbulence at the base of the cliff continued to churn. The white water maelstrom suddenly bulged in the center and expanded outwards. Slowly, a black metallic dome broke the surface and emerging from the water like a giant black leviathan rising from the ocean depths. Its glossy surface glistened in the morning light as water streamed from its rounded sides and cascaded back to the ocean below. The structure continued to climb the rock flank as it crept toward the apex of the cliff.

The dome was two hundred feet in length and fifty feet high. Apparently created from the latest nanocarbon compounds, the structure appeared incredibly lightweight for its size. A raised circular viewing platform surrounded by a safety rail was built into the dome's top. Below the platform, on the fourth level, a floor-to-ceiling window encircled the structure. Below the vista window, a thin water channel ran the circumference of the structure. The research and development laboratories, located on the other three levels, featured recessed balconies and intermittent portholes. The bottom level housed two giant doors—the transom to the lower floors. The dome's color and rail tracks matched the shade of the cliff face.

From a distance, it appeared that the structure had levitated up the side of the island. Hidden behind the dome and facing the cliff wall were dozens of giant girders supporting the structure. The crossbeams, mounted to an elongated plate, spanned the rear of the building. The plate attached to several rails running side-by-side, embedded in the cliff rock. The rails ran the vertical length of the cliff from below the ocean's surface all the way to the compound at the summit.

A figure emerged from within the dome's roof and stood at the platform safety railing. Jonathan Kane.

Kane faced the fleet of boats and aircraft before him. He spoke to the media, print and digital. He spoke to anyone concerned with the future of humanity, to anyone concerned with the future of Mother Earth.

Now was his moment.

"Thank you for your time. Thank you for your patience. Thank you for caring enough to listen to what I have to say. Sincerely, I thank you all. Your effort will be rewarded. People of the world, I give you— Neptune!" Kane raised his arms in a welcoming manner and smiled.

The blaring of safety horns, emanating from thousands of vessels at the same time, blasted across the ocean. Kane gloried in triumph.

• • •

On the landing, now far below the structure, the three men peered up at the massive building hanging from the cliff's apex.

Roland shook his head in awe. "Now there's something you don't see every day."

"Kane … you magnificent bastard." Lincoln stared, amazed at the sight before him.

Enheim, eyes wide with astonishment, absently caressed Napoleon under the chin. "I'll be fu—."

Two cables slammed into the rock wall beside them. Armed with machine guns, two security personnel landed on the pier. The guards released their rappelling harnesses and trained their weapons on the trio. One of the guards quickly disarmed them. The muscle-bound guard from the sentry tower grabbed Lincoln's cap and threw it aside.

"Good try," he said, grinning at Lincoln. "You nearly got away with it, too—except for one thing. Glenn, the guard you left in the cell after taking his uniform, is gay."

35

Surrounded by security, the three men were being marched across the compound when the plane thundered overhead. Lincoln stopped, midstride. His eyes lit up at the sight of the Bell V22 Osprey, a plane-helicopter hybrid with tiltrotor technology. The others almost ran into him as he gazed at the aircraft.

The plane turned laterally in mid-air, kicking up a storm of dust and dirt, then descended vertically toward the helicopter pad. The craft landed on the raised platform, its wing-tip mounted Rolls Royce turboprop engines slowly turning to a stop with a veil of swirling dust engulfing the craft. The rear cargo ramp swung down, and a slender woman wearing a helmet and padded motoring gear emerged, pushing a motorbike.

"This Kane has some serious money," Lincoln muttered, as the three stared in awe at the aircraft before them.

"These things start at seventy million. Then there's the maintenance—not to mention the fuel bill, you know," Roland said, equally impressed.

The muscle-bound guard shoved Lincoln in the back with the butt of his rifle. Lincoln winced but continued walking, his eyes on the magnificent aircraft just a few feet away. The helmeted woman shot him a sidelong glance as she continued toward the superstructure, now at ground level with the cliff's edge. A metal gangway, the width of a small truck, spanned the several feet between the cliff's edge and the entrance to the dome. She walked her bike over the bridge, stopped to glance back at the trio, and then disappeared into the shadows of the structure.

The guard shoved Lincoln in the back again, jerking his head in the direction of the dome. Lincoln tried to rub the pain away as he crossed the bridge. Despite the roar of the crashing waves echoing between the cliff and the dome, he forced himself to not look down and to focus on the towering black doors looming closer. Between the gaps in the metal grating, the waves were visible far below smashing against the rocks. He pushed the mental image to the back of his mind, preferring not to relive that tortuous climb and the gut-wrenching fear of falling.

Inside the dome, the guards marched them down a hallway that to Lincoln appeared practical and functional. The service elevator doors slid open, and the guards herded them inside.

The elevator doors opened to a world of five-star grandeur. The guards escorted them down a plush, carpeted corridor where paintings of seascapes adorned the walls, including several of Neptune wielding his mighty trident. Ornately designed sconces, their lighting perfect balanced, decorated the hallway at regular intervals. A well-dressed woman in smart business attire, her blonde hair tied back, sat behind a chic workstation at the end of the hallway. She looked up, tapped a key on her pad, and silently, a panel behind her glided opened. She nodded to the guards who ushered the trio into the adjoining room.

"Holy shit," Enheim exclaimed, admired the surroundings. "This is one classy bloody office."

36

The elegant design and furnishings in Kane's office exuded power and sophistication, presenting a perfect symbiotic relation between architect and interior decorator.

The opened shutters, mounted outside the floor-to-ceiling acrylic windows, allowed in the splendour of the late-morning glow. As the sun's rays refracted over the stone's perfect composition, light sparkled and danced across the marble floor, and the pastel-colored walls added to the soft ambiance of the space. Kane's imposing desk, positioned before the large window vista, would have been at home in the Oval Office.

Kane stood leaning against his desk, studying the motley crew before him. "These are the men?" he asked the guard.

The muscle-bound guard from the sentry tower nodded.

Kane walked over and closely examined each member of the trio, their ragged and torn clothes soiled with grime and dirt. Meeting with human odor that invariably accompanies a short time in the tropical jungle, Kane rubbed his nose in disapproval.

Kane had been flabbergasted by the earlier call from security, and now he found it difficult to imagine that these men before him had achieved so much in so little time. He turned to the tower guard. "These are the men who acquired my property and technology and found their way onto my island undetected? They evaded my security force, shot my chief security officer, managed to escape, and by chance were captured again. Then, to top it all off, you now inform me that two of them have escaped. Does that sum it up?"

Embarrassed by the events of the previous few hours, the tower guard discreetly lowered his eyes. "Mr Kane," he said, "Mr Maxwell has brought me up to speed with recent events and has asked me to take over his responsibilities while he is recovering in the infirmary. I have personally assumed all of Mr Maxwell's duties."

Kane glanced at the muscle-bound thug before him. "Understood." He walked around the group, his hands clasped behind his back, contemplating his response. "Your responsibilities are noted."

The guard grinned, pleased with his latest promotion.

"May I?" Kane indicated the pistol in the guard's shoulder rig.

The guard hastily withdrew the firearm and handed it to Kane.

Kane flipped off the safety and took aim at Lincoln's head. "Like my security personnel, I, too, have access to the security footage— sound and all."

Lincoln stared back into Kane's unblinking, emotionless eyes.

"You said—and I quote—'What a waste. We could have had some real fun with her.'" Kane kept his eyes on Lincoln while speaking to the guard.

This unrelated comment took the guard by surprise. "Why, yes. Yes, I did. I had to keep up the act, Mr Kane. I had to let them think that they were getting away. It worked, too."

"Yes, it did work. However, you didn't know it wasn't your friend Glen until Mr Monk here subsequently made the mistake of mock-shooting all the men in the group."

The guard had heard rumours regarding Kane—unsettling rumours. His confidence evaporated, replaced by uncertainty. "Y-yes, sir. Th-that's right."

"So, when you said, 'We could have had some real fun with her' before you knew of the deception, you meant it. That was your true nature."

The guard hesitated, unsure what to say.

Kane lowered the gun and confirmed that there was a round in the chamber. He locked the slide back in place and fired—at the muscle-bound guard. A crimson hole appeared in his forehead and he fell back, dead before he hit the floor.

The other three guards glanced sideways at each other and shifted uneasily.

"I do not want chauvinistic troglodytes in my organization. Women are to be respected." Kane turned to Lincoln. "Don't you just hate guys like that?" he said, waving the gun toward the body sprawled on the floor beside them.

Lincoln glanced down at the dead guard. "A real asshole," he agreed.

"Exactly. All muscle and no brains." Kane shook his head and continued with genuine sincerity. "I do not understand men of that nature. Don't they know intelligence is to be sought after, not this ridiculous alpha-male display?" He shook his head in disgust. "I have worked too hard and too long to have my vision of a new world jeopardized. I cannot and will not tolerate ignorance or failure. It's simply not an option."

Kane glanced at the guard closest to the body. "Take him away."

"Yes, Mr. Kane." The guard whispered into his earpiece and two more guards entered the room. As they dragged the corpse out of the office, they watched in disbelief as the body smeared blood across the polished marble.

Kane, emerging from contemplation, had lost his train of thought. "Where were we? Oh, yes. That's right." He leveled the gun again at Lincoln's head. "You and your friends have done remarkably well for men who were out-gunned and out-manned. I applaud you." He gave them all a small golf clap. "However, all good things must come to an end."

This guy is a real nut job.

"So ... How would you like to die? On your knees, or on your feet?"

Lincoln stood his ground, defiant, unwavering.

"Good for you," Kane said, impressed.

"Can I have a cigarette?" Lincoln asked.

"Of course you can. But only if I can have one, too." He grinned like a caught-out schoolboy. "Don't tell anyone."

Lincoln nodded toward the back pocket of his jeans.

Kane pulled out the pack of cigarettes. He handed one to Lincoln, then lit it and lit one for himself. "We have a lot in common, Mr. Monk. It's a shame it has to be this way."

Lincoln took in what may have been his last draw of a cigarette, and exhaled. Enheim covered Napoleon's head with his hand and swiped away the excess smoke.

"Ah, that ridiculous man with that ridiculous dog strapped to his chest." Kane went over to Enheim and gazed at Napoleon, still in the harness. He tried to remove Napoleon from the pouch, but the dog held tight. Kane nodded to the remaining guards. The first guard raised his pistol and held it at Enheim's head. The second guard yanked down on the pouch. The stitching tore as Napoleon came free. Kane gently lifted Napoleon from the harness. He turned the little dog around in his hands, studying the small canine.

Enheim's face became a mask of hate and furious restraint. "You hurt one hair on that dog's body and—"

"—and what?" Kane said. "You are in no position to make threats." He turned back to Napoleon, reminded of another time, another place. "When I was a young boy, we sometimes went for days without food. The hunger consumes your body, your mind, your soul. Soon, you will do anything to stop that hunger." He glanced from Napoleon to Enheim's steely gaze. "The cooked flesh is quite satisfying. If it's marinated for a few hours, it can be very delicious."

Enheim took a slow, deep breath to relax, then asked casually, "So you're the guy who gave the order to destroy my house and kill me and my family?"

Kane stroked Napoleon under the chin. "I'm the guy who wanted my property back. But if you put it like that, then yes. I'm the guy who destroyed your house and tried to kill you and your family," he repeated, mocking Enheim.

"Oh," Enheim shrugged. Before Kane could register his response, Enheim pounced. In one swift motion, he grabbed Napoleon and head-butted Kane square in the face. Kane staggered and clutched his bloodied face, open-mouthed in surprise.

"That's how cockneys deal with assholes," Enheim spat.

The guards leapt into action, pushing past Roland and Lincoln. Lincoln collided with the closest guard and fell to the floor.

Enheim was preparing to hit Kane again when the guard slammed his pistol butt into the back of his head. He collapsed to the floor, with

Napoleon still in his arms. The second guard kicked him in the ribs for good measure as the pistol butt came down a second time. The guard raised his gun again, but Kane waved them off.

The guards backed away, leaving Enheim moaning on the floor.

Kane wiped the blood from his face and knelt next to Enheim. "I'll give you that one. I was rude. I apologize." He nodded to the guards who lifted Enheim and dragged him back into place next to Roland and Lincoln. Enheim held his free arm to his ribs and winced. Roland offered to hold Napoleon, but Enheim shook his head.

Kane faced them again, still wiping blood from his nose.

"Do you know that all the dogs on the face of the Earth, right now, are descended from wolves?" Kane stared directly into Enheim's glaring eyes.

Lincoln, knew he had to diffuse the situation. "Humans from a distant past developed the ability to train wolves," he said. "Eventually the wolves became domesticated and bred to become what we know today as the canine species."

Kane laughed. "I really do like you, Mr. Monk. You are full of surprises." He nodded. "One hundred percent correct. Well done. Little dogs are … for want of a better phrase … just little dogs. They never make a difference. They are inconsequential. The big dogs of the world, however, they are the survivors. They do the real work—the work that must be done. The big dogs are the rulers of the canine world who will always command the little dogs. It's nature."

Kane turned to Roland and smiled. "Mr Pom. You are here for the spoils of war." Kane leaned over to Roland and whispered, "The technology is amazing. It will revolutionize the world, don't you think?"

"Yes. It most certainly vill. May I ask you a question?"

Kane waved his hands in a why not gesture.

"The V22 Osprey outside. Reports on them are mixed. Do they really handle that badly?"

Kane looked at Roland with admiration. "You know your craft." He paused to consider the question. "Let's just say that Osprey is my second one this year. I'm just waiting for the V280 Valor. It's far more practical and requires less maintenance." He winked in Roland's direction.

Roland nodded his approval.

Kane clasped his hands together as if preparing for work. "So, here we all are, full of surprises. Well, I have one more surprise that will knock your socks off, as they say." He spoke into his headphone. "Lana, I need to see Sophia please." He returned to his desk and leaned against the edge, waiting.

Sophia, the petite publicist, walked through the door, barely glancing at the men being held at gunpoint. She had seen captured activists and eco-terrorists in Kane's presence before. Today was just another day at the office.

Her back to the men, she stood before her boss. "Mr. Kane. What do you need?" Lincoln recognized something familiar about the way she moved and the sound of her soft, velvety voice.

Kane put out his cigarette and threw the butt in the waste basket beside his desk while Sophia waited for his request. "Please," Kane said, turning her so that she faced the group.

Sophia found his behavior odd, but she followed his lead.

Lincoln's jaw dropped.

Sophia froze as she locked eyes with Lincoln.

Her now-blonde hair was shorter and partially hid her face, and her tanned body was leaner. The oversized glasses perched on her delicate nose added to her changed her look. Still, Lincoln would have recognized her anywhere.

Kane was gleeful. "Sophia. I'd like you to meet my new associates. They know you as ... Sienna."

37

"I thought she was dead," Enheim whispered to Roland.

Stunned, Roland replied, "Ve all did."

Sienna's eyes widened with fear.

The shock of seeing Sienna alive brought Lincoln's mind and body to a standstill. He'd survived a high-speed helicopter chase, being shot at by canons and grenade launchers, and endured a raging ocean. He'd battled deadly creatures hell-bent on tearing him to shreds, and escaped the clutches of mercenaries. *All for nothing.*

Sienna stood before him, alive and well. The drive to find his ex-lover's killer had dissolved to nothing. He slumped, the energy drained from his tired and beaten body.

Kane addressed Sienna. "You have been an efficient publicist, and I thank you for that. However, because of the situation we all find ourselves in, I no longer require your services." He escorted her over to the prisoners and whispered to her, nodding in Lincoln's direction, "I suggest you do some explaining to your friends here, while you still have the time."

Gun still in hand, he addressed the group as if he was commanding a business meeting. "You all have impressed me by getting this far. You truly have. But the time of reckoning has come." He thought long over his next words, then smiled. "I just can't bring myself to kill you." Kane's admiration was genuine. "So—I'll let him do it for me." He indicated the open door behind them. They turned.

Maxwell stood leaning against the wall, a bandage around his mid-rift, and holding a pistol leveled at Lincoln's head. He frisked Lincoln and found the USB drive, which he tossed to Kane.

Kane smiled at the group, then dropped the drive onto the floor and crushed it with his heel. Roland groaned, his motivation gone as he beheld the now-trodden circuitry that had been the USB drive.

The dire expression on Maxwell's bloodless face said it all. "You should have killed me when you had the chance." For an injured man, Maxwell was quick. Lincoln didn't see the butt of the pistol, but he sure felt it.

38

Enheim and Roland stood apart in silence in the corner of the interrogation room. Lincoln couldn't bear to look at Sienna—the woman he once loved, the woman who betrayed him. He peered through the door's steel mesh window and observed Maxwell in the hallway giving instructions to the guards huddled around him.

Sienna sat at the metal table watching Lincoln. She understood the hurt in his green eyes. "All my peccadillos of the past caught up to me," she said softy. "Questionable decisions, life blunders ... My inexcusable behaviour was affecting not only my life but my job opportunities. I had to make a choice. I love technology and science, so my natural aptitude for secrecy was a perfect fit. I applied for a position, got lucky, and DARPA hired me."

"Defense Advanced Research Projects Agency," Enheim said. Sienna's explanation had piqued his interest.

"That's right. Under the direction of the United States Department of Defense, we develop and explore emerging technologies at home and abroad."

Lincoln turned from the door and reluctantly listened to her reasons for her actions.

"DARPA was the best job opportunity to ever happen to me. The department helped me leave all that emotional baggage behind and reinvent myself. They knew how to arrange for me to change everything: my name, the way I dressed, the way I looked. They helped me to stage my death such that if anything were to happen, no direct links would connect to the real me or my family. My staged death created a new beginning."

"So when we were together, you were working for DARPA?" Lincoln asked, beginning to understand.

"I was in training, which is why I would disappear for days on end. I was becoming a better operative by learning how to create a backstory and evade lines of questioning. I know my excuses weren't always the best. I apologize."

"And when you were with Michio?"

She nodded. "I had just been recruited."

Lincoln tried to comprehend the information pouring from Sienna. It was a lot to digest. *But it all makes sense now.*

"Quantum engineers were disappearing all over the United States and Europe," Sienna continued. "DARPA was called in to investigate. We knew Kane was building something, but we didn't know what. DARPA had a simple plan: Hide in plain sight and gather information. My past skills as a secretary and promoter came in handy. I managed to infiltrate Kane's organization as his publicist."

"Why did you send me the encrypted USB drive?" Lincoln looked her in the eye. "How did you know I could decrypt it?"

"First, I had to encrypt the drive. That way, if the drive got into the wrong hands, no one at Neptune would be the wiser because they'd think the data was still secure. I knew you'd have trouble decrypting it and would go to Michio for help." She paused. "You guys work well together. I knew as a team you'd figure it out."

She's right.

"Why did I send you the drive in the first place? Eddie, one of the engineers here on Neptune, helped create Kane's ultimate plan. In fact, Eddie was the chief engineer and designer. But when he discovered Kane's true intentions, he couldn't bring himself to participate. So he managed to compile the information and save it on the stick. But he couldn't get the stick out of here because they were watching him closely. I, on the other hand, come and go from the island freely. Somehow, Eddie discovered I was DoD. He told me what was on the stick and what would happen if Kane succeeded. I sent a copy of the drive to my department head back in Arlington, but it never arrived. Kane's web is global: shipping, transport, media, politics." Her tone changed from concern to tenderness. "No one could be trusted ... no one except my old friend, my former lover. I knew you would never give up. That's one of the reasons I loved you."

Lincoln gazed not at Sophia, but at Sienna. Even in the harsh fluorescent light of the interrogation room, her natural beauty shone through. His tone softened. Indicating his surroundings, he said, "All this secrecy, murder, and mayhem—and for what? Some glorified tourist attraction in the middle of nowhere?"

"Not the dome. The dome—Kane's gift to the world—is a distraction. I don't have access to a whole section of the island where Eddie works. The device is there, somewhere."

"Device?" Lincoln asked. "What device?"

"The specifics are beyond my understanding. Basically, Eddie has built Kane a machine that can destabilize any mass by matching the atomic frequency."

"Vhat does that mean?" Roland asked.

Enheim recalled the schematics from the drive that all made sense now. "It means the device vibrates and destroys everything within proximity of its set parameters," he said.

"Vhat does that mean?" Roland asked again.

"It means it shakes you to death."

"So Kane plans to shake Neptune Island to the ground? What would that achieve?" Lincoln asked. "And why?"

"Who knows?" Enheim shrugged. "Maybe because the guy's a friggin' nut job. And speaking of nut jobs, how's our chief security officer doing out there?"

Lincoln tried to process all the new information. He turned back to the door and peered through the security mesh. Maxwell had disappeared along with all the guards but two who stood outside the door, their backs to Lincoln. "We're down to two guards," he said.

Enheim's eyes darted about the room as he bounced his palms together. "What do you suppose he'll do to us?"

Without taking his eyes from the guards, Lincoln said, "I figure Maxwell's a sadistic bastard from the way he treated us and Big John, so he's probably rounding up more of his mercenary pals for a big show—with us as the star attractions."

"Meaning?" Enheim asked, not really wanting to know the answer.

"Most likely he'll kill us in some gruesome and horrific way in front of his goon audience."

"That's terrific. I always vanted a gruesome and horrific death," Roland said, his sarcastic tone mixed with apprehension.

Lincoln turned back to the others. "It's time to get the hell out of here."

"Really?" Enheim said. "And how do you propose we do that?"

"Remember when you head-butted Kane?"

"Ah, one of the highlights of my life."

"While you were doing that, I lifted this from the guard." Lincoln held up a small card from his jeans pocket. "I have the security card for the door," He smiled as he jerked his head toward the locked door behind him.

When their expressions of appreciation turned to fear, Lincoln followed their line of sight. Through the door's mesh window was Maxwell, grinning at the card. The door flung open and several guards surrounded them.

Maxwell stepped into the room and snatched the security card from Lincoln's hand. "Fortunately for me, we never turn off our cameras," he said, pointing to a small black covering nestled high in a corner of the room. "I think it's time for some fun, don't you?"

39

Eddie Ramirez peered through the large window overlooking the vast cavern before him. Built high above the cave floor and into the rock face, the office stations enjoyed all-encompassing views of the work being done below. As they took readings and made adjustments with their computerized notepads, dozens of engineers in lab coats scurried about the device that was positioned in the center of the cavern.

Eddie tried to focus on the task ahead—to make things right—and to forget the throbbing pain where Maxwell had severed his finger. He had tried to stall them for as long as he could despite fearing retribution, but their patience was at an end. His bandaged and bloodied hand was the sum of those fears.

He left the office and made his way to the catwalk sitting high above the cavern floor. The catwalk connected the offices with the other side of the cave, and its several tee junctions provided easy access to all points of the enormous area. Eddie stopped directly above the device and gazed down. With the top casing removed, he could see technicians working on the machine's inner circuitry.

Numerous Neptune employees and members of his staff had disappeared over the last two years, and now Faraday, his chief assistant, had vanished. Stories regarding the two divers and the geologist, all loners, circulated about the island. At first Eddie thought the stories were just rumors and idle gossip, but Faraday's disappearance confirmed his suspicion that time was running out. Eddie tried to push it all to the back of his mind, but he understood the reason for Faraday's disappearance. Faraday had discovered the truth and tried to expose Kane, and he had been killed because of it. The construction crew used to build the dome would not be harmed. They knew nothing of the project in the cavern, but the divers, the geologist and his crew of technicians, and Eddie all knew of the cavern's secret to some degree. Kane could never allow him and his team to live. Their knowledge of the real Neptune Empire and the work done in the cavern had sealed their fates long ago. Kane would kill them all and destroy all data related to the device. He couldn't let Kane get away with slaughtering innocent men. He wiped the sweat from his brow and contemplated the many reasons for his actions.

Eddie recalled Julius Robert Oppenheimer and General Lesley Groves, the architects of the Manhattan project. General Groves oversaw the project from conception to finish—a gruelling thankless task—yet Oppenheimer would be the man forever associated with the historical event. Oppenheimer corralled the scientists and encouraged them to be more creative and to work faster. He urged them to strive to achieve the ultimate goal, which they did—with deadly efficiency. The world changed forever on August 6, 1945 when "Littleboy," the nickname given to the world's first atomic bomb, fell on Hiroshima.

Following soon after the events of that day was the famous Oppenheimer interview. Oppenheimer quoted a line of Hindu scripture from the Bhagavad-Gita that haunted the world for decades to come: "I have become death, the destroyer of worlds." His quote gave the human race an insight into how tragically the Manhattan Project had affected Oppenheimer—not only on a physical level, but also on a psychological level. The device ended the war, but at what cost? A hundred thousand lives were lost forever, destroyed in an instant, by ideology.

Eddie could not and would not let those comparisons be made of him. The past was the past. Now was the time to rectify those mistakes. He prayed that he had made the correct decision to confide his information to the right sympathetic ear.

He made his way down to the device. The technician looked around, startled. "Mr. Ramirez. I wasn't expecting to see you down here."

"Just running over the last modifications. Nothing to be concerned about," Eddie said.

The technician looked confused. "I wasn't told of any last modifications."

Eddie patted him on the back. "Kane wants everything perfect, that's all. You know what he's like."

The technician nodded. He had heard of Kane's reputation for perfection. Every detail had to be exactly right, or suffer the consequences.

Eddie tapped keys on his note pad and began making preparations. He paused to consider the good men working in the cavern. They did not deserve to die down here. Any chance was better than no chance. "Our team has done well because you've all worked hard. Take a break. Get the team, go topside and enjoy some fresh air. Have lunch on me. I'll finish this."

The technician did not need to be told twice. "Thank you, Mr. Ramirez. The boys have been under a lot of strain lately, with the deadline and all. The outdoors and fresh air will do them good." He gathered the other technicians together and they headed toward the exit doors.

Eddie made the final adjustments. His thoughts turned to his retired mother in Washington, DC as Kane strolled towards him from the cavern's staff entrance to the dome.

Eddie studied the data on his pad as Kane approached him. Kane stood opposite Eddie, on the other side of the device and leaned over so as to get a better look at the inner workings within the casing. Tendrils of light curved and undulated within the confines of the clear casing, constantly swirling and changing length and color. Kane marvelled at the mesmerizing force of nature harnessed by man. "Wonderful."

Eddie continued to tap at the keys, not ignoring Kane but not wanting a conversation, either.

Kane glanced down at Eddie's bandaged hand. "How is it?" he asked with genuine concern.

"Doctor Mallory fixed it up and gave me some medication to ease the pain."

Kane nodded with approval. "Good." Kane could see in Eddie's demeanor the hurt and fear in the large man's eyes. "Eddie. To some my methods are extreme. But those methods get results." Eddie worked away but Kane gently pushed the pad aside. "Please Eddie. The work can wait for just a few moments. Look at me."

Eddie reluctantly looked away from his work and at Kane.

Kane smiled. "Ah, now I have your attention." Kane walked around the device and stood next to Eddie, putting his arm in a friendly manner around Eddie's shoulders. "Eddie, with your ingenuity and my vision, together we will alter the course of human history. Just think, a dream of many is about to become a reality. A new order will control the United States. In turn the world will be controlled by men with humanity at heart, not greed and corruption. A new world where we are free from the bonds of the old world and obsolete government control—free from the selfish ways of those who pretend to govern our once great nation. The hypocrites of Washington will be a distant memory. Imagine, no reliance on oil, no reliance on trade with other countries. We will be a totally independent nation in control of its own destiny.

"Eddie, we are on the brink of a new world where man will live in harmony with nature. The days of raping the earth and living beyond are means will soon be at an end. With your technology and my aspirations, we will nurture the human race toward a future of peace and self-reliance. We will give back to this fragile earth so that it can again breathe and be restored to its former self. We will have achieved a sustainable existence with our Mother Earth, ensuring the survival of our species. And you Eddie, have helped me to achieve that goal."

Eddie could see how easy it was to fall for Kane's rhetoric. His words were full of hope and optimism. Ideas for a better life for all of mankind and for the earth. No wonder his people would follow him to the ends of the earth. Eddie had heard this talk many times before in speeches given by Kane to inspire those around him. He forced a smile. "Yes, Mr. Kane. It's time for a change."

"Yes, it is." Content with Eddie's response, Kane smiled and patted him on the back. He surveyed the enormous cavern and the technicians scurry about creating his dream. At the far end of the cave, Kane spotted the second Osprey tiltrotor plane resting on the lowered platform—the delivery vehicle for his vision. "So, Eddie, the million dollar question is—how soon?"

"I have to run some preliminary tests, but ..."

Kane stared Eddie in the eye, his good nature and smile gone.

"... I'd say tomorrow at the latest. Possibly this afternoon."

Kane's eyes lit up and his smile returned. He slapped Eddie on the back. "Well done, Eddie, well done! I knew you could do it. I never doubted your abilities." He turned to go. "When you are ready, begin the testing immediately."

"Mr. Maxwell has instructed me to inform him when the testing begins."

"Don't waste any time trying to find Maxwell. I'll deal with him."

"Yes, Mr. Kane."

When Kane left, Eddie peered down into the core of the device. The glowing swirling light locked behind the casing was indeed mesmerizing. Eddie sighed and tried to rub away the throbbing headache pulsating through his brain.

40

"Oh shit," Lincoln muttered, as Maxwell's men lowered him by rope into the hole. Once his feet touched the ground, the men quickly retracted the lifeline and left him to fend for himself. Built for water catchment and storage, the circular pit spanned thirty feet with twenty-foot high walls. The water-stained and algae-covered concrete enclosure now served a darker, more twisted purpose.

Torn pieces of clothing, matted hair, and chunks of rotted flesh clung to the barbed wire lining the concrete walls. The wire encompassed the height of the wall all the way to the open rim, making escape virtually impossible. The overwhelming stench of putrefied meat drifted up from the knee-high water. Lincoln dry retched from the rancid odor. From around the rim of the pit, Maxwell and his mercenaries gawked down, laughing and cheering. Roland, Enheim, and Sienna stood held at gunpoint behind the taunting spectators, next in line. Lincoln ignored the jeering horde above and focused on Big John, the giant emperor crab in the pit with him, less than ten feet away.

The creature swung its claws back and forth with territorial menace. Lincoln spotted several burn marks across the creature's under-belly and shell cover, a dark reminder of Maxwell's stun gun. Two of its hind legs were missing, only their jagged shell edges remained. The creature battled on regardless of Maxwell's brutal legacy.

Lincoln backed away, but the barbed wire ripped into his clothing and skin. The sleeve of his stolen uniform caught on the wire. He tore the sleeve away, fearful of the creature cornering him against the wall. The torn sleeve triggered the memory of the alcove where he had outwitted one of the creatures by blinding it. He quickly removed his shirt. The crowd above wolf-whistled and whooped as Lincoln stood in the knee-deep water at the bottom of the pit—shirtless.

"What?" Maxwell snapped into his headset. "Fine, I'll be right there." He took one last look at Lincoln down in the pit, then strode across the compound, down the first loading ramp and into the belly of the complex below.

• • •

The plane rested on the lowered platform at the northern end of the cavern. Maxwell and the aviation engineer stood at the base of the extended ramp behind the Osprey.

"By the look of it," the Osprey engineer explained, plugging his diagnostic pad into the avionics port of the ramp, "the salt water in the air is corroding the hydraulic lines, which is causing the ramp here to malfunction." He tapped continuously on the screen. "It's not pretty. Some of the aircraft's functions aren't fully operational yet. Case in point: the doorway from the cockpit to the cargo-hold is electronically locked in place. Any access into the cab would have to be via the emergency hatch above the cockpit. We're still looking into that one." He indicated the rear ramp extending to the ground. "The ramp is locked down and we can't get it to retract. As I mentioned earlier, the doorway is locked in the closed position. But from a technical standpoint, I'd say the Osprey should be ready for flight sooner rather than later."

"What are you talking about?" Maxwell demanded. "Who the hell are you, and why have you called me down here?"

"M-Mr. Maxwell," the engineer stammered, taking a step back, "I thought you knew. Mr Kane asked me to call and brief you on the progress and status of the repairs."

Maxwell frowned. He couldn't comprehend why Kane would issue a command to a low-level employee. Then he caught sight of Eddie at ground level, working on the device. The machine hummed, its low reverberation echoing across the cavernous room. "Fine," he said to the engineer, "just send me a copy of the report."

"Yes, Mr. Maxwell," the engineer replied, wiping the sweat from his brow as Maxwell hurried down the catwalk to the lower level.

Eddie had just finished setting the maintenance panel in place when Maxwell appeared. Startled, he hesitated, then regained his composure and continued working. He tapped keys on his pad, trying to ignore Maxwell standing beside him.

"Ramirez, what are you doing? Why is the machine activated?"

Eddie worked as he talked. "We're running the preliminary tests today. We can only perform them if the machine is operational."

"Why wasn't I told?"

"Mr. Kane wanted me to inform him directly when the testing would begin. I did as he asked." Eddie took pleasure in knowing that this response, that Kane had given him a direct order that he would happily follow knowing it would upset Maxwell, would infuriate Maxwell even more.

Maxwell glared at Eddie, angered at his having gone over his head and at Kane's not having bothered to notify him of the test. "I'm the chief security officer for this company, and I need to be informed before trials are initiated, understand?"

"Sure," Eddie answered casually.

"You will respect the chain of command, Ramirez," Maxwell shouted, knocking the pad from Eddie's hand. He grabbed the hand and clamped down hard on the bandaged stump. Eddie shrieked and doubled over in pain as Maxwell reached for his sidearm. "Maybe another session in the room will show you some manners."

"That's enough." Kane's voice boomed over the cavern's internal speakers.

Maxwell stopped. His gaze darted among the security cameras installed around the cavern, and at that moment he understood. Kane blamed him for the mess, and this was his retaliation: having to endure subordinates passing on critical information without his fore-knowledge. Eddie's disobedience was Kane's punishment for the Enheim mansion debacle back on Saipan and for the escape of the prisoners here on the island.

Maxwell valued the bond he shared with Jonathan Kane and the knowledge that the extreme measures shown to others would never

168

apply to him. However, these were cold comfort knowing that his oldest friend still treated him as an inferior, much as a father would a wayward son. Maxwell despised knowing that Kane would always care for him while sympathizing with his weaker constitution. Maxwell's burden was to be regarded as second rate—as second fiddle to the brilliant and magnificent Jonathan Kane.

"Go back to your games now, Maxwell," Kane's voice commanded over the speakers.

Maxwell released Eddie, who fell to the floor, whimpering and caressing his injured hand. Maxwell fixed his hair, glancing up at the nearest camera and pondering what might have been had he never met Jonathan Kane. He straightened his suit and regained his composer. He glared down at Eddie one last time and left the cavern.

Kane studied the monitor before him. As Maxwell walked out of frame, leaving Eddie to nurse his injured hand, he murmured, "Even you, my dearest friend, must be punished for negligence."

41

Above the pit was a party atmosphere. The guards joked among themselves and made bets—not on whether Lincoln would survive, but on how long he would last before he was killed. A large, young guard pushed a smaller guard close to the pit's edge as the others laughed at the manly horseplay. The smaller guard pushed back, and the others laughed harder.

Lincoln sloshed through the grime and muck around the base of the pit, keeping as close to the wall as he could, careful to keep his distance from Big John who intermittently reared up, extended his claws, and slammed them down into the putrid water. The waves washed over Lincoln. Losing his footing, he slipped and landed in the sickening muck. He broke surface and scrambled sideways just in time to avoid the pincer as, inches away, it smashed into the wall beside him.

Lincoln regained his footing and circled behind the creature. He unraveled his shirt and prepared for his only chance of survival. Swinging his shirt around his head, he waited for the creature to turn full circle. He needed to be closer.

Big John lumbered around and faced Lincoln again, the frenzied snapping of his claws reverberating throughout the pit. As the creature's claws lashed out, Lincoln dived, and the claws struck the water. Lincoln tried to stand but slid on the slippery algae. Big John fully extended both claw arms and smashed them down, one on either side of Lincoln, trapping him between them.

From their vantage above, Sienna turned away, horrified, unable to watch the man she once loved die in this gruesome manner. Roland and Enheim wanted to look away but could not, knowing that this fate was to be theirs as well. Enheim covered Napoleon's eyes and pushed him down further into the pouch.

Lincoln had no escape. The creature moved in closer, his snapping mandibles inches from Lincoln's head. *Now or never.* Lincoln raised his arm and threw the shirt over the creature's eyes.

Big John paused. His undulating claws slowed.

Success! Lincoln scampered through the creature's legs as fast as he could and backed up against the pit wall behind Big John, wincing as the barbed wire punctured his skin and tore his flesh.

Big John reached with his pincer and ripped the shirt away from his head. The shirt fluttered down to the pit's water level. Big John grabbed the shirt with both claws and tore it apart.

The crowd peering down was roaring with laughter when Maxwell joined them again and peered down into the pit. "What did I miss?"

Big John was again maneuvering around Lincoln. His menacing claws glided in from both sides, trapping Lincoln as he prepared for the kill. Lincoln backed closer to the barbed wire despite the excruciating pain.

The large young guard pushed the smaller guard again—this time too hard. The smaller guard stumbled, and as the sand crumbled beneath his feet, he fell over the rim of the pit. His shinbones shattered as he bounced off the back of Big John and slid into the murky water behind the creature.

Angered by the intrusion, Big John reeled around, his claws snapping wildly in the air as the guard screamed in terror under him. Lincoln turned away as the creature's claws came down hard on the hapless guard whose cries were replaced by a soft gurgling sound, followed by complete silence. Even the sounds of the crowd above faded to whispers as the guard's lifeless body floated face-down in the filth and muck at the bottom of the pit.

Big John turned to face Lincoln, and again slammed his claws down on either side of him, removing any chance of escape. With nowhere to go, Lincoln braced himself against the barbed wire, fists clenched, ready for the fight of his life. *Come on you ugly bastard, give me your best shot.*

The rumbling was barely noticeable until the water in the pit rippled. Then the walls vibrated, and fine concrete dust choked the rotten air. Big John tilted his head skyward, confused by these new occurrences.

The rumbling stopped. Birds nesting in nearby palm trees took flight above the crowd surrounding the pit and disappeared into the distance. Silence filled the compound. In the distance, the ocean waves crashed against the cliff base.

The crowd, in shock from the death of the guard and now from the quake, carefully moved back from the pit's edge. The security force, unnerved by the silence and these new events, gave each other sideways glances, unsure of their next move.

Sienna's training had taught her many things, among them that seconds count. *Use them.* Keeping her eyes low, she scanned the compound, careful not to arouse suspicion. All four of the guard towers were empty. She caught Roland's attention and indicated the guard's firearm closest to him, then nodded toward the shelter of the raised platform near them.

Roland understood.

The ground beneath them shuddered violently as another tremor, closer and with deeper resonance, shook the compound. Several guards, taken by surprise, staggered with the sudden movement. Sienna seized her opportunity. Nodding to Roland, she grabbed her guard's pistol and in one quick motion, dove to the ground, took aim, and fired. He fell beside her, two bullets to the chest. Roland snatched the gun from the closest holster and did the same. The guard stumbled toward the pit, his hands clutching his bloodied chest. He dropped to his knees, and fell over the rim.

The entire pit shifted on its foundations. The earth beside the pit opened and a section of the pit's concrete wall collapsed into the gaping hole.

Inside the pit, all hell had broken loose. Lincoln clung to the barbed wire, not caring about the sharp spurs that dug into his skin. The putrid water swirled beneath his feet and emptied into the yawning crevasse before him. Dirt and rock crumbling from the ground above tumbled down into the pit, swallowed by the black abyss behind Big John.

The creature had just finished off the second guard when the ground under him gave way. Losing his footing, he crashed toward the angled floor, his pincers swinging wildly through the air, his legs clattering against the concrete. As he fell backward into the chasm, his claws flailed about and grabbed a section of loose barbed wire and held tight. Big John hung from the side of the pit—kept alive by only a few strands of wire still mounted to the crumbling concrete wall.

Lincoln kicked at the concrete chunk anchoring the barbed wire, hoping to dislodge it from the wall. He kicked again as the creature swung wildly below him. Big John snapped at Lincoln's feet. With all the energy he could muster, Lincoln held on to the barbed wire behind his back and used the strength of both legs to kick the concrete. The lump broke loose. The weight of the concrete and the creature tore the barbed wire strands free, and the section of wall and Big John disappeared into the blackness.

Above the pit, Sienna took aim and fired. As another guard collapsed, she peered around the corner of the square elevated platform with Roland beside her providing cover. Behind them, Enheim stood flat against the platform's sidewall, still carrying Napoleon in his harness, A hail of bullets tore into the earth at their feet, kicking up a cloud of dust and dirt. The security force took up fixed positions about the compound, including the towers, and returned fire.

Lincoln pulled away from the barbed-wire wall, groaning in pain, his back bleeding from multiple wounds. He yanked free a piece of torn shirt snagged on the wire next to him and ripped it in half. He wrapped each half around his hands, then clawed his way up the skewed barbed-wire wall to the rim of the pit and rolled over onto the ground, much to the delight of Sienna and the others. Their joy was short-lived as the earth around him exploded in a wave of bullets.

"Here!" Sienna yelled over the gunfire.

Lincoln turned in the direction of her voice and spotted Sienna waving to him from behind the platform. He scrambled to his feet and dashed toward her, diving behind the platform as another hail of bullets ripped into the ground behind him.

Roland smiled. "It's good to see you again, you know."

"Yeah, Napoleon missed you," Enheim added. "He thought you were a goner."

"I did too." Lincoln took a deep breath and tried to recover his senses. He peeked around the wall at the heavily-fortified compound. Guards had taken up positions behind maintenance buildings, parked trucks—anywhere with cover.

"How did you escape from the crab thing?" Sienna asked.

Lincoln spied the two choppers resting on the helicopter pads. "I'll tell you later." He turned to Roland. "Can you fly a chopper?"

"If it has vings, I can fly it," he replied, firing at a guard crossing the compound.

"Okay," Lincoln said. "Listen up, everyone. Here's the plan ..."

Moments later, they darted thirty yards across the compound toward the closest chopper. A strafing line of machine gun fire tore between them and the chopper. A guard had managed to get to the machine gun mounted in the northwest tower and opened fire on them, all nine hundred rounds a minute. Dirt and dust shot high into the air as the bullets tore into the earth before them, cutting off their escape route.

So much for that idea.

"Follow me!" Sienna shouted over the gunfire, and led the way to the first loading ramp. They leaped over the side of the loading ramp's half-wall and crouched down as another line of bullets shredded the concrete above them.

Two guards appeared over the parapet. They leapt down into the loading ramp, guns firing. In one movement, Sienna slammed the closer guard into the concrete wall, knocking him unconscious, and spun around and kneed the second guard in the crotch. He crumpled in agony, but the pain was short-lived. As he fell, she snapped his head back with a knee to the head. He didn't get up.

Lincoln winced at the sight of the two guards lying on the floor. Sienna smiled. "DARPA. Like I said, they changed my life."

"I'm impressed." He removed the guard's firearms and magazines and gave one to Roland and the other to Enheim.

Roland pocketed the magazine, while Enheim glanced at the gun. "Like I told you, I can't shoot." A bullet ricocheted behind Enheim's head and kicked a small fountain of concrete dust into his face. As he pocketed the magazine and readied the gun, Enheim spoke softly to Napoleon. "Daddy might have to kill bad men now. Don't look." He gently pushed Napoleon down into the torn pouch to cover the dog's head from sight.

42

Christina closed the door behind her and strolled over to Kane's desk. Kane studied the personal information displayed on her phone—information on Roland, Enheim, and Katya.

"Most interesting," he said, not taking his eyes from the screen. "They're here, on the island. Maxwell captured them a few hours ago."

"What?"

"He has them in the holding cell."

Christina sighed. "All that time back on Saipan, wasted. Maxwell got lucky. We both know it."

Kane gave her a nondescript shrug.

She swung his chair round, lifted his chin, and kissed him full on the mouth. He stared into her unreadable eyes. "I always liked the taste of strawberry," he said, admiring her full red lips. "Did you feel the tremor earlier?" he asked, changing the subject. "I can't get through to the team in the cavern. Eddie said they would be doing preliminary testing today, but he assured me the dampers on the dome would absorb any excess vibration."

"No, I didn't feel that tremor," Christina said, disinterested. "I've been preparing for … our tremors." Smiling, she unzipped her leather biker jacket and tossed it on the floor. Leaning against the desk, she slowly removed her leather pants, then tossed them in the direction of the jacket. Her lacy white lingerie contrasted perfectly with her trim tanned body. She tapped the secret keypad mounted under the lip of Kane's desk and watched the wall behind the desk slide open to reveal an elegant, tastefully decorated bedroom.

Tremors and bad communication links trailed from his thoughts as Christina presented herself to him. Gently she lifted him by the chin and guided his eager body to the bedroom. He followed her semi-naked figure without hesitation, and closed the door behind them.

Christina left him at the door. She crossed to the bed where her overnight bag still rested on the satin bedcover from the previous night and tossed it aside. Then she lay on the bed covering her nakedness with sexy and seductive movements.

Kane stood at the door transfixed by the beautiful and mysterious woman before him. He drew his gaze from the intoxicating sight and moved to the small bedside table. After searching for a few moments, he withdrew two flutes and a carafe from the bar fridge. He filled both glasses with chilled champagne.

"Tell me about Dr. Faraday," he said, "and the beach."

The question surprised her. "I took care of him," she said without emotion, sipping the sparkling wine.

"I would have mentioned this yesterday, but I was hoping you would have told me what went wrong."

"Nothing went wrong."

"Then why have I been fielding questions from my legal counsel for the last hour?"

"Faraday was a big guy with a big swing, and he sucker-punched me on the beach. He got away in a public area, so I couldn't use my usual choice of weapon. People were nearby. I chose to use my knife, and it worked."

"It didn't work."

"What do you mean?"

"Those people you mentioned called for help. Faraday lived long enough to get the attention of the local police."

"The local police are a joke. Nobody will listen. I know that, you know that."

"Yes, we all know that. However, Neptune does not need that kind of attention, not at this critical juncture."

"What would you have had me do? Kill the couple on the beach as well?"

Kane paused and stared at her with deadpan eyes.

"Not the innocent," she said, shaking her head. "I don't do that."

"The divers, the geologist, Faraday—they weren't innocent?"

"Maxwell hired freaks and perverts, just like him. The divers were known rapists, the geologist was a drunk who wiped out a family after a night of binge drinking, and Faraday was into kiddy porn, for chrissake. They all knew what they were getting into. Their pay-checks explained that." She paused. "Besides, your bidding was done."

"Yes, you're right. I did authorize the kill. Maxwell does hire undesirables, and the paycheck does justify the action." He leaned over and kissed her on the neck. "You were always my favorite. I will miss you."

The sound of the gunshot rang through the bedroom. Christina's eyes widened as excruciating pain swept through her body. She clasped the bloodied hole in her side and tried to stem the blood flow, still in shock.

Kane drew closer so that his mouth was inches from her ear. "For some of us, perfection is unattainable," he whispered. "I cannot accept failure, not now, not ever. Alas, our time is at an end." He shot her again.

Still in disbelief, Christina let out a final gasp.

Kane sat for a moment, engrossed by Christina's beautiful body, motionless on the bed. Her long hair had fallen over her face. Kane leaned over and gently pulled the hair back. "I never got the chance to understand you," he said to her still body, caressing the hair away from her temple.

He got up and withdrew the spare magazine from within the bar fridge. He took one last look at Christina's body on the bed, then walked out of the bedroom, closing the door behind him. "Busy day. Can't have any distractions now, can I?"

Kane tossed the gun on the desk and fitted the earpiece. "Maxwell." No response.

"Maxwell," Kane said again, irritated at having to repeat himself. Still nothing.

"Today of all days—surrounded by incompetence. Is professionalism too much to ask?" Fuming, he spoke into the headset again. "Maxwell!" No response.

Kane whipped out his notepad and tapped the keys. A grid of security-camera images filled the screen. He squinted with disbelief.

The central image showed a gunfight at ground level. Security personnel and maintenance staff were scurrying about to evade flashes of gunfire from the sentry towers and the main loading ramp.

Another tremor shook the structure. He glanced around as the walls shook and the ground trembled. The last natural tremor to hit Agrihan Island had occurred in the early nineties. Since then, the central volcano had been dormant. His thoughts turned to the device in the cavern behind him, and his eyes narrowed. "Eddie," he whispered.

43

Lincoln peered over the top of the wall bordering the loading ramp. Two helicopters sat on the helipads opposite the Osprey. A bullet tore into the earth inches from his face, and he ducked back to safety below the wall.

Lincoln turned to Roland and Enheim. "You two focus on the southeast tower, and Sienna and I will do the rest. Okay?"

They nodded.

Lincoln took aim and fired at the new guard in the southwest sentry tower. He missed. The return fire shredded the wall inches above his head. Sienna peeked over the wall, took aim, and fired. The guard spun and fell back out of sight behind the guardrail circling the tower.

"DARPA?" Lincoln asked, as he fired at another guard sprinting toward them. The guard stumbled and fell head first to the ground.

"DARPA," she replied, firing at another guard crossing the compound.%

Enheim, with left eye closed, took aim, and returned fire at the guard in the southeast tower.

The tower guard spun around and fell backwards through the air. His body snagged on the barbed wire fence and hung upside down. Roland gave Enheim a thumbs up. Enheim smiled, pleased with himself for a job well-done.

The concrete wall beside them erupted with semi-automatic rifle strafing. Two guards within the complex had taken cover behind a stack of pallet boxes, and were firing at the group from inside the loading dock. Lincoln fired into the security keypad. It exploded with a shower of sparks, and the heavy doors slammed shut automatically.

"That should keep them at bay for a little while," Lincoln said, scanning the area for permanent protection. Three forklifts sat at the top of the loading ramp. Lincoln grinned.

Lincoln slammed his foot down on the gas and the forklift, tines positioned at mid level up the mast, lurched forward at top speed down the ramp. Lincoln dove off the forklift a moment before impact and landed heavy on the concrete floor. The forklift continued and slammed into the heavy security doors. The force of the impact tilted the vehicle forward. The tines lodged into each of the doors, effectively locking the entrance shut. Lincoln returned to Sienna's side and continued firing at guards darting across the compound.

"Nifty trick," Sienna said. "Defensive Vehicle Training?"

"No. Walmart forklift operator for two years."

The sentry in the northwest tower swung his M240L machine gun toward the loading dock. He set it to level three, unfolded the leaf sight, took aim, and fired. The parapet evaporated in a cloud of dust and debris as 950 rounds a minute torn into the concrete wall.

Dirt and cement dust choked the air. Between coughing bouts, Sienna asked, "Any more tricks?"

"Maybe." Lincoln followed the tower's line of view, and the position of the helicopter. He smiled. "When I say go ... run as fast as you can to the chopper."

Everyone nodded.

Sienna gave him a sideways glance. "And how do you propose to get us off this loading dock?"

Lincoln picked up a chunk of shattered concrete. "With this."

The forklift rumbled toward the northeast tower, driverless, with a slab of concrete pressing down on the gas pedal. The tines slammed into a 44-gallon drum of fuel, tearing two holes in the container's metal skin. Highly flammable liquid spilled from the puncture holes in the drum, pinned to the front of the forklift, leaving a trail across the compound.

The sentry in the northeast corner followed the forklift as it closed in on his tower. The forklift careened into the tower and skidded sideways out of control, crushing the support girders. The tower lurched violently, and the guard fell. He survived the fall only to watch the tower topple through the security fence and crush him.

"Spectacular. But how does that help us again?" Sienna asked, unconvinced.

"You're a better shot than I am. Shoot the drum," Lincoln replied.

"What?"

"Just shoot the damned drum pinned to the forklift."

She took aim, sighted the drum still embedded in the tines of the forklift, and fired.

The drum exploded. The forklift vaporised in a fireball of flame and black smoke. Burning fragments scattered across the compound, raining down on any unsuspecting soul caught in the open. The fuel trail left behind from the punctured drum ignited.

A wall of scorching fire shot across the compound, from the burning wreck of the forklift to the loading ramp. The diagonal line of churning flames, six feet high, cut the compound in two, the view from the northwest tower to the helicopters obstructed by a wall of flame.

Sienna patted Lincoln on the back. "Well done, Monk."

Lincoln gave Sienna a wink and a smile, then turned back to the group. "Ready?"

Roland and Enheim were more than ready.

"I'll cover you," Sienna said, still focused on guards scurrying about the compound.

Lincoln shook his head. "No. We all go together."

A security guard appeared from a nearby maintenance building and fired in their direction. Sienna returned fire. He staggered, a bullet hole through his head, and fell to the ground.

"I'm trained for this type of situation, you're not. I'll cover you. Don't worry about me, I'll be right behind you. Go," she commanded.

Lincoln's police training only went so far. She handled herself like a professional—choosing her targets, calmly and methodically. Her abilities obviously surpassed his in more ways than Lincoln could imagine. His talents, for now, were better-suited protecting Roland and Enheim. "Okay." He turned to Enheim and Roland and indicated the chopper. "Go."

The three dashed across the compound toward the helicopter, running parallel to the firewall. Bullets whizzed past as Lincoln flung open the chopper's sliding door. He ushered Enheim into the cabin while Roland climbed into the pilot's seat.

Roland prepared the helicopter for take-off. The blades above Lincoln's head came to life. They turned, lazily at first, then faster and faster, until they became a blur of speed and motion.

Sienna turned at the sound of the chopper preparing to take off. Lincoln stood next to the open door, beckoning her over. She took a deep breath, resolute in knowing that she had done her best to keep them alive. She braced her legs against the concrete ramp and prepared for the run, when the loading bay doors exploded outward.

The blast tore the disabled forklift from the metal doors. The forklift somersaulted backwards over her and crashed down to the ground just a few feet from her location. The force of the concussion threw her backwards. She lay on the concrete incline, stunned and winded.

Several of Maxwell's men stormed through the smoking charred doors and surrounded her, all guns trained on her hapless form. She dropped her gun in a show of non-resistance. As they converged on her like vultures swooping on prey, one of the guards recognized the three fugitives and opened fire on the helicopter.

The northwest tower guard could only hear the fire fight. Frustrated, he slammed his hand down on the M240 machine gun. The wall of flame dividing the compound obstructed his view of the other side. He heard the distinct thump-thumping of rotor blades and grinned with satisfaction. He swivelled the gun on the tripod, lined up with the sound of the rotors, and fired.

Bullets whizzed across the compound through the firewall, puncturing the chopper's sleek airframe. Lincoln, stunned at the sudden turn of events, moved toward Sienna.

Enheim held his shoulder. "It's suicide." More bullets slammed into the chopper.

"Ve haf to go," Roland shouted over the idling turbine.

A bullet clipped Lincoln's ear. He spun from the pain, stumbled back against the chopper, and clutched his bloodied ear. Meanwhile, the guards dragged Sienna up the loading ramp toward the dome's gangway.

More bullets ripped into the chopper's fuselage. The windscreen spider-webbed from the impacts. Roland twisted in his seat as bullets ripped into the co-pilot's chair next to him. Another stream of bullets tore into the avionics beside him. Roland ducked as sparks flew about the cockpit.

The window on the chopper's sliding door shattered, inches from Lincoln's head. Lincoln sighted the gas bottle on the last forklift at the loading ramp and fired. The 7.2mm round tore through the air, punctured the bottle, and ignited the pressurized gas. The forklift blasted sideways, bounced over the parapet wall, and crushed the remaining guards at the base of the ramp.

Lincoln ducked into the chopper's cabin. Enheim sat in one of the plush leather chairs, his arms wrapped around Napoleon offering protection.

"Go," he yelled above the roar of the rotor blades above him. "I'm staying."

"What?" Enheim yelled back. "Are you kidding me?"

Roland whipped around.

"Just go. Get out of here. This is the last chance you're gonna get."

"Not vithout you, ve don't," Roland yelled.

"Hey! In the movies, the hero always saves the girl. It's my job."

"This island is tearing itself apart. You'll never make it," Enheim bellowed.

"I'll see you all back in Saipan," Lincoln shouted.

Before Roland or Enheim could answer, bullets tore through the air, splintering the oak panelling behind Enheim's head. Another round of gunfire strafed the engine cowling below the blades. Thick black smoke billowed from the damaged fuselage.

Lincoln slammed the sliding door shut and dove behind a nearby maintenance shack. He gave Roland the whirlybird take-off gesture.

Roland glared at Lincoln but reluctantly agreed. He pulled back on the stick and the chopper lifted from the helipad. The damaged turbines struggled to perform as Roland fought to keep control of the craft. The helicopter spun laterally over the pad before Roland corrected for pitch, then, with a trail of black smoke in its wake, took off across the compound, over the dome, and into the southern horizon toward Saipan.

Bullets passed way above Lincoln's head. *He's firing blind.*

The ground shuddered, and a low rumble reverberated throughout the island. Between Lincoln and the dome, a section of land gave way, creating a crevasse ten feet wide, spanning the width of the compound.

Lincoln felt a vibration in his pocket and pulled out the dosimeter. The LED orb, now brighter, flashed continuously. Lincoln swiped the radiation meter over the crevasse. The meter lit up as it detected high-energy emissions from the chasm below. Lincoln calculated that there must be a connecting entrance from the cavern to the dome, a separate underpass for staff on the lower level, possibly a short cut directly to Kane. The answers to Kane's secrets lay below in the unknown, amongst the dust and debris—and Sienna was on the other side.

44

Lincoln landed heavily below the ground level of the compound and rolled into a pile of broken concrete and shattered building material. The ceiling, partially collapsed, still supported a few flickering fluorescent lights. He dusted himself off. Daylight streamed through the opening, the sky above choked by a cloud of black smoke.

A series of tangled and warped catwalks crisscrossed throughout the vast cavern. Smoke and dust filled the air. Natural light flooded in, giving the room an unearthly, ethereal quality. Another tiltrotor Osprey aircraft perched on an elevated platform near the far side of the cave, its engine cowling and several panels removed.

Lincoln's dosimeter lit up, its readout panel flashing several warnings.

Tendrils of electricity arced from a smoking crater in the center of the cavern and attached themselves to random rock formations around the walls. The tendrils, searching for breaks and cracks in the rock, disappeared into the larger fractures. Blue light glowed from the deeper fissures as strands of charged particles searched the cavern's structure. The tendrils of light mapped the subterranean foundation and the surrounding bedrock, profiling the substrata below the island.

Moaning whimpers caught Lincoln's attention. He pocketed the dosimeter, and climbed over several slabs of concrete. A heavy-set man, wearing a lab coat, lay on the floor. Part of the ceiling had collapsed and he lay beneath it, among the dirt and debris. A chunk of concrete pinned his crushed legs. Blood from a neck wound poured across his chest. He groaned as Lincoln attempted to lift the concrete, but the concrete slab held firm. Lincoln propped him into a comfortable position and read the nametag fastened to his lab coat. "You're Eddie. Eddie Ramirez."

"Who are you?"

"Lincoln Monk."

"Let me guess. You're here because of Sophia."

"She sent me the drive."

Eddie smiled at a job well done. "She said you wouldn't give up. She was right."

"Marcus Enheim figured out your location. We have him to thank, too," Lincoln said.

Eddie grimaced. "Enheim." He spat the name with disdain. "What an asshole. I suppose he told you I owe him five hundred bucks."

"He mentioned something about it."

"When you see him, tell him I won the bet fair and square … and he should stop being a pussy about it."

"I'll let him know," Lincoln said. He wanted to ask about the bet, but given the circumstances, decided against it. He removed the dosimeter from his pocket and presented it to Eddie, with a look of concern.

"Your fine," Eddie said, dismissing Lincoln's apprehension. "Short term exposure, nothing to worry about." Eddie struggled to stay conscious, but after seeing the dosimeter his thoughts turned to his greatest achievement. "The prototype is a magnificent machine, a beautiful synergy of technologies." He smiled to himself. "The applications were endless. It would have changed the world for the better." His smiled faded to a frown. "Instead, Kane wanted it for … other things. Death … destruction … experiments. To change the world into his sick twisted vision."

The cavern shook. Another quake rocked the bedrock of the island. A section of the catwalk collapsed and crashed onto the floor below.

"What are you talking about?" Lincoln asked.

"This island was the testing ground for the device. Kane and his geologists chose Agrihan because of this cavern. We needed to test and refine the acoustic boundaries of the device. The cavern's dimensions, size, and shape are perfect for our requirements."

"How does this machine work?"

"The quantum computer calculates every known detail of its surrounding mass, air and quantum space volume—the space between the trillions upon trillions of atoms within its boundaries. Acting like an amplifier, the quantum computer agitates the mass and uses it against itself."

"What does all that mean?"

"It means that the quantum computer undermines the atomic structure and destabilizes the molecules. It finds and exploits the structural integrity of the bond between atoms. It creates space where there wasn't any."

Lincoln frowned, still not understanding.

"You set this device under a large structure and it uses the structure's size to destroy itself."

"You mean like a bomb—a bomb that implodes, not explodes?"

"Kind of." He coughed. "The structural integrity is weakened. Position the device under a building. Give it a few minutes, and it collapses into itself. No chemical trace, no remnants of explosive material, nothing. It creates a perfect natural disaster—completely untraceable."

Lincoln took in the deadly information. This accounted for the back-door access to the data on the drive. Once the device is delivered, Kane wipes out all the data—the perfect crime. Nobody would ever be the wiser.

"Kane used Agrihan for many things, but it was never the target." He coughed up blood again. "La Palma in the Canary Island chain, off the coast of Africa, was the perfect target. Kane's plan was to set this device inside the mountain range and destroy it."

"What would that achieve?"

"The volcanic mountains on La Palma are a pressure cooker waiting to explode. If they collapse in the right sequence of events and at the right velocity, the mountains will slide into the ocean. Imagine, sixty square kilometres of rock falling into the ocean at terminal velocity. The tsunami following the slide would be catastrophic across the world—devastation on a global scale. The wave would not only wipe out parts of Africa and Asia, but the entire eastern seaboard of the United States. Washington, D.C., gone—under water.

"That's when Kane and his followers step in," Eddie continued. "Congressmen, Senators, law enforcement officials, media tycoons—all working for Kane, all striving for a New World order."

Eddie reached for the laptop beside him. He flipped open the screen and tapped a key. Lincoln watched as a 3-D computer-generated-image of the device appeared on the screen. The machine was the length of a coffin with a metallic outer casing. The image zoomed inside to reveal thousands of small metallic plates maneuvering around a spherical core of white light. Data scrolled down the left of the screen—the computer calculations for the surrounding mass, volume displacement, and energy required for maximum yield. When the calculations finished, the plates realigned, allowing small spaces between them. Strands of pure light flowed from the apertures. The image zoomed out to reveal a mountain with the device represented by a small pulsating point. Like veins in the human body, erratic paths of light radiated from the flashing point and spread throughout the interior of the mountain, slowly engulfing the mass. The mountain image transformed to red, indicating critical mass had been reached.

The frame zoomed out to a topographical view of the mountain and the surrounding geography—LaPalma Island. The mountain flank collapsed into the ocean creating a giant tsunami radiating out across the Atlantic Ocean. The wave hit Canada, South America and the United States, engulfing New York, Washington, D.C., and the entire eastern seaboard.

Lincoln felt sick to his stomach as a list of estimated death toll statistics and property damage reports from the individual regions rolled down the screen. He turned away, unable to comprehend the catastrophic nature of such an event. He shook his head. "This can't be real."

"It is," Eddie lamented.

"Why would Kane do this?"

"As Kane puts it—governments only act when faced with catastrophe. But if the government doesn't exist, then his new order takes control."

Lincoln still couldn't believe what he was hearing. "He's insane."

"More than likely—yes."

Stunned by Eddie's confession and the scope of Kane's plans, Lincoln needed time to absorb the information. "Enheim said the data on the drive was incomplete."

"I completed the equations, but no one will ever have the algorithm." Eddie tapped his forehead. "It's all up here. The device down there in the cavern was the working prototype, the only one. I made sure of it. Kane can't build another one, not without the final formula. I reset the test parameters for Neptune Island. This whole island will implode in one hour."

"When this island collapses, won't it cause a tsunami?"

"Possibly a minor wave, but it doesn't have the mass or the elevation of La Palma. It can't reach the velocity needed to trigger a major wave." Another cough drew more blood. "Get off this island now. Tell the world who Jonathan Kane really is."

"I don't have the USB drive anymore. Kane destroyed it."

Eddie tapped the laptop. "Remove the drive. All the information you need is on it."

The ground opened inside the crater in the cavern. Dust and smoke choked the air.

Eddie convulsed violently and drew his last breath. Lincoln placed his fingers over Eddie's bloodied neck and checked for a pulse—nothing. He carefully lowered Eddie's upper body and rested him on the floor.

Quickly he set his stopwatch for one hour. The walls around him cracked and swayed from the vibrations deep within the island. Lincoln grabbed the laptop and turned it over. Using one of Eddie's pens, Lincoln levered off the drive panel. He removed the drive and placed it in his pocket. *Time to go.*

Lincoln scanned the area and quickly found the secondary passageway to the dome. The roof had collapsed, obstructing the passage. An elevator stood at the other end of the corridor, built into the rock face. Lincoln climbed over the debris and made his way down the hallway toward it.

Damaged and buckled, the closed doors refused to open. Lincoln grabbed a nearby sliver of concrete mesh and wedged it between the locked doors and pried them open. Inside was an empty void in the elevator shaft. Lincoln peered down into the cavity. The bottom of the shaft disappeared into the shadows below. Above him, lodged into the side of the shaft, the shattered carriage rested on a precarious angle, ready to fall with the next tremor.

"Shit," he said aloud. *Think ... If there's an elevator, there's a stairwell.*

Lincoln glanced around. He spotted a solitary door marked STAIRS at the end of the hallway and made his way toward it, stumbling over more chunks of concrete and building debris. In the right hand corner of the testing area, a section of the upper compound crashed into the cavern. Time was running out.

Lincoln failed to notice the air shimmy and distort around the metal frame as he opened the door to the stairs. A thunderous roar, like that of a freight train passing, filled the corridor, as a jet flame shot out of the stairwell and down the hallway.

With milliseconds to react, Lincoln threw himself to the ground as the blazing inferno raged overhead. He rolled away from the fireball through a doorway and into another office, kicking the door closed.

Scrambling to his feet, he took a deep breath. He leaned on his haunches and assessed the situation. With the elevator out of order, the stairwell on fire, and the cavern disintegrating before his eyes, the only way out—was the way he came in. Back up into the compound.

He sighed with resignation.

45

56:00 minutes to implosion

The catwalk's tangled handrail had fallen against the rim of the crevasse. Using the railing as a ladder, Lincoln climbed from the dark hole. His pistol, tucked behind his belt, caught on a jagged steel pipe and dropped into the dust cloud below where the offices crumbled and disappeared into the depths of the island. Shattering glass and collapsing concrete thundered around him. As a gush of compressed air forced its way up and out of the crevasse, the white cloud of cement dust cleared.

Lincoln hung for a moment, peering into the inky blackness below. His thoughts turned to Nietzsche. "When you gaze long into the abyss—the abyss will gaze into you."

You got that friggin' right.

A short time later, Lincoln climbed out of the chasm and back into the compound, glad to be above ground. The fuel was burning itself out, so the wall of fire had subsided, giving the guard in the northwest tower a clear line on anything moving throughout the compound. He caught sight of Lincoln getting to his feet, swivelled his M240 machine gun around, and opened up.

Lincoln sprinted the short distance to the gangway at the entrance to the dome. He charged over the ramp and rolled into an alcove behind the giant doors as nine hundred rounds a minute shredded everything in sight.

The outer façade of the dome, surrounding the main entrance, bore the full brunt of the barrage. The shells ripped into the dome's polished black surface, tearing it to shreds. Dust and smoke filled the air as the volley of bullets continued to pummel the dome. Lincoln covered his head as shards of metal splintered from the wall around him.

The island reverberated with a deep, ominous rumble, and the sound of rock grinding against rock resounded through the air. Engineers and maintenance personal scurried about, confused and frightened and unable to comprehend the recent events, whereas security personnel understood the dire situation—a remote island in the middle of nowhere, and probably no help on the way—and sought a means of escape.

The last chopper, aside from the Osprey, sat idle on the second helipad. The rotary engine came to life and the blades spun at full rotational speed, ready for takeoff. Desperate men hung from the land skids. The overloaded Eurocopter lifted, hovered for a few moments, and dropped to the pad. The men scrambled from under the chopper, but quickly returned, anxious to escape. They thumped and punched the chopper's fuselage with clenched fists, their faces filled with anger and terror.

A fight broke out in the chopper's cabin. The sliding door swung open and several mercenaries, still in the throes of wrestling for a place on the chopper, fell to the landing pad.

Seeing this as their last opportunity for survival, the men outside trying to gain entry stormed the opened door. They scrambled aboard as the frightened pilot tried to take off again. He throttled up on the stick and the chopper lifted.

Terrified men clung to the landing gear as the chopper swayed from the extra weight. The balance ratio destabilized, and the right side of the chopper angled downward. The spinning blades tore into the concrete slab of the helipad and sent up a swirling shower of sparks and concrete shards. Wildly out of control, the chopper spun laterally. Nose down, tail up, the chopper careened across the compound and slammed into the rear of the dome. Its fuel tank ignited and the aircraft exploded in a fireball of smoke and flame. Charred bodies and ragged pieces of flaming metal exploded outward from the blast, scattering across the compound like some macabre rain of death and destruction.

Without warning, the ground beneath the parked trucks within the compound lifted. Shipping containers behind them tumbled over each other and rolled into the jungle. A chunk of earth the size of a house rose in the air, its back end higher than its forward section. Slanted at a crazy angle, the trucks, one by one, rolled down the slope. The first truck swerved out of control, ripped through the compound's barbed wire fencing, and disappeared from sight over the cliff's edge. The second truck moved through the compound unobstructed, picking up speed.

The earth under the northwest guard tower opened up. As the tower swayed back and forth, the guard lost his footing and fell. His machine gun ripped from its mounted tripod, swivelled downward, and crushed the guard's skull. The metal posts supporting the platform buckled from the severe vibration, and with the sound of screeching metal filling the air, the tower toppled into the deep crevasse.

Another quake of greater magnitude shook the island. The giant backing plate mounted to the rear of the dome supporting the section of the giant structure attached to the rails along the cliff face, buckled and warped from extreme pressure. Two of the five supporting rails tore away from the cliff. The dome lurched forward but held fast to the remaining rails, its front section angled down toward the ocean. The lighting inside the dome flickered, then blinked out. The back-up system kicked in and the lights returned, this time with a dull, reddish glow.

Beneath Lincoln's feet, the ground shuddered and he lost his balance. He slipped and fell into full view of the open doorway. The latest tremor had shaken a nearby maintenance building to its foundations. The roof, a single sheet of interlocking girders, fell sideways to the floor, holding its form, and then slid over the crevasse, creating a makeshift bridge.

The second truck rumbled over the makeshift bridge and careened over the gangway. It shot through the open outer doors of the dome, passing inches from Lincoln's head.

After barreling past, the truck veered sharply, tilted to one side, and rolled over. It skidded on its side across the loading dock and crashed into the inner entrance of the dome's viewing level. The rear doors of the truck swung open. Dozens of guns, boxes of ammunition, and several long metal cases fell to the floor, scattering behind the wreckage, hidden from Lincoln's view through the crushed wall and inner entrance to the enormous adjoining room beyond.

The third truck skidded as it crossed over the makeshift bridge, dislodging the weakened crossbeams from their precarious hold over the crevasse. The truck slammed into the metal gangway, jack-knifed, and crashed sideways into the framework of the main entrance. The wreckage of the truck wedged into the open doorway, with the crushed cab between the doorframe and the trailer behind it. Within the compound, the roof and bridge structure slipped from the edge of the crevasse and tumbled into the cavern.

Finally, the metal support struts beneath the gangway gave way. Weakened and worn from quakes and the weight of trucks, the gangway buckled from the center out, collapsing inward and crashing between the cliff face and the dome down to the ocean below.

Lincoln scrambled to his feet and surveyed the destruction around him. *Holy shit.*

A familiar voice boomed from the dome's internal loudspeakers. "Lincoln, get out of here," Sienna's voice sounded strained as it echoed around him.

"Hello, Lincoln. The outlook from the viewing area is quite breathtaking, don't you think?" Kane's voice taunted him.

After having climbed around the wreckage of the truck and through the remains of the wall, Lincoln found himself in a truly spectacular setting—the dome's viewing level.

"Mr. Monk, I believe I have something you want ... Too late."

The sound of gunfire reverberated throughout the dome.

46

51:00 minutes to implosion

Maxwell hid behind a maintenance shed when the tremors and the gunfire began. The quakes continued, but the gunfire ceased. He peeked around the side of the small shed. "Shit." He punched the wall's thin aluminium siding and cursed himself for believing Ramirez. The preliminary test was only a trial run for the main event on La Palma. That data calculated tremors measuring only 2.0 on the Richter scale at most— not the destruction he was witnessing now. Ramirez had triggered the device. "I should have shot that fat asshole when I had the chance."

Maxwell pondered Kane's reaction and the consequences of his oversight. Many mistakes littered his life, but nothing compared to the disaster zone surrounding him. Friends since school, he and Kane had seen good times and bad, with Jonathan trying to create a new way of life for them and the world. Neptune was Jonathan's dream—and Maxwell's failure. Jonathan would never forgive him for this monumental error in judgement.

Maxwell took a deep breath. Kane would only take so much disappointment from his closest friend, his friend who had killed his chance to create a new world. Maxwell's life was in danger—not only from Kane, but from the island tearing itself apart around him.

The Osprey sat on the elevated landing platform, the pilot's accommodation beside it. The concrete bunker featured a makeshift porch and a small garden bed, giving it a homey touch.

Maxwell trampled the row of flowers and flung open the front door. He found the Osprey pilot hiding behind the shower curtain. A long-haired reject from the sixties, the pilot wore a Grateful Dead T-shirt. He raised his hands in the classic surrender gesture.

"Prepare that thing for takeoff. Now," Maxwell ordered.

"I need Mr Kane's authority before I can do that," the pilot said, quivering.

Maxwell raised his gun and fired at the wall, inches from the pilot's head. Concrete slivers and tile fragments bit into the pilot's face. He flinched from the pain.

"Now!"

The pilot nodded hastily. "Okay." He scurried past Maxwell and out the front door to the waiting Osprey.

Maxwell followed close behind. Passing through the filthy living room, he noted white powdery lines on the coffee table. Next to the cocaine was a DVD of *Salò, or the 120 Days of Sodom*. "My type of guy," he declared.

When the rotors came to life, Maxwell climbed the Osprey's rear-loading ramp. The downdraft pulled at his suit and he spotted a long rip down his coat sleeve. "Damn it," he snarled. He removed the coat and threw it out the back of the aircraft. The coat undulated through the air before catching on the guardrail surrounding the raised platform.

The Osprey lifted from the staging, glided above the remains of the compound, and thundered over the jungle. Maxwell studied the destruction below him and considered the last hour's events. If Sophia, Sienna, or whatever she called herself, had not sent Lincoln Monk the drive, then Eddie would never have triggered the machine. His friendship with Jonathan Kane was over because Monk had interfered. So Lincoln Monk had destroyed his life, and now it was his turn to return the favor. Despite the confusion in the compound, he recalled Monk, very much alive, heading towards the dome.

"Get us a safe distance away, but stay close to the island," Maxwell commanded to the pilot over the headphones.

"W-What?" the pilot stammered, glancing down at the jungle canopy that was still shuddering and swaying from the continual earthquakes.

Maxwell placed his gun to the pilot's temple.

47

The architects and interior designers understood the emotional impact of a breathtaking experience. The viewing level, the size of a soccer field, was an elegant blend of classic architecture mixed with ultra-modern design.

The level spanned the entire floor of the dome. Acrylic windows three-stories high wrapped around the curved design of the structure, allowing in the panoramic seascape. The overhead support beams, designed to appear like bulkheads, crossed the width of the room, giving the room a nautical feel, while the pastel walls and parquet flooring perfectly reflected the warm glow of the sunlight flooding the cavernous space. A row of Corinthian support pillars ran the length of the room, with circular leather-clad benches fitted around their bases. The back wall, in line with the main entrance, housed a café, restroom facilities, two restaurants, a gift shop and a fully stocked bar—all of which overlooked the stunning panorama beyond the windows.

The magnificence and splendour reminded Lincoln of the wonder and adventure he'd felt reading Jules Verne's classic *Twenty Thousand Leagues Under the Sea*. In another time, he would have loved to be here. He pushed those thoughts to the back of his mind and concentrated on the task at hand.

Several of the support pillars had split and cracked, causing the room to tilt at a thirty-degree angle toward the ocean floor three hundred feet below. The angle also caused the wrecked truck to slowly edge across the room toward the panoramic windows.

Kane stood before him, using Sienna as a shield, a gun jammed in her back. He made his way around the room toward the inner

198

entrance, his eyes fixed on Lincoln. "The sound of gunfire is attention grabbing, don't you think?"

Lincoln followed his movements across the room.

When Sienna lagged, Kane pressed the gun deeper into her back, prompting her to move forward. Sienna had no choice but to obey. "All the money I've spent bringing the wonders of the oceans to the unwashed masses, bringing this truly stunning structural achievement to the people—the Eighth Wonder of the World—all gone."

King Kong will always be the Eighth Wonder, asshole. "You can't win," Lincoln said.

Kane smiled and dug the gun deeper into Sienna side causing her to flinch. "Really?"

"Eddie told me everything."

Kane leaned his head out from behind Sienna, only his face visible to Lincoln. "Did he now?"

"I know about the machine—the prototype. Only Eddie and no one else knew the complete equations to make it work. Without them, the schematics are useless. That information died with Eddie in the cavern. I know about the Canary Islands and the politicians in Washington. With the media on your doorstep, it's only a matter of time before the world knows what happened here. It's over, Kane."

Kane paused to consider his options. "That's the thing," he said. "The advances made here and the subsequent series of events could easily be misconstrued as the work of a man with gambling debts, a man battling dark demons within himself. A man so fundamentally flawed, in his mind, that this was the only way out. All that talent, and he used it for death and destruction. Oh, Eddie, what a waste of a beautiful mind."

Lincoln understood where this was leading: the lone gunman ploy, blame Eddie.

"You think this is the end? This is only the beginning," Kane said cryptically.

Another tremor pulsed through the dome. The structure lurched forward, increasing the slant of the floor. As the truck slid further toward the glass divide, Kane edged closer to the entrance. "I could give you a big speech about how I'm trying to change the world for the better, how I'm trying to get the human race to take responsibility for its actions—how I'm trying to create a new world. I could explain all these things, but I fear time is not on our side."

Kane tightened his grip around Sienna's head.

"Wait," Lincoln pleaded. "You don't have to do this."

Kane whispered in Sienna's ear. "Oh, but I do. Not only did you acquire data belonging to my company, you acted on this private information." Kane's tone became manic. "An employee of mine broke my trust and betrayed me. I simply cannot tolerate this type of behavior. I can't and I won't."

"It doesn't have to—"

The sound of gunfire echoed throughout the viewing level. Sienna's back arched, her eyes widened in pain and disbelief. From across the room Lincoln reached out into thin air, helpless to protect her. Kane fired again. Sienna moaned and fell to the floor.

Kane lifted the gun and took aim at Lincoln's head. Lincoln, stunned at the sudden shooting, stared in disbelief at the woman he loved lying on the floor. Blood matted the lower part of her back as she lay motionless at Kane's feet.

Slowly, Sienna turned her head toward Lincoln and smiled. "You never gave up."

Lincoln couldn't find the words to comfort her as the life ebbed from her body. Blood seeped from her mouth and ran down the side of her neck. Her eyes closed for the last time.

"Touching," Kane admitted.

His anger and hatred for the man before him took control as Lincoln turned his attention from Sienna's lifeless form to the man responsible for the death and ruin of so many lives.

Kane gazed dispassionately at Lincoln and at the body on the floor. "That's the third one today."

Lincoln leapt at Kane. Kane fired. Lincoln twisted and fell as the bullet struck his hip.

As Kane squeezed the trigger again, the dome lurched. The bullet, missing Lincoln's head by inches, whizzed through the air and ruptured the truck's fuel tank behind him.

The truck exploded throwing Lincoln to the ground as the shock-wave pulsed through him. In a fireball of smoke and flame, the wreckage lost its grip on the polished floor. The truck slammed through the panoramic window, shattering it into a million pieces before tumbling over the edge and dropping from sight to the ocean below.

48

Still anchored around the southern end of the island, thousands of boating enthusiasts witnessed the listing dome and the truck crashing through its glass wall. Phones and cameras captured every second of the spectacle playing out before them.

Two beer drinkers lazed on the deck of a cabin cruiser. Even with the no-go zone now resumed to three miles, they still enjoyed an unobstructed view of the day's events. The first beer drinker spat out a mouthful of beer. " Did you see that?" He angled his phone for a clearer shot. "First the dome tilts over, and now this."

"Yeah," the second drinker gasped. "I saw it." He stood, hoping to get a better view of the dome. He placed the phone in a small pouch in the front of his baseball cap, still recording, and continued drinking.

A father and son in a nearby sailing boat watched in amazement as the last waves settled from the truck impact. The father rubbed his eyes, unable to comprehend the sight before him. "Did I just see a truck smash out of the big window and plunge to the ocean?"

The boy grinned with excitement. "How cool was that!"

Marie, enjoying her morning coffee, peered through the cabin window of the KSPN2 News helicopter as it flew high over the flotilla of boats. Her eyes locked on the truck as it disappeared below the surface. She lowered her sunglasses so she could witness, with her own eyes, the events unfolding before her. When the assignment desk at the television station had offered her the chance to cover Jonathan Kane's grand revealing, she had accepted graciously but was less than enthusiastic about the assignment. She knew it was a fluff piece for the masses with little or no journalistic merit—just a piece designed to push the Neptune brand, to get the ratings up, and to charge the advertising clients accordingly. Her assignments were becoming more inane and frivolous by the week. It would only be a matter of time before her childhood dream of becoming a real investigative journalist was a distant memory. Now, however, she could smell a story. Her journalist's instincts kicked in. She spoke into her headphones. "Tell me you're getting all of this," she said to Roy the cameraman beside her, his camera inches from her shoulder.

"Never stopped rolling," he answered.

49

38:00 minutes to implosion

Kane sprinted toward the inner doors and disappeared down the main corridor. He climbed over the truck lodged in the outer entrance and stopped.

The gangway rested in a heap of crumpled metal at the base of the cliff, leaving a gap of several feet between him and the compound. Black smoke drifted throughout the compound, creating a hazy cloud of soot and ash, while intense fires scorched the battle-scared grounds.

He peered down at the crashing waves three hundred feet below, then across at the gaping divide and nodded, satisfied that he could make the jump. He took a deep breath and leaped across the abyss, rolling to a stop on the other side. He dusted himself off and smiled with satisfaction. His smile faded when he saw the crevasse crossing the compound and the Osprey landing platform—empty. Flapping in the wind, snagged on the platform's guardrail, was Maxwell's coat. Kane put his hands on his hips and shook his head in a genuine display of disappointment. "Leon," he sighed. The ground wrenched apart beneath him and tore open. He lost his balance and tumbled backwards, arms flailing into the chasm.

• • •

Lincoln awoke to the sound of screeching metal and the whole world askew. Building debris rolled across the floor—still at a crazy angle—and through the shattered window frames. Sienna lay motionless on the floor before him. He shook his head, trying to clear his mind. This wasn't some wild dream or bizarre nightmare. This was real.

Lincoln crawled across the floor toward Sienna, careful not to slip down the incline to the edge. A circular chair at the base of a nearby pillar broke free and tumbled toward him. He braced himself as the chair bounced along the floor, passed above his head, and over the edge.

He continued crawling until he reached Sienna. He cradled her in his arms and squeezed her lifeless body close to him. The world could tear itself apart, but this moment was his and his alone. As a tremor shook the dome, he rocked her gently in his arms and kissed her lightly on the temple. "I'm so sorry," was all he could say.

A track rail mounted to the cliff face broke free and buckled from the weight of the structure. The rail swung wildly away from the cliff and slammed into the back end of the dome, crashing through its exterior facade. As the rail sliced through the rear wall inside the viewing area, the café and gift shop exploded. Refrigerators, tables and chairs, clothes racks—anything not nailed down hurtled across the observation deck toward the glass window.

The café's counter top tumbled end over end until the wreckage slammed into Lincoln still holding Sienna. Catching him across the upper body, the counter top flung him away from the falling debris. Lincoln watched in horror as Sienna's body vanished over the side with the debris, trapped within the tumbling furniture shattering the viewing window. The dome swayed and edged further from the cliff face.

Lincoln pushed his grief to the back of his mind and turned from the shattered window frame, knowing he could mourn Sienna's death later. He spotted a clothes rack lying at his feet, grabbed a random T-shirt, and put it on. The black shirt had a white Neptune logo emblazoned across the chest. He snagged a black baseball cap and slipped it on his head.

He examined the surrounding carnage and scorched flooring, and the previous location of the truck that was now at sea level. The hit from the counter had thrown him back toward the center of the room, in line with the inner entrance doors. He peered toward the open doorway at the second truck wedged in the main entranceway beyond the end of the corridor. The Pacific Ocean filled the window with a panoramic view, while the observation deck lay at forty-degree angle. The only way out was up.

Lincoln braced his legs against the tilted floor and made his way, staggering, toward the inner entrance. Systematically, he clawed his way up the incline when another quake shook the island. The dome swayed, and the sound of tearing metal filled the air. Then the screeching of tortured metal ceased, and the rumbling died away.

A long silence enveloped the room. For the first time, Lincoln could hear the boom of the ocean swell rolling against the cliff below. He tasted the salt of the ocean air washing through the observation deck, a welcome sensation from the events in the jungle.

Lincoln watched with curiosity as an office chair rolled across the floor and over the edge.

50

The roar of colliding bedrock thundered in the morning air. The island shook with the largest quake yet. The northern end of the island shuddered violently and lurched upwards. A plume of black dust and dirt rocketed into the air as the terrain collapsed in on itself. A cloud of dirt charged across the island, engulfing everything in its path.

Lincoln stumbled but managed to steady himself. Down the corridor, the main entrance gave way. The truck tore free from the framework and tumbled toward Lincoln and the observation deck.

Lincoln had nowhere to go and no time to scramble from the juggernaut's deadly path. He spun around to the shattered window frame behind him and glanced at the ocean. A small chance of survival was better than none. In a split second Lincoln prepared himself for the final battle with Neptune Island. As the truck crashed through the inner doorway and barreled across the viewing floor toward him, Lincoln stepped through the broken window frame and into the blue void.

51

30:00 minutes to implosion

Marie stared open-mouthed, stunned by the series of events taking place before her eyes. While earthquakes rocked the ground, the northern tip of the island exploded, causing the dome to list precariously from the cliff. A truck fell through the observation level, and a man hung from the open deck three hundred feet above sea level.

Roy the cameraman continued recording every moment of the spectacle as it unfolded before him. Marie smiled. This was turning into a momentous day for her career and for journalism.

Not far away, the first beer drinker steadied himself on the deck of the cruiser. He lowered the can from his mouth and stared at the front of the dome. "Hey," he called to his buddy. "There's a dude hanging from the vista window."

As the sailboat swayed with the swell, a boy tugged at his father's shirt. "Hey, Dad, there's a man outside. Look." He pointed to the vista window.

"Well, I'll be damned!" his father said, adding, "Poor bastard."

• • •

Lincoln's fingers had caught on a small rain channel circling the observation deck. He hung on with all his strength as the truck passed inches from his face, sailing through the air and tumbling down to the ocean. The truck crashed cab-first into the water then slowly sank beneath the waves.

Taking a moment to regain his composure, Lincoln breathed deeply. Now for the really hard part. With nothing between him and the raging ocean three hundred feet below, he clenched the rain gutter tighter.

Don't look down. Don't look down.

He glanced down.

Oh, shit.

Focus on the gutter.

By picking up his right hand, reaching further right and gripping the gutter, then moving his left hand nearer to the right, he clawed his way around the outside of the dome to the cliff face behind the structure.

He stopped above a small balcony one level below. He dropped, landing heavily on the balcony deck with his right foot collapsed beneath him. Rocking back and forth he clutched his ankle. Then, with the pain coursing through his leg, he managed to hobble to the balcony rail and peered across to the cliff face just a few feet away in time to see the last of the rail tracks supporting the dome rip away from the cliff face. The backing plate crumpled in on itself, and the crossbeams below buckled and collapsed. The dome swayed violently from side to side, gaining momentum until the sound of metal tearing apart reverberated through the sky. Slowly, inexplicably, the dome released its hold on the cliff and made its final journey downward.

The gap between the dome and the cliff was widening by the second. Lincoln had no time to think. Ignoring his ankle pain, he climbed onto the railing, focused on a small ledge running along the cliff's edge, and jumped.

The dome crashed down the side of the cliff and plummeted to the swirling sea below.

Its lower levels crashed against the hard-jagged rock as chunks of concrete and metal broke apart, filling the morning air with sounds of destruction. The dome's roof collapsed and crashed through to the observation deck, blasting out a shower of metal, glass, and debris. The dome slid along the cliff face, leaving a trail of devastation before nose diving into the ocean and sending up a giant wall of frothing white water. The sea quickly flooded into the remains of the mega-structure causing the dome to heave and groan in response to the ocean's final assault. Within minutes, the wreckage sank below the crystal blue surface of the Pacific.

Beneath the waves, the dome glided to a darker region of the ocean. Like a leviathan eager to return home, the dome disappeared into the inky blackness of the deep waters. Several bubble streams made their way up through the murky haze until they, too, dissolved into nothingness.

Marie was speechless.

"You still want me to record?" Roy asked, feigning nonchalance.

"Are you serious?" she spluttered.

52

Lincoln clung precariously to the side of the cliff face, his outstretched hands gripping the craggy rock. As the rock crumbled beneath his feet, his trekking boots struggled to find a foothold. He warily peered down at the school of sharks circling in the blue water and at the ocean swell crashing against the base of the cliff—more reminders of the fate below.

Another tremor shook the island causing a small avalanche to tumble down the cliff face. Lincoln flattened himself against the ledge as the rocks plummeted around him. A cloud of earth and sand followed the falling rock, and Lincoln found himself covered in dust and dirt. To his left, huge chunks of rock wrenched apart from the cliff face and crashed into the sea. To his right, a section of the cliff gave way. The metal ladder they had used disappeared in the thundering mass as it slid into the ocean, sending a mountain of frothing water into the air. The cliff's summit crumbled to dust, shaken to its core by the constant vibrations. The tremors arrived with greater frequency. It was only a matter of time before the island imploded.

Amidst the cacophony, Lincoln heard the distinct thump thump of rotor blades. Battered and bruised, he sighed from exhaustion and relief. Beyond the southeast corner of the island, the tiltrotor Osprey appeared in the sky, banking around from behind the cliff face. It maneuvered into position before him, hovering less than fifty feet away, his line of vision level with the cockpit.

Maxwell sat in the co-pilot's seat, his glaring eyes locked onto Lincoln clinging desperately to the crumbling cliff face. Maxwell nodded to the pilot as the Osprey edged closer, its dual rotor blades spinning just a few feet from Lincoln's hapless form. The pilot flipped the safety cover for the firing switch, prepared the side-mounted canon, and took aim.

What an asshole. As Lincoln braced himself against the rock, ready for the final assault, his thoughts turned to his friends. At least they were safe, free from Kane's reign of terror and madness, even if he faced certain death.

He grimaced with determination. *This is it. Oh, well, you take the good with the bad.*

He looked again at the circling sharks below. This time, the height did not bother him as it had in the past. The distance sent shivers down his spine, but the all-encompassing fear had disappeared.

The force of the rotor wash pummeled him as he readied himself for the final leap.

Fuck it. He closed his eyes, took a deep breath, and prepared to allow gravity to take control.

A high-pitched whistling sounded above him. Behind the cliff's summit, a trail of white smoke streaked across the sky. The helicopter lurched sideways as its fuel tank erupted. The left tiltrotor exploded in a fireball of flame and smoking metal. The blades dislodged from their mounts on the rotor engine and swung wildly. Lincoln ducked as a flaming blade embedded itself in the rock above his head. The other blades finally tore free from their mounts and hurled themselves in all directions.

Fear etched across Maxwell's face as he looked to the pilot who was struggling to regain control of the Osprey. A second stream of white smoke rushed across the sky. Maxwell turned from the pilot to the view beyond the windscreen in time to see the second rocket hurtling toward him.

The cockpit exploded and tore away from the fuselage of the failing helicopter. Smoke billowed from the gaping hole as the twisted chunk of metal that was the cockpit plummeted to the ocean below. The rest of the chopper followed, crashing into the burning cockpit as it hit the ocean waves. The fuel tank on the starboard side exploded. The helicopter tore apart with the force of thirteen thousand pounds of fuel igniting at once. The fuselage, wings, and tail evaporated in a blinding thundering flash of white light.

A line of thick rope unwound next to Lincoln and slapped against the rock face. The other end was out of sight over the crest of the cliff.

He grabbed the rope and began to pull himself up, hand over hand. He dragged himself up the last section of rope and hauled his body over the ridge of the crumbling cliff. He rolled on the ground, relieved and happy to be alive. He wiped the dust and sweat from his eyes and gazed at the beautiful woman kneeling before him.

Her auburn hair was tied back, and she wore loose fitting sweat pants and a baggy T-shirt caked with blood. She moaned, and when she clutched her side, fresh blood appeared on her hand.

"I remember you. The café."

"Christina," she said, wincing. "Now we're even."

Lincoln eyed the bloodstain on the T-shirt. "What happened?"

"Gunshot wounds," she explained, "courtesy of the psychopath, Jonathan Kane." She compressed the wounds with her hand, and tried to stop the bleeding. "I gave myself a shot of adrenaline, so I should be all right for a while."

Lincoln spotted the rocket launcher beside her. A waft of smoke still trailed from the weapon's rear exhaust port.

Christina followed his line of vision. "I found the rocket launcher at the observation deck. It's amazing what you find just lying around this place." Another earthquake shook the island, this time closer. The edge of the cliff turned to dust and vanished from view.

"Eddie Ramirez, the chief designer, triggered the device. We've got—" Lincoln glanced at his watch, "—twenty-two minutes left to live. Time to go."

Beyond the compound's security fencing, an acre of jungle shuddered violently. Branches swayed and millions of fallen leaves ebbed and swirled through the humid air. Flocks of birds scattered into the sky. As the ground lifted, the trees lurched sideways, and the earth disappeared from sight, swallowed by the giant abyss opening below.

To the north, the island collapsed before their eyes. The south side led to hungry sharks at the bottom of a disintegrating cliff face. The east and west flanks of the island had sheared off and slid into the ocean, leaving unpassable gaping wounds in the island's topography.

Lincoln helped Christina to her feet, keeping an eye on the fractured and crumbling ground around them. "By chance, you wouldn't know a way off this island, would you?" he joked,

Christina stared into Lincoln's eyes. "As a matter of fact, I do."

53

Lincoln and Christina made their way down into the cavern via the crevasse dividing the compound. At ground level, they found themselves before a mountain of crumpled catwalks and mounds of loose rock.

The section of the cavern's floor where the device once operated had fallen into the earth creating a large gaping hole the size of a house that blocked their escape route. Rocks and debris surrounded the rim of the void, and Lincoln determined it would take too much precious time to traverse around it.

Lincoln and Christina searched the cavern for another way to the other side. Lincoln spotted a piece of the skywalk lodged in a pile of rubble. He dragged it to the edge of the abyss and maneuvered the catwalk so that it spanned the gap, creating a makeshift bridge.

Christina sprinted over the catwalk and quickly made it to the other side.

Lincoln groaned at how easily Christina made it across, and shamefully followed on all fours as another tremor shook the island. The catwalk shifted on the loose rubble and slid sideways. Lincoln gripped the metal as the catwalk rolled over. Again, he found himself dangling perilously over an abyss. *You've got to be shitting me.*

Christina grabbed the end of the catwalk and steadied it as best she could.

Lincoln hung on tight. Using the metal grating floor of the walkway as monkey bars, he swung from grating panel to grating panel until he reached the outer rim of the hole. Christina gave him a hand as he climbed up and over the rim.

"Thanks," Lincoln said, dusting himself off. "I'm just about done with heights today. I really am." They pushed ahead through piles of torn metal and broken concrete.

"It's not too far now," Christina said.

"If you don't mind me asking, what did you do for Kane?"

Christina paused for a long while. "Personal assistant."

"Wow." Lincoln's tone was tinged with cynicism. "A personal assistant who knows how to give herself an adrenaline shot and fire a rocket launcher. You're one very talented personal assistant."

Christina spun around and grabbed Lincoln by the throat. Her glaring eyes locked onto Lincoln's startled face. "Mind your own business."

"Sorry," Lincoln said sincerely. "I didn't mean to pry." She loosened her grip and continued making her way through the debris. Lincoln rubbed where her hand had left a red print on his throat. *That's one tough lady.*

They passed the second tiltrotor Osprey still sitting on the lowered platform. The rear-loading ramp was down and the escape hatch above the cockpit open. Several fuselage panels sat beside the craft and wheel chocks wedged the plane in place. Behind the Osprey, toward the dark recess of the cavern, a shaft of light illuminated the dusty, hazy air. Lincoln calculated that they must be near the pit at the northern end of the compound. He gazed up at the plane as they picked their way around piles of loose rock. "By chance, you wouldn't know how to fly one of those things, would you?"

"If I knew how to fly it, I wouldn't be leading us down into the depths of a crumbling island now, would I?"

"Good point," Lincoln conceded.

"Besides, they're making repairs on it. Last time I heard, it was still grounded."

A small tremor hit the cavern. Lincoln picked up movement in the cockpit, and stopped for a moment to study the plane. Small concrete chunks dropped from the cavern's ceiling and hit the plane's fuselage, causing it to scatter over the hull and fall to the floor.

Christina turned and followed Lincoln's line of sight to the cockpit. "You see something?"

Lincoln waited for a moment but the movement didn't recur. "My mind must be playing tricks. It was probably just dirt and sand falling from the surface. Let's go."

As they clambered over more mounds of dirt, Lincoln asked, "How do you know there's a way out down here?"

"Below this cavern there's a second one at water level. Inside is a pool that empties out to the ocean through a fissure in the rock."

"How do you know about the fissure?"

She gave him a steely-eyed stare. "I just do."

Lincoln understood when to back off. "Okay. So how do we get down to the second cavern?"

Christina climbed to the top of the next knoll of debris and studied the darkened rock wall. After a moment she found what she'd been looking for: the familiar shape of a doorway.

"Hold on." Lincoln stopped her before Christina could open the warped stairwell door.

She shot him a curious glance as he ushered her behind him and then analysed every square inch of the metal door and the doorframe. "Had a bad experience with a door—I'll tell you later." He gently tapped the metal surface and found it cold to the touch. He nodded an okay to Christina, turned the handle, and pushed. The door stood fast, buckled within the framework.

"My turn." This time, Christina ushered Lincoln back. He stood a few paces behind to let her do her work. Christina lined up her right leg with door just above the handle, and kicked hard. The door tore off the hinges and flung open.

"Well done."

"Let's go." Christina made her way into the stairwell and down the stairs.

"Let's." Lincoln smiled, impressed by the skill and power of the woman before him.

Lincoln and Christina stood at the base of the stairwell overlooking a giant cave twice the size of the one overhead. The cave's only light source came from the gaping hole in the floor above. The light shaft illuminated a pile of debris in the center of the lower cavern, but the outer walls were still swathed in shadow.

Lincoln coughed on the choking dust that filled the air as he followed Christina down a descending pathway along the cave's wall. They entered a rock tunnel and emerged in a smaller cavern. Near the center of the cave was a pool of swirling, ebbing water.

"The water comes in from under that rock wall," Christina said, indicating the wall on the far side of the cave. "From there, it flows out to the ocean."

Lincoln understood what she had in mind.

Christina turned to Lincoln. "How long can you hold your breath?"

54

10:00 minutes to implosion

The tremors and quakes had stirred the foundations of the island, causing silt and sand to cloud the seawater in the fissure. With visibility low, they swam toward a faint light in the distance.

Lincoln felt something brush alongside him. A baby shark glided next to him, its black eyes watching his every move. Christina panicked and tried to swim away from the predator. Lincoln punched the shark hard on its snout. The shark writhed about and retreated into the murky water. With their oxygen running low, Lincoln indicated for Christina to follow him. She needed no encouragement.

They passed the fissure's oceanside entry and they kicked their way to the surface. They broke through the water at the same time, gulping in mouthfuls of clean fresh air.

"Thanks for the help back there in the fissure," Christina said, gasping for air. "How did you know that would work?"

Lincoln grinned. "What can I say? I love Nat Geo."

Christina swam toward the cruiser anchored at a small landing by the base of the rock wall. The name Christina ran along the side of the bow. She climbed aboard saying, "If I were you, I'd get out of that water as soon as possible. If baby's swimming around then mom can't be too far behind." She turned. "Nat Geo." Lincoln didn't need to be told twice.

Christina throttled up, glided away from the floating dock, and headed for open water.

Giant whirlpools had formed around the island, cutting off any planned escape route for the open ocean. Frothing water circled inside the maelstroms funnels and disappeared into the dark abyss of the crushing ocean. The whirlpools churned the ocean bordering the island, rendering any attempt to pass between the roiling waters suicidal.

"What the hell?" Christina surveyed the surrounding waters.

Lincoln looked at the funnels of swirling water and shook his head. "Eddie said this would happen. The device is searching for all the cavities on the island and surrounding bedrock. The device weakens the rock until it can't support itself anymore. Huge caverns must exist below the seabed too, not just on the island. The ocean is pouring into those caverns."

Christina had no choice but to turn the boat around and follow the island's rocky coastline. Lincoln trusted they would find a safe channel between the whirlpools, but he crossed his fingers anyway. The cruiser hugged the sea cliff as it ploughed through the rough ocean at the island's base. They held on tight as the cruiser reeled when Christina swerved to avoid falling rocks and debris crashing into the water. Without warning, an ominous cracking filled the air as the cliff face swayed and teetered.

With seconds to react, Christina yanked hard on the wheel. The cruiser swung sharply and rocketed into a small alcove in the rock face just as a sheet of rock the size of an office building crashed into the ocean behind them. The swell picked up their small boat and slammed it into a rock wall inside the alcove. The cruiser crunched hard against the jagged rock. Lincoln and Christina leaped overboard as the boat splintered into thousands of pieces. The wave engulfed them and hurled them against a far wall inside the alcove before washing back out into the ocean.

They found themselves on a natural rock landing, coughing up seawater, gasping for breath, and trying to comprehend their situation. *This is the end*, Lincoln thought. *Our bodies have been through hell, and exhaustion is setting in.* He wiped the burning seawater from his eyes and breathed deeply.

He looked over at Christina who was still trying to regain her breath. He couldn't tell for sure, but he thought he saw a tear roll down her cheek.

Not now. Not like this.

We've come too far for it to end this way.

Never give up.

He dragged himself to his feet and tried to formulate a plan. He scanned the alcove for inspiration, for anything to help them get away from this damned island.

Think.

The empty cave looked familiar, very familiar. He turned back toward the entrance to the alcove. A grin spread across his face.

55

00:05 seconds to implosion

The Duck maneuvered between two of the smaller whirlpools, shuddering violently from the choppy water below her beam. The Duck shot through to the calmer ocean beyond and headed south, away from Neptune Island. The sturdy amphibious vehicle was speeding across the water when an ear-splitting thunderous crash exploded, causing the water to shimmy and quiver as the sound wave pulsed over and through the water.

Lincoln throttled down and the Duck slowed through the water, drifting with the tide. Lincoln and Christina turned to watch the spectacle behind them.

A deep rumbling shook the boat, then faded with the afternoon breeze. An ominous silence filled the air. Christina turned to Lincoln for an answer. Lincoln's gaze was fixed on the island, hoping that Eddie had miscalculated. The eerie quiet and peaceful calm filled them with a sense of dread.

A sight and sound neither observed nor heard by another human being since the eruption of Krakatoa more than a hundred years earlier unfolded before them and before those aboard the flotilla on the distant horizon. The loudest thunderclap Lincoln had ever heard, like a detonating atomic bomb, exploded across the calm ocean. They covered their ears as the shattering sound wave resounded all around. The deep rumbling returned with a vengeance. The ocean chopped and churned as the Duck heaved with the swell of the undulating waves.

The island buckled and lifted from the seabed. The three-hundred-foot cliff surrounding the island shuddered and collapsed. A cloud of black dirt and debris shot into the air as the island succumbed to the forces of gravity. The land lurched downward with another thunderous roar, sending huge chunks of rock and earth exploding into the sky, before sinking below the ocean's surface. The island disappeared behind a swell of white churning waves as a cloud of ash spread over the Pacific.

Awestruck, Lincoln and Christina gaped as the ocean swallowed Neptune Island, leaving a swirling mass of black churning water in its wake. "Whoa," is all Lincoln could think to say.

Christina stood shaking her head, pondering the ramifications of the event. Finally she took a long deep breath and sighed. "It's all over."

As Lincoln nodded, his peripheral vision picked up an unusual form. He squinted and focused on the thin black line crossing the horizon. "Oh shit," he muttered.

Christina groaned. "What now?"

"Tsunami."

56

Lincoln swung the Duck around and took off at top speed away from the oncoming wave.

The amphibious craft raced across the ocean, heading toward the thousands of boats at anchor, unaware of the oncoming disaster. Lincoln knew the Duck could never outrun the wave. Even with Roland's modifications to the engine, the wave would be on them in no time.

Warn the spectators. Warn them now. Seconds count. "We have to warn those people, save as many as we can!" Lincoln shouted to Christina over the din of the engine, nodding to the flotilla of boats still a distance away. With one hand on the tiller, Lincoln searched the console for a speaker system and microphone. *Roland must have installed one somewhere. All tour boat operators have a voice amplification device so the tourists can hear them.* Lincoln hunted frantically under the console, then gave the wheel to Christina and threw open the bench seats that lined the deck behind the cabin. Nothing. "Come on, Lincoln, come on," he said to himself, annoyed that he couldn't find the microphone.

With one hand fighting for control of the Duck, Christina reached with the other and fumbled along the inner nooks of the cabin. Next to her feet, tucked back into the folds of a canvas pouch, she found the small hand microphone and tossed it to Lincoln.

He grabbed the plug and rammed it into the console socket, then turned the volume to maximum. "Attention all craft! Attention all craft! A tsunami is headed this way. I repeat: A tsunami is headed this way. Maneuver your craft accordingly. I repeat: Maneuver your craft accordingly."

Roy saw the tsunami first. He lowered the camera and squinted, trying to comprehend the black line, growing larger and higher on the horizon. He whipped the camera up again and focused as best he could on the distant skyline. Through the camera's viewer, he witnessed the front of the wave getting higher by the second. He nudged Marie and pointed toward the horizon. Marie followed his gesture and gasped.

On a nearby boat, the first drinker asked his companion, "Did he just say tsunami?"

The second beer drinker peered closely at the black line growing higher across the horizon. He dropped his beer can, his eyes wide with terror. "Oh shit! shit! shit!" He jumped from his deckchair and stumbled toward the wheel.

"What?" the first beer drinker asked, watching his pal fumble the keys into the ignition.

The engine spluttered, coming to life. The first beer drinker looked back toward the horizon. "Holy fu—"

As the second drinker yanked on the wheel, the cabin cruiser swung around and gunned through the hundreds of boats in its path. He grabbed the intercom and flipped it to external speakers. "Tsunami! Tsunami! There's a tsunami coming!" Desperate to get through the congestion, he slammed up against anchored boats.

Lincoln repeated the message but to no avail. His voice was drowned out by blaring horns and revving engines. The pleasure boats sat, idly drifting, transfixed by the spectacle behind him—unaware of the impending disaster. Lincoln felt helpless, unable to think of any other way to warn the thousands of boaters. A deafening roar filled the sky above him.

Overhead were two long pontoons attached to a camouflaged C-47 Dakota. The aircraft soared overhead then set down on the ocean's surface between the Duck and the flotilla. The plane skimmed the water and slowed, but continued to move away from the Duck.

The external speaker, mounted to the cockpit's roof, came to life. "Lincoln, hurry up, vill you? There's a big vafe coming, you know."

Lincoln recognised the voice instantly. "Ha, ha, ha, ha. Roland, you're full of surprises, you son of a bitch!" He shouted to Christina,

"They're with me. Head toward the plane." She nodded and made a beeline for the plane.

As the cargo doors of the C-47 swung wide, Enheim, with Napoleon still in the harness around his chest, appeared through the hatch, beckoning Lincoln to hurry up. "Come on!" he shouted over the roar of the twin Stratton engines.

"Why doesn't he slow down?" Christina yelled to Lincoln.

"He can't," Lincoln shouted. "If he does, the plane will stall. He'll never get it back up again in time."

Nodding, Christina yelled, "We need to lighten the boat!"

Lincoln gave her a thumbs-up and started jettisoning anything not nailed down. He hauled the spare batteries from under the seats and heaved them over the side. He wrenched the bench seats from their mounts and tossed them over the gunwale. The Duck picked up speed, shortening their distance from the C-47.

The vibration from the plane's skimming across the water nudged the cargo bay door from its locked position. The door swung back toward Enheim, who managed to catch it in time, but Napoleon's harness snagged on the hatch's framework, and the stitching gave way. "NO!" Enheim screamed in horror as he watched Napoleon fall to the ocean.

Katya appeared next to him with a questioning look. She followed his line of sight and gasped. Her hand covered her mouth as she stared in shock.

Enheim leaned back into the cabin. "Stop the plane!" he shouted.

"I can't," Roland yelled. "If I do, ve all die."

Enheim frantically ran his hands over his bald head as he watched Napoleon drifting further away.

Meanwhile, below the surface of the ocean, the mass of the tidal wave crashed into a coral reef. The swell, still moving at top speed, built up behind the wave. The wave doubled in height, and crashed down over the reef. A wall of white churning water, twenty feet high, rushed toward the flotilla at one hundred miles an hour.

57

Everyone in the flotilla heard the unmistakeable boom and thunder and witnessed the wave breaking on the reef. Panic and terror set in as thousands of desperate boaters maneuvered away from the wall of water. Boats crashed into one another trying to escape. Smaller craft capsized from the wakes of the larger cruisers. People fell into the water, screaming and yelling for help.

Lincoln spotted the little dog in the water, paddling bravely. He looked back toward the rolling white wall closing in on them and climbed over the Duck's port railing.

"What are you doing?" Christina yelled.

Lincoln indicated Napoleon in the water. "Get me as close as you can," he shouted.

Christina paused—then swung the wheel so that the port side lined up with Napoleon.

Lincoln gripped the rail and leaned down as far as he could.

Enheim and Katya watched, wringing their hands, knowing that this was their only chance of getting their baby back. Enheim threw his arm around Katya's shoulder and hugged her with all his might. She kissed his cheek and gripped his hand.

Roland eased back as far as he could without stalling the engines. The revs slowed and the engines spluttered. The plane dropped speed and slowed, but not enough to prevent the plane from being prepared for take-off. Michel, the mechanic from Roland's hangar, sat in the co-pilot's seat looking worried and fumbling in his pocket for a pack of cigarettes. His hands shook as he lit one and inhaled deeply.

Roland reached out. "Could I haf one, too?"

As the wave thundered on, its momentum unstoppable, Lincoln and Christina felt the forward spray from its wall of water now less than a city block behind them.

Marie spotted the Duck approaching the C-47. She elbowed Roy and pointed. Roy swung his camera from the wave to the Duck as she made her way toward the plane.

With Napoleon just ahead, Lincoln stretched his arms as far as he could, one hanging from the Duck's railing, the other just inches above the water. As Napoleon flew by beneath his hand, Lincoln grabbed his collar and pulled the little dog from the water. Lincoln hauled himself back onto the boat and slumped down on the deck with Napoleon licking his face. Lincoln smiled. "You know your mom and dad are worried sick about you." He hugged the little dog, stood up, and showed the world that Napoleon was still alive.

Enheim and Katya screamed with joy. They hugged each other and laughed, with tears rolling down Katya's cheeks. Below, the Duck closed on the plane. Katya lowered a rope ladder out the bay doors while Enheim secured it to the safety rail above the hatch.

Christina brought the Duck in line with the left pontoon opposite the cargo bay doors, struggling to maneuver toward the doors with the boat handling badly in the choppy water. She was fighting for control when, to her surprise, Lincoln passed her Napoleon and took the wheel to keep the boat on course.

"Time to go," Lincoln yelled.

"You sure?"

"I'll be right behind you."

Christina carefully tucked Napoleon down her sweatshirt and tied a knot in the bottom end around her waist. She was about to leave, then hesitated.

"What's wrong?" Lincoln asked.

Christina kissed him lightly on the cheek and smiled. She climbed out of the Duck and onto the pontoon, grabbing its rear strut supporting the float. Katya swung the rope ladder over. Christina grabbed it with her free hand and released her grip on the strut. She climbed up the rope ladder and, with help from Enheim and Katya, through the hatch and into the cargo bay.

Enheim and Katya stood over her, watching, waiting. Christina realized who owned the little dog. She reached into her sweatshirt and pulled out Napoleon, all safe and sound.

Enheim cradled the little dog and kissed him all over. "Daddy will never ever let that happen again." Katya smothered the dog with kisses.

Christina scrambled to the hatch. She grabbed the rope ladder, and prepared for Lincoln. Enheim and Katya joined her with Napoleon firmly between them.

Lincoln steadied the Duck and timed the swaying of the C-47 as best he could.

It's now or never.

He leaped onto the Ducks gunwale and jumped.

Just as Lincoln landed chest down on the pontoon, the C-47 lurched in the rough water. Lincoln clawed the air but missed the strut and slid toward the backend of the float. His boot caught on a small cleat, stopping his fall. Christina calculated the length of the rope. It would never reach that far along the pontoon. The Duck, now without a captain, followed the wake of the waves made by the C-47 and drifted away from the plane.

"Lincoln's on the pontoon," Enheim shouted to Roland.

Roland peered through the cockpit's windscreen and gulped. The distance between the C-47 and the flotilla was closing fast. He throttled up the engines. The C-47 picked up speed as it approached the fleet.

Marie was riveted to the events below. From the corner of her eye, a black form flying low over the white water caught her attention. "What the hell?"

Slowly Lincoln dug his rubber soles into the smooth side of the float and did his best to keep his hands flat on the surface. He edged his way up the slippery pontoon in line with the hatchway.

At the same time, Christina lowered herself from the plane. She climbed down the rope ladder as far as she could go and reached out to Lincoln. Lincoln leaned over the rushing waves between them and reached for her hand. Their fingertips touched—as a strafing round of bullets tore through the left wing.

Lincoln rolled back onto the pontoon, but this time he managed to grab the strut and hold on tight as Christina backed up into the hatch for protection. They both looked in disbelief as the second tiltrotor Osprey cruised behind the C-47, keeping ahead of the white water. A few of the outer panels were missing, but the black Osprey was definitely flight worthy.

Calm and collected, Jonathan Kane sat at the controls of the Osprey. He straightened his back and stretched his neck, as if preparing for a workout, his unblinking eyes glued on Lincoln clinging to the pontoon below the C-47.

With its nose down, backend up, and a churning wave of frothing water filling the background, the image of the Osprey was a sight Lincoln would never forget.

Christina pulled a Colt 45 from her sweatpants and returned fire. Kane flinched as cracks spider-webbed across the Osprey's windshield, but the sight of Christina in the hatchway, still alive, surprised him. "Ah, my darling Christina, you're alive—but unfortunately, not for long."

The cannon mounted under the Osprey came to life and another barrage of bullets ripped into the left wing. A damaged panel section from the C-47's wing broke free, flew backwards through the air, and passed just inches above the Osprey's cockpit. Kane grinned. "That was exciting."

The flotilla of boats filled the view from the C-47's cockpit. "Ve haf to lift off now," Roland shouted into the planes intercom.

Christina emptied her gun at the Osprey. She climbed out of the hatchway and down the rope ladder where she wrapped one arm through the rope and reached out with her other arm. Over the roar of the engines she screamed to Lincoln, "It's now or never!"

The C-47 skimmed along the surface of the ocean and slowly lifted from the water. Lincoln braced himself against the strut, like a runner about to leap from the starting post.

"Holy shit, the guy's gonna jump," Roy said to Marie.

Enheim and Katya hugged each other tighter. "Come on mate, you can do it," Enheim whispered.

"Come on, Lincoln darling." Katya squeezed Napoleon.

Lincoln smiled at Christina—and jumped. He sailed through the air, over the rushing water beneath him, and caught hold of her outstretched hand. She swung him around and into the rope ladder. He caught the rope and held tight.

"Yes!" Marie screamed in delight.

"Bravo. Bravo—" Kane said, congratulating the daring leap, "—and goodbye." He edged the Osprey closer to the ascending plane and aligned the cannon with the open hatchway. His thumb hovered over the trigger.

The cockpit door beside him buckled inward and flew backwards into the rear cabin. A huge claw appeared through the doorway, followed by a bulbous head with black and yellow stripes running down its exoskeleton. Stalked eyes scanned the cockpit and settled on Kane.

Big John was back.

"Well," Kane said in surprise. "I didn't see this coming."

Lincoln and Christina watched as blood sprayed across the inside of the Osprey's cracked windscreen. The Osprey, wildly out of control, lost speed and swung around laterally. The right wing dipped low, the ocean caught hold, and the tiltrotor plane disappeared in the churning white water of the tsunami. As the C-47 soared over the flotilla, its pontoons clipped the mast of a luxury yacht and its engines screamed in protest.

The energy from the wave had dissipated after hitting the coral reef. The swell didn't have time to build behind it, so when the wall of water reached the flotilla seconds later, its momentum had all but disappeared.

The white water washed through the flotilla, with the larger crafts faring better than the smaller ones. Yachts, schooners, and cabin cruisers managed to roll over the surging wave, while the runabouts and day-trippers weren't so lucky. They disappeared in the churning wash as the white water crashed over them, only to reappear seconds later, capsized.

By the time the wave passed through the back end of the flotilla, its height had diminished dramatically. The boats at the rear of the fleet rocked and swayed with the tail end of the surging water but stayed afloat.

The first beer drinker pulled another tsunami casualty from the water. Frightened and wet, a dozen survivors huddled on the deck of the cruiser. The second beer drinker opened the fridge and pulled out two six-packs. He faced the group with a big grin. "Okay, we've all been through a lot today, so who's up for a beer?"

Roy lowered his camera. He wiped the sweat from his face and sighed in relief. "What happens now?" he asked.

Marie stared out across the ocean and up at the old plane as it disappeared over the horizon. Smiling to herself she said, "Now we get the story of a lifetime." She turned to the helicopter pilot and shouted into the headphones. "Follow that plane!"

58

The C-47 transport climbed high in the sky over the shimmering blue waters of the Pacific Ocean. Lincoln climbed into the cargo hold and collapsed on the metal floor. Christina followed as Enheim and Katya helped Lincoln to his feet. She closed the hatch behind her and locked it shut.

Enheim patted Lincoln on the back. "Well done, Monk."

Katya gave him a big kiss on the cheek. "Lincoln darling, I'm so glad you're alive." She shifted so Napoleon could lick his face.

Enheim turned to Christina. "I have no idea who you are," he said, giving her a big hug, "but I thank you."

Katya stepped in and kissed Christina on both cheeks. "We haven't been introduced yet. I'm Katya, and this is my husband Marcus," she nodded toward Enheim. "And this is our very grateful Napoleon." She lifted Napoleon to Christina's face.

"I'm Christina." Christina smiled as Napoleon licked her cheek.

Lincoln took a moment to catch his breath. Then he peered through the hatchway window at the aftermath of the tsunami. Hundreds of people drifted in the wash of the wave, shouting for help, their arms flailing about. "We have to help those people down there," he said.

"They'll be fine," a familiar voice said from the front of the cabin. Lincoln spun around to see Michio resting across two seats, his arm and leg wrapped in fresh bandages. Michio indicated out the window.

Lincoln and the others gazed down at the scene below. The larger craft, not affected by the wave, was moving among the survivors, helping them out of the water. Lincoln scanned the surface of the water searching for the Osprey—nothing.

Michio laughed. "To quote one of your classic movies, 'I'd kiss you, but I just washed my hair.'" Lincoln turned back to Michio and grinned. Then he hugged Christina and smiled.

"Thank you," he said, "for everything." She hesitated, then hugged him back.

Enheim leaned over and whispered to Lincoln. "Look, Roland and I didn't know how to handle the situation between you and this Sienna woman, so we've said nothing."

"Thanks." Lincoln made his way along the aisle and slumped down in the seat opposite Michio. "How's the arm and leg?" he asked.

"Nothing a shot of tetanus and antibiotics couldn't fix."

Lincoln grinned.

Michio turned and gazed out the window. "Is he dead?" he asked.

Lincoln thought over the events of the previous two days: the highs, the lows, the complications of Sienna's life—the revelation that she'd faked her death and was still alive, only to be brutally murdered by a sick psychopath. Michio had been through hell over the past twenty-four hours, and Lincoln didn't want to put his friend through any more grief if he didn't have to. He would tell his friend the truth soon, when he was in better health—but not today.

Lincoln's serious tone conveyed his genuine sincerity. "The man who killed Sienna is dead."

Michio nodded in approval. "Did you find that Eddie Ramirez character?"

"Yeah. He didn't make it."

Michio nodded.

Lincoln paused, recalling the events of the last few hours. He leaned closer to Michio. "Before he died, Eddie referred to a technology that ties in with something Kane hinted at. Eddie said Kane was using the technology for other things, for experiments. Later Kane backed up Eddie's statement by saying this wasn't the end, that it was only the beginning."

"You're talking about that creature on the island?"

"Big John was certainly a hybrid of some kind." Smoke from Roland's cigarette wafting down into the cabin distracted Lincoln from his unfinished thoughts. Eager to have a cigarette Lincoln reached into his empty back pocket. He laughed. "Son-of-bitch."

"What?"

"Kane stole my cigarettes."

Michio dug into his pocket and tossed a small packet to Lincoln. Lincoln caught it and checked out the packaging—nicotine gum.

"Try it," Michio ordered.

Lincoln shrugged and opened the packet.

Roland stepped out from the cockpit and rested his arm on Lincoln's seat. "Nice to see you again, Lincoln," he said with genuine warmth.

"It's really good to be here," Lincoln replied enthusiastically. "How did you get back here so fast?"

"As you know the helicopter we borrowed was damaged, you know, so we made a forced landing on the ocean."

Enheim heard part of the conversation from the back of the plane and felt the need to chime in. "Crash landing," he called out.

Roland ignored him. "Once ve vere outside the communication scramble zone, I contacted Michel back on Saipan and told him to get his ass here and rendezvous with us at a predetermined location. I also gave him the approximate heading and estimated location of the runabout from the landing, so he picked up Katya and Michio, too. Oh, Michel said the runabout owner demands a date with Katya."

"Over my dead body," Enheim added.

"We'll deal with that later. And Michio's health condition?"

Michio piped up. "Roland keeps a comprehensive class-one medic kit on board for such emergencies. He also has an inflatable lifeboat, parachutes, a fully stocked bar, and—nicotine gum."

Roland smiled. "For the tourists, you know." He struggled with his next sentence. "I hate to be the materialistic person in the group, you know, and I realize this is bad timing and all, but uhhh…did you manage to come across another drife by any chance?"

Lincoln grinned and removed Eddie's hard drive from his pocket. Enheim, Katya, and Christina made their way down the aisle and hovered next to Roland. They all looked on as Lincoln raised the hard drive to eye level so everyone could see.

The hard drive had the tip of a bullet embedded in it. The casing was shattered and small chips of metal dropped to the floor. As Lincoln turned his hand to get a better look at the drive, it broke in two.

Lincoln recalled the shots fired by Kane on the observation deck. One of the rounds struck his hip. The bullet struck the hard drive in his pocket, which accounted for why he was still walking—and still alive. He slumped back in the chair and wiped his brow, exhilarated at being alive, yet frustrated at not having brought the drive back in one piece.

Disappointment swept over the group as Roland sighed in defeat.

The ends of Michio's mouth turned up in a small grin. He turned to Enheim. "Professor. May I?" He pointed to Napoleon.

Curious at the request, Enheim lifted Napoleon from his pouch and handed him to Michio. While Napoleon licked his face, Michio carefully removed the necklace from the dog's neck. He passed Napoleon back to Enheim and separated the pendant from the chain. He flipped open the clasp on the love-heart shaped locket and pocketed the heart-shaped picture of Sienna and himself.

Lincoln leaned forward and peered closely at the pendant. A small metallic plug protruded from the top centre of the heart design. It took him a few moments but he recognised the design of the plug. His previous despair turned to astonishment. The pendant was a micro USB drive in the shape of a heart.

Bewildered, Lincoln said, "You made a copy back at the bungalow, right?"

"Once I got past the encryption, the drive was like any other drive on the market."

Roland's eyes lit up.

Lincoln stared at the heart-shaped drive long and hard, and considered everything it represented. He looked Michio in the eye and spoke solemnly. "It was never about the money."

"I know."

Lincoln saw the dollar signs flashing before Roland's eyes as he leaned closer, wanting to get a better look at his future. "Roland, it's not ours to keep. The world has to know what happened here. We have to hand the drive over to the authorities."

Roland moaned. He stared longingly, like a heartbroken lover, at the small drive in Michio's hand.

"Mr. Pom." Michel's voice interrupted from the cockpit.

"Yes?" Roland replied, still transfixed by the small device between Michio's fingers.

"The oil pressure is dropping. I need some help reading the gauges, please." Roland managed to tear his eyes away from the locket and return to the cockpit.

"That bloody thing would have changed all our lives," Enheim said to the group.

"It already has." Lincoln glanced over at Christina and smiled. She casually returned the glance with a look of uncertainty, yet with a hint of a smile. The sound of Roland clearing his throat emanated from the cabin's speakers. "People, I haf good news and bad news, you know."

Everyone in the cabin turned to the sound of his voice through the speakers.

"The good news is Michel just got his pilot's license." They cheered as Michel leaned out through the cockpit doorway and grinned, a cigarette hanging from his mouth.

And the bad news? Lincoln could already guess the answer. Everything that could have gone wrong in the last forty-eight hours had gone wrong. He wasn't having a good week.

"Well, the plan vas to get us back to Saipan, but—" The plane lurched and the muffled sound of an explosion from the left wing filled the small cabin. They turned to the port side windows and gazed out over the left wing. Black smoke billowed from the engine cowling and streamed past the fuselage. The cowling suddenly tore away and disappeared behind the plane. Flames shot from the engine and ran down the wing. The plane banked left as more pieces of engine broke away and shredded the tail fin. Lincoln sighed.

Life never goes according to plan.

EPILOGUE

The wreckage of the dome slammed into the seabed, churning the silt into a cloud of murky haze. The emergency lights still worked, causing a red glow to surround the structure. The bedrock below the dome cracked and gave way. The front of the dome tilted downward and split from the rear section, revealing the inner lower floors, before tumbling into the blackness and disappearing into the Pacific's deep waters.

The rear section of the dome hung on the edge of the bedrock cliff, its inner levels exposed. The dozens of tanks and cages that had lined the walls of the lower floors were all smashed and broken beyond repair. Human bodies floated lifelessly among the walls and corridors of the flooded levels, drifting with the ebb and flow of the tide. Through the cloudy haze, shadowy forms appeared, gliding, pulsating, and undulating amid the structure's buckled girders and crumpled metal.

Some sought the safety and shelter of the darker water below, while others made their way toward the light, far above.

ABOUT THE AUTHOR

I'm an avid reader and film junky. So, inspired by the works of all the great action adventure writers and film makers, I put pen to paper and started writing. Because my brain works in a cinematic way, certain actors sprang to mind when writing the novel:

When writing Lincoln, my thoughts turned to Chris Pratt (*Guardians of the Galaxy*) and Josh Duhamel (*Transformers; Las Vegas*).

Chiwetel Ejiofor (*2012; The Martian*) was always Jonathan Kane, and David

Hyde Pierce (Niles Crane from *Frasier*) was the inspiration for Roland Pom.

Only Jason Statham (*Snatch; The Expendables*) could play Marcus Enheim.

Olga Kurylenko (*Quantum of Solace; Hitman*) was in mind for Katya Enhiem.

John Cho (*Star Trek*) was Michio.

Maggie Q (title role in the TV series *Nikita; Die Hard 4*) was the only actress I thought about for Christina.

However— don't let my inspirations interfere with your imagination.

I hope you have enjoyed reading *Neptune Island* as much as I enjoyed writing it. I love to get feedback on my novel, so please feel free to leave a review, and if you wish to contact me— TonyReedAuthor@gmail.com

Made in the USA
Middletown, DE
22 September 2018